THE
STARS

EMPIRE
PUBLICATIONS

First published in 2014

EMPIRE PUBLICATIONS
1 Newton Street, Manchester M1 1HW
© John Ludden 2014

ISBN 978-1-909360-23-5

Printed in Great Britain.

For Mum x

'Who is that in the red?'

ACKNOWLEDGEMENTS

I would like to thank the following people for their help in the writing of 'From the Stars'. Ashley Shaw of Empire Publications, Dad, Christine, Roy Cavanagh MBE, Mel Esson, Danny Lovelock, Rachael Moores, Jane Durbin and the rest of the red army who have encouraged me to get this story told. Thanks all and I hope you find it is worth the wait. And last but not least my little boy Matthew. My star.

CONTENTS

THE BALLAD OF THE HOLY TRINITY

While the plot of this novel is based on real events, the thoughts, motives and conversations are fictionalised and should not be construed as a verbatim record of fact.

Introduction

Sir Matt Busby sits amongst the Old Trafford faithful watching, as Manchester City's Denis Law, backheels his infamous goal on the late afternoon of Saturday 27ᵗʰ April 1974.

OH DENIS, DENIS, what have you done, son? I cannot bring myself to shed a tear because this is not a tragedy. Around me grown men are crying, many I know. Many who should know better because they were around when the real thing occurred.

A voice behind shouts down towards me, 'Matt this is a tragedy!'

This comment makes me mad. I turn around but cannot catch his eye. Don't talk to me about tragedy! Nobody has died here today. There is no blood in the snow. There is no German priest handing me the last rites. There are no screams from boys whom I thought of as my own sons. Boys that died amid scenes of terror.

Dry your eyes for United will go on. We have lost nothing that cannot be replaced. Nothing except our First Division place and, shamefully, as thousands of our supporters run onto the pitch, our self-respect. But I can live with this because there are no crumpled bodies lying deathly still. No sobbing wives, sons, daughters, mothers and fathers.

My time has gone. I want to scream. How did we make such a mess? How did we destroy everything it took so long to build? The foundations I believed we had laid to last for generations to come have crumbled to sand in less than six years.

Who is to blame? Is it me? Am I fallible? I know there are those who believe I still hold the reins of power. But I do not. This is not of my doing. I plead to all who will listen – I am an innocent man!

For I will tell you now how we fell from the stars…

MUNICH

Thursday 6ᵗʰ February 1958: The roar of the engine grows deafening as ice and snow flies against the porthole. I clasp hold of my seat. Something is terribly wrong. Then an almighty bang, like an explosion. We have gone through a perimeter fence. I brace myself. For what, I have no idea.

'Please God save us!' I hear a voice shout.

We start to spin round and round. Like a rollercoaster in hell. Then everything goes black, the terrifying sound of tearing metal. Something hits my head. There are sparks, my chest is cracked and I can't breathe.

So this is how it ends. On a snow bound runway in Southern Germany.

In Munich.

The plane is spinning, there are sparks igniting. There is fire and smoke. Round and round, we are upside down. Everything is going slower now. There is silence. I am drifting, I can see the sky and the snow is coming down.

I think I am dying.

I regain consciousness; I am lying flat in the freezing snow. I open my eyes to scenes no mortals should have to witness. This is the pits of hell. I see friends bleeding, open wounds, pleading for life, screaming for loved ones.

Others lying dead. This is not fair. You say you are a rightful God, a peaceful God? We survived a world war, your war. You invented that. And we served and survived. We kissed our loved ones on return in joy and hope that we could live simple, peaceful lives. But oh no, you just had to twist the blade a little deeper.

Has Manchester not suffered enough?

Fire and flames... I am so very cold. My chest feels like it is set to explode. It is so hard to breathe.

There is blood coming from my mouth. I prop myself up on one arm. I can see the aeroplane fuselage still smoking, it lies twisted and smouldering. I see bodies in the snow. 'Are you okay boss?' I hear a voice. It is Bill Foulkes. Bill leans down.

'It is my chest son, I can't breathe.'

'You hang on in there,' says Bill, 'I'm going to get help.' And then he is gone. I wake up once more. I am in a vehicle, the pain is agonising. We seem to hit every bump on the road. I hear a familiar voice. It is young Bobby Charlton. His face covered in cuts, his eyes watering. He is holding my hand.

'We are going to the hospital, boss. Hold on, everything is going to be alright.'

Then another voice. It is Big Bill. He is shouting. I see him hit the driver over the head, not once but twice. He is close to tears with shock and anger. 'Slow down you German bastard, slow down. And watch your driving. He is dying back there, dying back there...'

I can hear screams and crying and loud voices. Men shouting. I am on a hospital stretcher being taken down a corridor. It is brightly lit. Lights that blind my eyes. There are strange faces staring down at me. White figures, blurred white figures. Angels maybe? They are chattering in German. They appear concerned over somebody or something. I see one make the sign of the cross. Then I hear somebody speak in English. He is whispering. It is like he does not want me to hear.

'Many dead, it is a disaster,' he says, 'they are all but wiped out.' What is he talking about?

I cannot feel my legs. My chest is heavy like a dead weight. My breathing is slowing. I close my eyes and don't expect to open them again. I am so tired. Is this heaven?

I am in the hospital bed. I can feel no pain, but something tells me I must not sleep for I will never wake up. I can make out a man in a white collar. A priest is stood over me. He takes hold of my hand and starts to speak in English.

'Through this holy anointing may the Lord in his love and mercy help you with the grace of the Holy Spirit.' I recognise these words. This is the Holy sacrament of the last rites. The Priest has a kind voice. His fingers are cold as he anoints the top of my forehead.

'May the Lord who frees you from sin save you and raise you up.'

So be it. But it appears my body is strong where my will is weak, for it is refusing to die. As I drift in and out of consciousness this hazy mist in front of my eyes does not lift. And yet through the fog I can make out a familiar face. My old friend the Priest has returned. Once was not enough, for I am still around and I am to be given the last rites again.

My collapsed lungs and chest prove to be too badly damaged and so I feel his cold, kind hands on my forehead once more. This time I shall gladly go. I want to go. It does no good to keep the Good Lord waiting. The Good Lord? I must remember to ask him one question when I walk through those big white gates.

Why?

★

I was born into a loving family on 26th May 1909, in Orbiston, Bellshill. A tiny mining village near Motherwell, east of Glasgow. I lost my father to a German sniper, curse him, in the First World War, leaving my mother to raise four children in a two room cottage. Come my early teenage years we almost ended up immigrating to America. Fate decided otherwise and now aged forty eight, in the early days of 1958, I lie here in a German hospital bed. By all reckoning, after twice being given the last rites I should be dead, but for a reason known only to the almighty he has spared me.

Still, I have no idea who has been lost in the crash. Father forgive me for my sins. I never meant it to be like this.

Now who has perished. I must know. Tell me the cost of a fallen dream?

★

I would recognise that Welsh growl anywhere. Jimmy Murphy is here. I open my eyes. He is gripping my hand tight. I try to talk but find the words won't come. I have so many questions – Who is alive? Who is dead? Am I the only one? Jimmy notices.

'Save your energy old pal.'

He strokes my forehead. What does he know that I don't?

I look into his eyes hoping they may give me a clue. But they are empty. He appears tired, so very tired. I try to push myself up on the bed, I must talk, and I have to tell him. Somehow I have to find the willpower to make the words come out of my mouth.

Jimmy leans close and I whisper into his ear.

'Keep the flag flying until I get back Jimmy.'

★

To know or not to know. The realisation, the pain of loss. The guilt, all measured up against the terror and sheer frustration of not knowing. I fear for my sanity and so I ask Jean.

I tell her 'I will say a name and you either nod if they are alive. Shake your head if they are not.' I have heard whispered names already in hushed German conversations. Jean has tears in her eyes, but I must insist. I have to know

'Okay Matt' she replies.

Who do I mention first? Who do I wish to have lived more? This is evil, cruel and unfair. I begin and decide to go from the goalkeeper onwards.

'Ray Wood?' Jean Nods. 'Roger Byrne?' Jean shakes her head. 'Mark Jones?' Jean shakes her head...

I am on the hospital balcony looking out over the grounds. It is a beautiful clear blue German sky. The birds are singing, it is early morning. Yesterday I was told that Duncan had gone. His was a truly courageous struggle for life that left doctors and nurses heartbroken and in tears. So typical of the boy. Sadly this is one battle Duncan lost. That takes the total of the boys lost to eight. Eight mother's sons. Then there are Bert Whalley and Tom Curry and the poor journalists.

It is my fault. I could have said we are not getting on that damned plane. I should have done something.

I should have done something. I should...

★

The radio man hands me my speech. 'When you are ready Matt. 3, 2, 1.'

'Ladies and Gentlemen, I am speaking to you from my bed in the Rechts der Isar hospital in Germany, where I have been since the tragic accident at Munich, just over a month ago. You will be glad, I am sure, to know that the remaining players here and myself are now considered out of danger. And this can only be attributed to the wonderful treatment and attention given us by professor Maurer and his fine staff.

'I am obliged to Empire News for giving me this opportunity to speak to you. For it is only in this last two or three days that I have been able to be told anything about football. And I am delighted to hear that the club have reached the semi-finals of the FA Cup. And I enclose my best wishes to everyone. And finally may I just say. God bless you all.'

'Well done Matt' says the radio man with tears falling down his cheeks, 'Well done.'

★

The German surgeon Doctor Georg Maurer has been invited by the club as guest of honour for a forthcoming home match. The very least we can offer for a man whose surgical skills have saved and healed so many of our people. I swear this man has not slept since the crash. He is taking over to Manchester a tape recording I made earlier today to be played over the tannoy at the stadium. But also in my absence, performing a most terrible service.

'Matt, I just wanted to say thank you for this wonderful if sad honour. It will be my privilege on your behalf to visit these people and express condolences.'

Earlier today with Jean's help I had written for him a list of the bereaved families and their addresses.

'Doctor Maurer,' I say, 'you are a wonderful man and truly sent to us from God.'

He shakes his head. 'What we did to try and save all your boys was nothing to do with God. In what I witnessed during the war and again this last month. Young men suffering so called God's will? No.' He smiles. 'I prefer my Scottish friend to think our actions were just common human decency.' This man raged against all the carnage, hell and furore wreaked by Munich.

Myself and Manchester United will owe him forever more.

★

In the early afternoon of Sunday 18th April 1958, I arrive home in Kings Road, Chorlton. Alongside me in the back of the car is Jean. She holds my hand tight. A large crowd has gathered to welcome us back. Well wishers along with pressmen and photographers mill around.

How normal everything looks.

I have been to hell and this place has not changed at all. I can see our two children Sandy and Sheena stood at the door. I have to hold it together. I am home now.

'Everything is going to be okay now Mattha,' says Jean whispering into my ear. People are waving. There are shiny happy faces. I slowly manoeuvre a way out with my sticks. I smile wide to our audience. A little girl steps forward and hands me flowers. I bend down and kiss her on the cheek.

'Thank you young lady' I say. 'They are lovely.'

I turn to the reception committee. 'Are you alright ladies and gentlemen. How have you all been whilst I have been away?'

In the pits of hell.

★

Saturday 3rd May 1958: Manchester United have, against all unholy odds, made it to the FA Cup Final against Bolton Wanderers. There are simply no words for what Jimmy has done. 'Murphy's Marvels' I have seen them referred to. More like 'Murphy's Miracle.'

I am here on sticks but in all honesty I wish I was a thousand miles away. I simply cannot face this. Jimmy has asked if I wished to say a few words to the boys before kick off. I am stood outside the dressing room waiting for him to come out and say they are ready. What do I say, what do I do? They are not my lads. My boys are shadows and dust. Jimmy appears, he smiles.

'The boys are ready Matt.' I enter and look around at their faces. Some I don't even recognise. I blink and my boys are back. They are staring at me: Duncan, Roger, Tommy, Eddie, Liam, Mark, David and Geoff. I have to leave. I break down. I turn to Jimmy.

'I am sorry but I can't stay.'

I so miss my boys.

With a glass of fine Spanish wine in hand, I am sat on Don Santiago Bernabeu's spacious balcony overlooking the city of Madrid. Santiago is sat opposite. He has generously invited me and the other survivors to his beautiful city to recuperate and to use the club's magnificent facilities. The man will not accept a penny.

'You are our friends Matt. It is the least we can do.'

His kindness touches my soul and must never be forgotten. Once we were genuine rivals, friends but sporting adversaries, now I fear his majestic Real Madrid are too far beyond the stars for us to even dream of competing with them for many years. Then I have an idea.

'Santiago, your kindness has already been overwhelming. But may I be so bold as to offer you a proposition. We cannot afford your match fee but can pay in instalments over time. Would you be willing to accept such an offer?'

Don Santiago smiles and raises his glass. 'My dear friend, you pay us only what you can afford. Ours is a shared bond. A Tale of Two Cities shall we say.'

We raise our glasses. 'To Champions of Honour' he toasts, 'to Manchester United.'

There are no words.

If there is such a thing as a footballing visitation then 60,000 have experienced it here tonight at Old Trafford. With a sense of wonder and awe and, I admit, blind despair, we watch as Real Madrid destroy Manchester United 6-1 with the ease of someone swatting an annoying fly with a newspaper. Tonight we have witnessed football from the heavens: Di Stefano, Puskas, Gento and Didi have cast white scorch marks on our pitch. I, like others, cannot help but think – what if?

These wonderful boys from Madrid would have found themselves in a battle royal tonight. For we were close, so damn close before hell overtook us and now we start again. But will there ever be enough time? Do I possess the strength and will to carry the fight on? These magnificent *Madrileños* gather in the centre circle and salute the crowd and the reception they receive from the Mancunians is as if these lads were our own. A reminder of happier times. Of paradise.

We were close. So very close.

★

A late February morning in 1960 and on a rain lashed Old Trafford forecourt we stand as the Munich memorial clock is officially unveiled. Jean is next to me and grips my hand tight.

Words are said, kind words about those we lost. But words mean nothing. I look in the eyes of the bereaved families. I can still see the pain. Time they say is a good healer. It ebbs away over the years until the grief is just numbness in the heart. Always there but you can live with it. It has been two years since and I am still on the plane. In my dreams I still feel the cold of the ice and snow. But it is a beautiful clock and there is polite applause as the curtain draws back. I tell myself I must not cry. For one day I swear we will win the European Cup.

1 - WONDERFUL WORLD

Wembley Stadium, Wednesday 29th May 1968:
One thought is in my head as Eusebio runs through
to beat Alex Stepney. It is that my God possesses a
cruel streak and despite how you bow before him, if
the mood arises, if you catch him on a bad day he will
destroy you.

Now, I am a religious man. My faith is both my
saviour and my crutch. It has saved me both physically
and mentally. It has been my greatest weapon in the
battle to keep going. To not look back onto that
runway. To survive the nightmares and the echoes of
dead voices in the Old Trafford corridors. I believe I
have been a good man. A righteous man. Faith should
not be a toss of the dice. A deflection or a rebound.

Please God if you are good, just let him miss. Do
not let me view you as a cruel God with a twisted
sense of justice. For we do not deserve what is about to
happen. I close my eyes;

I hear Jimmy Murphy's voice: 'Miss you bastard,
miss!'

And then the roar of the crowd. The sweet sense of
relief. Alex saves it: Eusebio has tried to burst the net
instead of picking his spot and we are still alive. We are
still alive! Jimmy is off the bench screaming at Nobby
Stiles.

'Concentrate Nobby, Just bloody concentrate!' The
boys are exhausted. Everybody has given their all. We
need that full time whistle. I am sweating, I can feel

my heart beating loudly. Eusebio has the ball again. He senses it, the Panther senses blood. Our blood. Oh no, have we not given enough?

'Nail him' screams Wilf McGuinness, 'Bloody nail him!'

As Eusebio prepares to send us home in tears, big Bill Foulkes, Good old Bill, gets a foot in and we get the ball back.

Now keep it, give it Paddy. Take your time Paddy lad. The referee, Señor Concerto Lo Bello, has the whistle in his mouth, he blows, 1–1.

My boys need encouragement.

On we go to soothe tired legs and ease shattered minds. I need to lift hearts because we are still fighting for this trophy. Kicking and screaming, we will not give up. Not whilst I have a living breath in my body.

Ten years on we are still fighting.

I tell them, 'Don't sit down. Don't let the Benfica players see you are tired.' Jimmy does similar. I can see the fire in his eyes. Welsh flames. Jimmy is United through and through. I love him, though I never tell him. They say I am a good man, a great man. Well Jimmy is a better man. Always has been. He is my brother, my brother in arms. I have to put things right.

As ever Wilf, my Wilf, Collyhurst lad. He is on the list. He cried a thousand tears when my boys came home. He grieved over his mates, no more than over little Eddie Colman. Wilf loved Eddie, I love Jimmy.

We are all United and we are still fighting for this European Cup. 'Don't let the bastards see you are tired boys. They are finished; I can see it in their eyes.'

Wilf claps his hands. 'Come on now, let's have them in this next thirty minutes.'

Jack Crompton hands out massages. Good old Jack, he came back from Luton Town after Munich to help Jimmy. To help us when we were almost down and out. He deserves this trophy tonight for he has suffered too. He knows what this means. Jack knows. He just knows.

I speak softly to Bobby. I whisper in his ear:

'Just give me a little more son. A little more and we are done.' Bobby has little left in the tank but I know from somewhere he will find more. He nods. 'Good lad' I say.

Paddy is chatting with Nobby about Eusebio's near miss

'He came from bloody nowhere Pat, I didn't see him.'

'No surprise there Nob,' laughs Paddy.

Nobby smiles. My boys. I lean down speaking to Paddy.

'You have to keep the ball, Pat. Make them work. Keep it simple.' How many times has he heard this from me? A thousand, ten thousand? Yet still Paddy listens like it is the first time.

'Okay boss.'

'We are almost there Pat.' I clench my fist. 'Just a little more.'

Another one on my list. loyal and red to the core. A man like Paddy will always fight your corner. He will fight in any corner on any street or field in the world if he feels the cause is just. The cause is red. He is one of us. But he is tired, they are all so tired.

George Best is sat on his haunches. My George. This wee boy from Belfast who regularly drives me to despair and yet equally lifts my tormented soul with moments of wonder. This boy's heart impresses me equally as his bewildering skills.

Tonight the Portuguese have taken it in turns to kick George up into the air. Yet he has continually bounced back down to carry on torturing them. George has had better evenings but he has kept going.

'Listen son, they are scared to death of you. Now they are exhausted, so keep chasing. You scare them George, your talent scares them. They remember the Stadium of Light. It haunts them, you haunt them. Haunt them one more time. For me George. For me. Keep going lad, run their bloody socks off.'

George smiles like only George can.

'Will do boss. Don't worry, I will win this for you.'

I ruffle his hair. My George. My genius.

It begins again.

I look across to Jimmy to catch his eye, to share this, what we have both given and strove for, but he has eyes only for the pitch. Wilf cannot sit still, he decides to stand, arms folded, quietly praying. Around us Mancunian accents scream loud.

'Come on you reds!'

The ball goes long over the halfway line from Alex's kick and David Sadler flicks it on. It falls to George, please, go on George.

'I will win it for you boss,' he promised.

Go on George! He soars into Benfica's penalty area. He takes the ball around Henrique.

Please, please.

He scores!

Around me bedlam reigns! I punch the air, Wilf hugs me and people slap me on the back. We lead again. Jimmy remains calm, he knows. He is straight to the touchline. He shouts over to Nobby and Bill. He points to his head, the meaning obvious.

We attack again. We have a corner. The ball is loose; it is in the air, a scramble, a free for all.

Off the crossbar!

Then Brian Kidd heads back goalwards. I can't see, it is a melee as we stretch our necks. A roar goes up like I have never heard. Like an approaching train. It is in! Our Brian, the nineteen year-old Collyhurst boy. 3-1!

A cauldron of noise. Benfica have collapsed. It is nearly over.

Brian is crying.

I look over to the Portuguese bench, they sit like statues. For them the game is up. For a second I feel sympathy but the emotion is such I cannot think of anything but elation and relief. Please God don't take this away from me now. End the pain.

End it.

With tears still in his eyes Brian races down the Benfica wing and reaches the touchline. 'Give it to Bobby' screams Jimmy.

Kiddo does so and Bobby with his right foot smashes it high into the net past a flailing Henrique.

I can't breathe. I am embraced by Wilf.

'We have done it boss. By Christ we've bloody done it!'

I see Bobby gaze toward the heavens, he falls into Paddy's arms. He makes a gesture to suggest that he knows, he understands, we all do.

The European Cup is ours. The noise from the terraces reaches a crescendo. A sea of smiling, joyful faces.

The first half of extra time ends and we switch around. 'No bloody stupid business' urges Jimmy.

'Keep it tight lads' shouts Wilf.

'Almost there' I add. 'Almost there.' We stay calm and the final whistle blows. I take a deep breath and head towards the pitch. I am surrounded by goodwill. Swamped in back slapping, bearhugs and embraces. I shake more hands but I see no faces. I look into no eyes. I compose myself: cameras flash in my face. They are blinding me.

'Congratulations Matt', 'you've done it Matt', 'we love you Matt', 'you deserve it Matt'. Inside my stomach churns. Ecstasy was not supposed to be like this.

I look around swiftly for Jimmy but he is not to be seen. He will be celebrating with ghosts. Red ghosts.

Jimmy is in a crowd of one. He needs a minute alone. He rubs his eyes, he sees Duncan and Tommy and Eddie and Roger and the rest of the boys stood smiling back at him. Still in the beauty of youth, spared the ravages of Munich and age, they too can now be allowed to rest in peace.

He and I have grown apart. It can never again be like it was. I like the power, the boardroom battles. Jimmy lives for the game. The passion and the beauty. Busby's babes, Jimmy apples. Together from the beginning but never truly close. This is now sadly how it will end. How it was written. A football tragedy with a happy ending to suit the audience.

Myself and Matt. Together but apart. He never wanted it to be like this. Never.

★

I see Eusebio in the centre circle. He is a good lad, I must shake his hand. He deserves at least that. But immediately Bobby falls into my arms. He cries, he sobs. 'We have done it boss, for Duncan and the boys. We have done it!' Eusebio smiles and slips away.

'Oh Bobby.'

I close my eyes and hold him tight. Nobby and Brian join us. Paddy also. I embrace Alex. I shout into his ear, 'you saved us son. You saved us.'

Celebrations unbridled.

Stood behind applauding Busby wildly with tears streaming down his beaming face is United's assistant reserve team coach and former babe, thirty year-old Mancunian Wilf McGuinness.

A career cut short by injury, he was taken in by the boss. Kept in the fold, kept close for Wilf is United through and through. He loves Busby and remembers so vividly the pain of Munich. The trauma of Manchester. The aftermath. The dead and the dying. The shattered faces of the survivors. The looks of incredulity and despair. He still feels it like it was yesterday. The newspaper billboards screaming out across the city:

UNITED IN PLANE CRASH:
MANY FEARED DEAD.

Wilf tries hard not to cry. He dries his eyes and smiles. 'Thank God it is done' he says quietly to himself. 'Now we can rest.'

The crowd are chanting my name, 'Busby, Busby, Busby' rings out from the massed terraces. I wave and then my thoughts suddenly turn to my wife Jean. Somewhere amid this red sea of emotion she will be crying too. This is for her as much as anyone.

Without her love and strength I would not be here tonight, I would have ended this torture years ago. She is my reality, she has seen the truth. The doubts and the agonies, the pain and the torment. For her this is no Hollywood ending, it has been a journey from hell.

We clap the brave Portuguese up those long Wembley steps to receive their medals. Gallant but rather them than us. Paddy and the boys crowd around me. 'It is only right you go up boss,' says Paddy, 'this is your time, your trophy; you go and pick it up.' They are insistent.

'Where is Jimmy?' I look around. He is watching proceedings twenty yards away stood on his own. I nod and he smiles back. Tonight we will talk, build bridges, we will toast Duncan and the boys. We will cry and we will laugh.

'No,' I say eventually, 'it is not right lads; Bobby will go and get the trophy. He has earned the right.' I look over to him and he smiles. From a boy to a man he has struggled in silence since the horrors of that German runway. His smile is not one of joy, it is sheer unadulterated relief. Not a rainbow's end but rather the closing of a door on a howling, shrieking wind that threatens to blow away your very heart and soul.

My Bobby is close to exhaustion. Bobby's journey is almost over. Through the blinding smoke a red phoenix emerges to finally spread its wings, and now the European Cup is won. Through the fire and the flames Bobby raises the trophy above his head. We are champions. I look up and the London night is full of stars. Northern stars up for the cup. A heavenly red sky littered with my angels. My boys. It is over and I can do no more.

I have paid my dues. I have given everything and more. This piece of silverware has almost cost me my faith, my family and my life. And Jimmy. I hope I have not lost Jimmy.

I don't want to do this anymore. I am tired, so weary. I feel old. Tomorrow I will talk to Louis and the board. I have my list of names. The time is right, the time is nigh. Let someone else keep the Red Devils flying high. But for tonight I will drink and be merry.

Please God, let me have this one night free of bad memories.

★

The Russell Hotel in the West End: My good friend Joe Loss is there with his orchestra. As I walk through the door carrying the trophy the packed room stands to applaud and the band plays 'Congratulations.'

So many friends and faces. I lift the cup high and exclaim, 'Up the reds!'

Everyone cheers loud. My friend from Manchester, dressed as elegantly as ever, Paddy McGrath appears to shake my hand. He has tears in his eyes. Paddy comes from a world I only dip in and out of. He's a real character. 'I am so happy for you Matt. You deserve it,' he says. We shake hands.

The party is already in full swing. Brian Kidd, goal scorer and birthday boy, is being presented with a huge cake. All present serenade him with 'Happy Birthday.' The champagne corks pop. They toast him, 'cheers', a hundred glasses raised high. Kiddo looks embarrassed. He glances over to his mum and dad, their faces beaming with pride. A different world to Collyhurst. A long, long way from St Patrick's church and school. A United loyalist area, a breeding ground: the fearsome nuns, fire and brimstone. Sensing Kiddo's discomfort

Nobby Stiles steps forward to place an arm around his fellow Mancunian. 'Come on lad, to the bar.'

Myself and Jean are led over to a table where waiting for us are Jimmy and his lovely wife Agnes. The wives embrace: Jimmy kisses Jean, I kiss Agnes.

'I am so pleased it is over Matt,' she says.

I sit down next to Jimmy. He is looking at me. He passes me a glass of champagne. 'Let us have a toast' says Jimmy. 'To our boys back then and now.'

I smile. 'To the boys.' We raise our drinks. Now we will talk. We will sort everything out.

'Jimmy look I need to say a few words.'

'I'm listening Matt.' He puts his glass down on the table. I look in his eyes.

'I want things to go back like they were. I…' I am interrupted by a hand on the shoulder.

It is Joe Loss. 'Matt you have to sing a song.' Suddenly the entire room is looking at me. A table of the players and family start to chant.

'We want Matt, we want Matt.'

Soon everyone is joining in. I am not keen. Jean grabs my hand.

'Go on Mattha. Give them a song.' I turn to Jimmy.

'We will speak when I get back yes?' He smiles. I stand and the room goes wild with applause and cheers. I walk to the stage with Joe alongside me. I stand at the microphone.

'I think there is only one song don't you?' I say to him.

Joe smiles. 'I think so.'

He turns to his orchestra and says quietly. 'Matt is going to be singing 'What a Wonderful World.' They take up their instruments. I face the crowd. They go quiet.

'Ladies and gentlemen, I would just like to say this trophy we have with us here is not just for the players who have done us so proud at Wembley tonight. But for those who can only be here in spirit.' I catch Jimmy's eye. He nods in acknowledgement. 'And it is with those boys in mind I will now try not to sting your ears too much with what I consider Satchmo's finest moment. If you are listening out there Mr Louis Armstrong, please forgive me. My friends I give you, 'What a wonderful world.'

The band starts up

'I see trees of green, red roses too.......

I finish with my eyes closed and tears fall down my face. There is rapturous applause and not a dry eye in the house. I wave and leave the stage. I need to speak to Jimmy. I reach the table but he has vanished.

'Where is he Agnes?'

'Oh he got a little upset Matt. He had to leave the room.' I have to find him. Suddenly there's an arm on my shoulder. It is Paddy.

'There is someone here who would like a word Boss.'

'Can it wait Pat? I need to find Jimmy.'

'Well it is Duncan Edwards' Mum. She was asking after you but was too shy to come over to your table.'

I smile 'Of course. Where is she?'

Pat takes my arm. 'I'll come with you.' He leads me over to Sarah Ann Edwards. I can see Duncan in her, around the eyes. She sees us coming and goes to stand.

'No please,' I say. We all sit down.

She grabs my hand and clasps it tight. 'My Duncan loved you Mr Busby, he really did.' I don't think I can hold things together much more. Paddy is close to tears also. 'I just wanted you to know that.'

'He was a wonderful boy Mrs Edwards. He was like a son to me. They all were.'

She keeps hold of my hand. I wonder what has happened to Jimmy? 'Mr Busby, do you know that whenever United play in the Midlands fresh flowers are placed on my Duncan's grave. They come and visit in their droves. It is a great comfort.' I can do nothing but stare at her heartbroken eyes. She continues: 'You sang before about a wonderful world Mr Busby. Maybe once.' Her voice trails off sadly. 'Maybe once but it is not a wonderful world anymore.' She shakes her head 'Not for me.'

'Me neither Mrs Edwards,' I reply.

She smiles and holds my hand even tighter. 'You are a good man Mr Busby. God bless you.' Mrs Edwards grabs Paddy's hand too. 'You remind me of my Duncan Mr Crerand.'

'Please call me Pat,' replies Paddy. 'And Mrs Edwards you could not give me a finer compliment.' The granite faced but huge hearted Scot whose fists can move infinitely quicker than his feet is crying.

Paddy tells her he watched Duncan play several times before the crash and if it was not for Munich it is unlikely he would have joined United. For him the small talk is painful as he too sees up close still the pain and grief in Sarah Ann's eyes. Her Duncan.

The light of her life snuffed out and taken from her in a manner no mother should have to suffer. I look around. Every eye in the room feels like it is upon me. I am so tired and only pure adrenalin and the whisky and champagne is keeping me awake. I dread to be alone with myself and my feelings. To open a door to these thoughts swirling around my head. Everything is so raw.

I don't want to go back to that runway. Not tonight, not ever again. With the drink there are no bad dreams, just sleep, so I am not going anywhere.

Another whisky, another glass of champagne. Another toast.

Not just yet.

Shattered both physically and emotionally Bobby Charlton does not even make it downstairs from his room to the banquet. He does not want to let the old man down. Let Manchester United down, but he can't get off the bed. Each time he tries he simply collapses. Does he smile or laugh or cry?

Bobby is torn. He is beyond exhaustion. He gives up and falls back on the bed. Tears in his eyes. His wife Norma shrugs off her disappointment. She says she will go alone. 'It's not worth embarrassing yourself,' she tells him. 'Or the old man. I will explain.'

Norma speaks with just a hint of disappointment for this was to be her moment. To walk in to huge applause with her husband, her man Bobby Charlton. World Cup winner for England and Captain of the European Champions. Her moment. Hers. Norma plays her game with wonderful aplomb. She smiles and charms. She offers apologies for all who inquire about Bobby's absence. 'My Bobby is not feeling well. It has all been too much. He is exhausted but sends his love.'

Meanwhile upstairs, with the party and revelry going on and echoing through the floorboards beneath him and the sound of the Joe Loss orchestra resonating loud, Bobby is crying. Now he remembers. He sees their faces. His many pals ripped apart and thrown about like rag dolls in the crash. The blood in the snow. 'Bobby Charlton was a lucky boy' they said. 'Bobby Charlton had the luck of the devil. A red devil.'

Well as the tears fall Bobby does not feel lucky. On this night of 29th May 1968, with the quest for redemption over, Bobby wishes only to think of those no longer around to be greeted by 'Congratulations'.

How he still misses them so.

Present and reluctant to enter the party atmosphere are crash survivors Johnny Berry and Kenny Morgans and many other family members of the Munich dead. Invited along by United as a goodwill gesture, one can only imagine their thoughts and feelings on this strange, wonderful and, some might even say, macabre evening.

Wrought emotions, guilt wracked at feeling happy in victory, with thoughts of loved, long gone fathers, brothers, pals forever on their minds.

No closing of the grief for the sad tables. Just a momentarily glimpse of a rainbows' end.

'Where is George?' so many ask. It is not a party without 'Georgie boy'. At the start of extra time with United in grim need of a stiff livener to raise spirits it was the bewildering kid from Burren Way on the Cregagh estate in East Belfast who dropped a shoulder and cast a spell over the Benfica defence to put his team back in front.

Now George has gone. The night calls his name.

He and his entourage, after paying due reverence to the great and the good at the Russell, shaking hands and enduring the backslapping, have made a swift exit. A smiling George counts down the minutes to his disappearance. He looks at his watch. He cannot wait to leave, it is Georgie time.

Time for a drink, a proper drink. Only then can he truly relax. One, two, three, four then he can be himself. That gentle haze, the confidence to be who they want him to be. And who when drunk he loves to be, 'Georgie boy!'

George and his Mancunian posse, including his best friend Malcolm Wagner, lead the way. The once only dreamed of delights of the West End await the boys from up North. Playing away.

'We are with George' their very own key to the city.

Later George vanishes once more. The boys look all over but he has decided to spend the rest of the evening with his latest girlfriend – the beautiful and blond haired model Jackie Glass. No goodbyes, he simply disappears. Typical George.

But where would they all be without him?

THE HOMECOMING

Late next morning it is a hungover but joyful United party who disembark from Euston Station on a private train to arrive home on Platform 11 at Piccadilly, Manchester. On board the carnival continues. A free bar. More photographs, beaming smiles with the trophy. Two security guards watching its every move.

'Glory, glory Man United!' Supporters at every stop on the way back north, waving and cheering,

Bedecked in scarves. I smile through the window and wave back.

Finally, we hit Manchester and it is utter bedlam. To take us from the railway station to a civic reception at the town hall a twenty year-old red and white open top bus is dusted down. Outside an entire city is close to hysteria. Word gets out, we are back. United are back!

The noise deafens, the excitement mounts.

The short journey to Albert Square from Piccadilly promises to take an eternity as the red throngs occupy every vantage point along the way. Up lamp posts, on top of bus shelters, hanging for grim life onto window ledges.

The bus appears in sight, the players wave and the European cup is held up for a city to see. Manchester goes mad! Seven policemen on black and white horses clear the way.

A smiling Crerand holds the trophy on the front of the bus whilst clasping tight on my shoulders. Paddy is making it clear - this is for me. This is for the old man. The crowd's affections knowing no bounds for they believe I have made their dreams come true.

After a long, drawn out glorious parade myself, the players and officials and family members are ushered off the bus and into the relative sanctity of the town hall. Here we meet and greet the Lord Mayor Alderman, Harold Stockdale.

All dressed up, splendid in traditional black hat and red flowing robes. An important figure on any other day but utterly insignificant on a day like this. I shake Stockdale's hand. Pleasantries and speeches abound. Niceties are exchanged. A short speech. 'I said last night was the greatest of my life, but I don't know whether today is the second greatest as well. I feel very deeply for the enthusiasm which the crowd has shown to the boys.'

The noise from outside remains deafening.

'We want the cup.' They shout my name. So loud it resonates through the walls. A specially erected platform has been set up outside the town hall for us to speak to the 250,000 crowd. Again the cheering: They drown out the Mayor's words, he gives up. There is only one man they wish to listen to.

I step forward to the microphone. I have not slept. My eyes are glued open. The time for weariness has long past. When I rest now I will simply collapse into what I hope is a passage of sleep I come round from. Who was I kidding yesterday. Retire? I look across this vast sea of red and white all chanting my name. I have given everything and sweated blood for this moment. Why should I leave it all behind? No. I am going to go again. I want to retain this beauty and win back the First Division title from Manchester City. This is a red town; I want to keep it that way. For I am not yet ready to slip gently away and write my memoirs. This is my kingdom, my club. My people. I lift up the trophy and declare to all

'I have brought this trophy back to the best supporters in the world. Let us hope this is not the end. Let us hope this is just the beginning.' Manchester goes wild, 'Up the reds' I roar.

Paddy is alongside me. Always loyal. I hand him the trophy. Typical Paddy, he pays tribute to lads like Denis Law out through injury. He thanks Jimmy. I should have done that. Jimmy watches on. He is smiling.

Quiet. No one is chanting his name. Too late to talk now. Too busy, I will speak to him during the summer. Not now, for now is not the time.

So many hands to shake, people to meet and greet. My city needs me, my city wants me. Manchester is me and I am them. My adopted home. For thirty years and more. 'Busby, Busby' they sing. They have embraced and taken me in. This city that has given shelter with open arms to Catholic, Protestant, Jew and Gentile. To Irish, Scot, Italian and Pole and so many other immigrants from near and far. All welcomed with great charm and reverence. This murky half visible cottonopolis that is forever engulfed in smoke and mist from the billowing chimneys poking towards dark miserable skies.

My Manchester.

Where people work hard, love their families, drink their beer and adore their football in equal measure. This place of hope that never gave in. Not to poverty, the Great Depression or Hitler's bombs.

I am going nowhere, for this is my hometown.

2 - AN ILL WIND BLOWS

In the glorious red summer of 1968 I travel to London once more, this time to meet with Her Majesty Queen Elizabeth at the Palace and receive a knighthood. It is a proud moment for me and my family.

Jean beams. I look splendid if I say so myself in top hat and tails. Her Majesty is delightful. So charming. 'Mr Busby' she addresses me as. 'Congratulations on that wonderful victory at Wembley.'

'Thank you Ma'am, it was a long time coming.'

She looks me straight in the eyes. 'Those poor boys that were killed at Munich. They would have been very proud.'

I smile. 'We won it for them Ma'am. I could feel their presence.'

When Jean asks me what we spoke of I fill up. She understands and simply takes my arm to greet the many cameras and photographers waiting outside. We pose outside the palace. 'Can life get any better Sir Matt?' shouts out a reporter.

'Oh yes!' I laugh, 'I have not quite finished yet.'

★

Meanwhile, in sun drenched Majorca, Busby's jewel in the crown is having a riot. Georgie boy and his chaps, 'the Mancunian posse', 'the Best set,' including friend and sidekick Manchester City star Mike Summerbee, are letting their hair down.

Under Spanish skies this Irish pied piper is followed

by hordes of girls wherever he goes. On the beach George take his pick then everyone grabs seconds.

The beer and wine flows, the photographers never stop snapping and the party continues until the sun comes up once more. It is paradise on earth for the shy unassuming Belfast boy whose mesmeric balance, dancing feet and explosive shooting have catapulted him amongst the world's best. There have been footballing superstars before but never like George.

Never like George.

But as night falls and the music starts up and the girls crowd around, such plaudits can wait. Too much fun to be had. So many girls, so little time.

So little time in the glorious red summer of 1968.

★

Before the new season begins I find myself in Ireland with my good friend and United scout Billy Behan. We are in his house and good old Billy has dug out a grand bottle of Johnny Walker as we speak about what lies ahead. I am laying out to him my aims, my ambitions.

'I want to prove Bill that there is no such thing as a rainbow's end. I want to go on and do it all again.'

Bill smiles. 'Rainbow's end' he says quietly and shakes his head. 'There is nothing magical about them. Rainbows just fade away and die. You have to ensure that does not happen to us Matt.'

I put down my glass and Billy immediately goes to refill it. I am concerned; my old friend has something on his mind. 'What is bothering you Billy?'

He pours himself a stiff one and looks me straight in the eye. 'There is a storm coming Matt, there is an ill wind blowing, I can feel it. We desperately need new blood. We must buy, we need to freshen up. They can't go on forever. Denis is injury prone, Nobby too. Bobby, Paddy and Bill are not getting any younger. As for George? He can't do it all on his own. It is time to act. Alan Ball and Mike England, they are the ones for us.' I listen intently at my old friend's words. I smile. Bill continues: 'They are United class, they have huge hearts, they have fire in their eyes, and they pass and move on the ball and know the game. We could have reared them ourselves Matt. These boys were born to be red devils.'

I suddenly realise this is Jimmy talking. It seems my pals think I need a nudge. I try hard not to look insulted. But Billy has irked me. I don't say anything. I am fifty-nine years old. I have been knighted and I am the manager of the European Champions. And I know what I am doing. Winning the cup put £250,000 in United's coffers. My coffers. The money is there to spend if needed. Louis will do as he is told. Louis is my man.

It has been his money but I have made him into the man he is. I gave him respect. He recently put a new ten year contract in my pocket. I never had to ask. 'Thanks for everything Matt,' he said. 'Stay as long as you want.' Because he knows I know what I am doing. I am happy with my lot. I am content. The team does not require major surgery. No matter what Billy or Jimmy or those outside these walls declare. Old Trafford is my footballing Camelot. So let them come and try to topple us from our perch. Let them come.

Right or wrong I owe a fierce loyalty to those whom have delivered me the holy grail of the European cup. I am nowhere near yet of sufficient heart and mind to even contemplate ending relationships with these boys. Maybe I am blinded by a father's love?

This ill wind Billy spoke of. Maybe it does blow unnoticed in my eyes and is heading ever closer north. Maybe it will turn into a hurricane and blow our walls down? We shall see.

This season the challenge will come on three fronts. Firstly, we have to win back the league title off Manchester City, to shut Malcolm Allison up. Then we must retain the European Cup. Also we must prepare for the exciting but equally daunting prospect of a two-legged showdown for the World Club Championship against Argentine and South American champions Estudiantes.

My good friend Jock Stein has already marked my card to watch our backs over there. Last year his Glasgow Celtic side experienced a bloodbath. He also told me a story of how the referee was pulled out of a hat of three names but later he was informed each piece of paper had the same name on it! They were spat at, mauled and bitten and his boys fought fire with fire. He swore never to take part again and has urged me not to play them.

'It will happen to you Matt,' he claimed. 'They want it so badly, they cannot help themselves.'

But despite my old friend's advice I feel we must rise above such concerns and do what is right. We will play the Argentines.

★

The curtain draws back: it is Saturday 10th August 1968 and 61,310 supporters are packed into Old Trafford to witness our first league game of the season against

Everton. The European Cup is on show. It is shirt-sleeve weather; a beautiful day and the sun is casting dancing shadows over the pitch and grandstands. Our mood is one of supreme optimism. Ten of my team who played in the previous May against Benfica will start, with one exception. A royal exception. Blow the trumpets for the return of the king. Denis is back. Denis Law, king of the Stretford End has recovered from injury.

The line up: Stepney, Brennan, Dunne, Crerand, Foulkes, Stiles, Best, Kidd, Charlton, Law and Aston.

I wave to the crowd, they sing my name and I take my place on the bench next to Jimmy. They don't sing Jimmy's name. Jimmy is quiet.

Everton have come to attack. The wise and the good of football fancy them to go close this year to the championship. My pal Harry Catterick signed Alan Ball to reinforce an already strong team. He needs him, we do not. They start well and are all over us.

Their midfield trio of Howard Kendall, Colin Harvey and Alan Ball pass and move. Pass and move. We cannot get near them. They are lightning quick in both mind and action. In comparison we appear cumbersome, pedantic. For twenty minutes it is a mismatch. Only Alex Stepney keeps us alive. Thirty-six year-old Bill Foulkes is being given a torrid time by the visitor's young, powerful centre-forward Joe Royle. Bill is struggling, the crowd are agitated.

'Come on you reds, sort it out,' they shout. Wembley memories are fading fast 'Get off the pitch Foulkes, you are useless,' somebody screams behind me. Poor Bill, have they forgotten Madrid already?

Others just shout 'Give it to George. Just give it to bloody George!' Suddenly as if sparked by a rush of electricity beneath their feet Best, Law and Charlton come alive. Bobby accelerates over the halfway line. The roar goes up; Denis pulls wide taking worried blue shirts with him. Nobody spots George Best but Bobby spots him, he reads George's mind. Best races towards Everton goalkeeper Gordon West who looks around for help but he is alone and helpless. George picks his spot and with effortless aplomb he despatches the ball into the net.

We lead after being outplayed. All is well again as Old Trafford relaxes and normal service is resumed. But all is not really well for Everton are coming back hard and are all over us. It has to happen and who else but Alan Ball, playing with a point to prove, who smashes home past Alex Stepney. He stares across at me as if to suggest 'I could have been yours'.

'He wanted to come' Jimmy mumbles under his breath. 'We could have had him.' I hear it but ignore him. Four minutes is all it has taken. But I have George. He picks up a loose ball and sets off. Old Trafford rises once more: Past one and two, George goes on, tackles slipped like a child dancing through raindrops. Bobby Charlton finds space, he shouts 'George, George over here, George please. George gives me the bloody ball!' Bobby has his hand raised; he gets the pass and thunders a ferocious shot past a diving West. 2-1. Old Trafford erupts and we lead again. Half time comes and goes and Everton press and press.

Wave after wave of blue shirted attacks. We buckle but hold. Just. I am worried at what I see. The final whistle brings victory but plenty of doubts. The crowd chants my name and, thank God for George, we have been lucky. The cheers from the terraces come tinged with relief. United are ragged, second best. Foulkes, Crerand, Stiles, Law, all are off colour and look more grey than red. Only George, always George. He has played Everton on his own. FA Cup holders West Bromwich Albion are up next. A battle at the Hawthorns. The Baggies will be waiting. Keen for a red devil scalp. Just four days till then and thank the heavens for George.

Wednesday 14th August 1968: I keep the same line-up and after twenty minutes we have been blitzed. On a warm evening in the West Midlands, with a home crowd delighting in the dismemberment of the reigning European champions, the Baggies rip through our defence at will.

A fourth minute header from centre forward Jeff Astle begins the rout. Two more swiftly follow from Astle again and Tony Brown. Crosses rain in from all angles. We are under siege and cannot get going. Alex Stepney has the look of a man ducking bullets. Bill Foulkes is exposed. Poor, poor Bill. Age cruelly takes no prisoners and he is run ragged.

The entire defence is indecisive and outgunned. This is embarrassing for our travelling supporters. As half time approaches Bobby fires one back to give the scoreline a modicum of respectability but in all reality it has been a rout. In the second half we rally but to no avail.

A huge roar greets the final whistle. It is a famous night at the Hawthorns. The great Manchester United have been slain. Myself and Jimmy rise from our seats. The red shirts slump off the field. Heads down.

Defeated. Great names, huge names but games are not won on reputation. I need to have a word for this cannot go on.

I can feel Jimmy's eyes in the back of my head. He says nothing but says everything. I don't turn around but a part of me feels feel like doing so and screaming at him. 'Where are your apples? Your bloody ripe apples to help my boys out! Why has the well run dry?'

Maybe he hasn't got it any more, maybe he has lost it? A bad night at the Hawthorns. A bloody awful night.

★

The champions are next up. Manchester City at Maine Road: The derby. Bell, Lee and Summerbee. Last season's dramatic last day finale when our defeat at home to Sunderland and City winning at Newcastle conspired to send the title to Maine Road still cuts deep.

The wound is deep and painful. City, champions of England and kings of Manchester.

We have injuries and changes will have to be made. Fresh blood and young legs. Big Bill and Law have knocks and will not play. Paddy Crerand will be rested as will Shay Brennan. My boys will be hurt but I have no choice. I admit it, I erred. We should have bought fresh blood, red blood.

Derby day: Saturday 17th August 1968. The newspapers are hailing this the biggest Manchester derby ever. The European Champions versus the League Champions. The pride of Manchester at stake. I meet my opposite numbers Joe Mercer and Malcolm Allison. Myself and

Joe are good friends, not pals, wartime friends. Malcolm is younger, He is brash. Malcolm likes to talk. He is outspoken, loud but a talented coach. He and Joe do not always see eye to eye but they make a good team. Like me and Jimmy once. I adore Joe; my generation, a proper football man. A man of substance.

City are not just looking to take our mantle domestically, they are aiming to also win the European cup. Malcolm has already declared, much to Joe's concern: 'We will win the European cup. European football is full of cowards and we will terrorise them with our power and attacking football.' Malcolm has no fear but we will have to wait and see on that. City are a fine team: Mulhearn, Kennedy, Pardoe, Doyle, Heslop, Oakes, Lee, Bell, Summerbee, Owen, Young. They are confident and cocky. After so many years in United's shade. Now they rule Manchester. For the moment. We must get it back. Must.

63,000 cram tight inside Maine Road for our visit. The atmosphere is tense, poisonous almost. I hate it. Bottles are thrown by both sets of supporters. There is fighting outside the ground.

I make four changes. Youngsters Frank Kopel, John Fitzpatrick and Alan Gowling come in. Plus David Sadler. It is good to have John back. I have told Fitzpatrick to stick tight to Colin Bell. John is no Nobby but he has a good temperament.

I have told him make the contest ten against ten. But I am worried, the stakes are high. Bell, if on form, can rip my boys apart. A draw will suffice to keep pride intact. Mancunian pride. A stand off occurs. Like us, City are more intent on not losing and a goalless if volatile affair suits all. Fitzpatrick handles Bell's midfield breaks with impressive tenacity. And I have to admit in a sometimes brutal manner.

City fight fire with fire. Doyle, Summerbee and Lee kicking anything in red when the chance arises. Despite this being no classic contest, there remain moments of high drama. And sadness. My twenty-two year-old Wembley hero against Benfica, John Aston, breaks his leg after an accidental collision with Francis Lee. All the players feel sick, we all do. John is carried off, his season wrecked.

During the ninety minutes one flash of genius stands out. One that takes the breath away. One worth tenfold the entrance fee for red or blue. One that causes grown men to watch open-mouthed in wonder. It's the reason I cannot give this game up. And it comes from the dazzling feet of George Best. A wandering, seemingly uninterested George suddenly ignites into life and scares the living hell out of them. Roaming on the edge of the City penalty area he takes a sorcerer's touch to kill the ball stone dead. Then in the same movement unleashes a savage strike that almost breaks the Manchester City crossbar.

Many spectators behind the goal cross themselves and thank God for the woodwork, for if George's hit had been five inches higher it would surely have ripped somebody's head clear off.

This apart we are shot shy. I admit it - we are struggling and need reinforcements. I need more firepower. I mention this to Jimmy in the dressing room. He agrees and tells me we have received a phone call off a friendly journalist to say Leeds United and Don Revie are on the verge of signing Burnley's exciting twenty-three year-old Scottish right winger Willie

Morgan. He wants to know if we would be interested because Willie wants to come here. He fancies the glory. Needs must – I move fast. I am a big admirer of the fast, elusive and skilful Morgan. He is one for us.

'Ring Jeff Mitten,' I say to Jimmy, 'ask him to get hold of Morgan. Tell him to hold tight and that we are coming.'

Jimmy nods. 'It makes sense Matt.'

He goes to ring Mitten who is a real old fashioned Mancunian character. A fixer of deals both in business and sport. He gets things done. Mitten visits Morgan and his head is turned. He agrees to come and stalls on Leeds. I now have to speak to a man who makes my blood boil: Burnley chairman Bob Lord.

We have history, bad blood. In Munich's dark aftermath Bob Lord claimed 'United should be left to live or die. It is not up to anyone else to save them. Let them live or die.'

'Live or die?'

Well we lived and he is quick to accept our club record of £117,000. A deal is struck but I don't shake his hand. I will never shake his hand. It is simply a question of needs must and I don't wish him or his club well.

So it is Old Trafford not Elland Road for Willie Morgan. I shake Willie's hand and I ask him what swung the deal? Willie smiles. 'It was easy' he replies. 'It was Jeff's opening line. My name is Jeff Mitten and I have been sent by Manchester United and Matt Busby.'

This boy will do for me. Willie asks for the number seven shirt, 'George's shirt.'

'No problem son' I tell him. 'George won't mind, he can have eleven.'

'Also, Mr Busby, in the past I have had problems with Nobby Stiles.'

Jimmy laughs. 'You and the rest of the world. Well your problems are over now Willie lad.' He puts his arm around Willie's shoulders. 'Nobby is on your side now.'

I make Willie our highest paid player. I warn him 'Talk of money at Old Trafford causes bad blood and will not be tolerated.' He shakes his head. He knows, Willie is not daft. I would hate George, Denis or Bobby to learn he is earning more: £165 a week, £20 a point plus bonuses for playing in the cup and scoring goals. A sign of the times I am afraid.

Crazy money.

Willie feels his boat has come in. He fancies the big stage and there is no bigger stage than Old Trafford. Willie fancies the glory. Willie fancies himself. No one has a bigger love of Willie Morgan than Willie Morgan. Willie looks in the mirror and he sees George Best. He hates this and tells all who will listen and those who won't.

'I am as good as George Best. I am better than Bestie. Me, Willie Morgan. I will show them. Wee Willie Morgan on the wing.' Willie Morgan signs for Manchester United and on the same day, Saturday 24th August 1968, with wee Willie watching from the Old Trafford stands, gazing around at his new kingdom, a desperate United are duly hammered 4-0 by a rampant Chelsea. It is our biggest home defeat since 1959.

Suddenly Willie wonders, 'What the bloody hell have I done?' Happily four days later he makes his debut at home against Tottenham Hotspur and along with George runs riot as United beat the visitors 3-1.

Willie waves to the adoring Stretford End as they chant his name. His name, not George's, he loves it. Best, Law, Charlton and now Morgan.

In Willie's opinion not necessarily in that order. Just give him time…

3 - WELCOME TO BUENOS AIRES

It is late evening on Saturday 21st September 1968. After beating Newcastle 3-1 at Old Trafford, with two goals from George, who else, and one from Denis we begin our epic journey across the globe to face Estudiantes in the first leg of the World Club Championship.

Four wins in our opening fourteen games means it is good for us to have a break. But this is taking it to the extreme. I am sat next to Jimmy. He is staring out of the window. He does not appear in talkative mood so I close my eyes. Then I hear his voice.

'Have you ever thought what you are going to do when this is all over?' I open my eyes, I am shocked but happy Jimmy wants to chat. An air hostess appears.

'Two large whiskies please lass.' I give Jimmy a sideways glance and he nods. We take our drinks.

'Ah Jimmy, it will never be over for me. It is like a drug, I could not just walk away. You are no different; they will have to carry us both out of Old Trafford in boxes.'

Jimmy smiles, 'Aye,' he says, 'even then they better make sure the coffins are nailed down.'

We both laugh. I sigh. 'I know I am in the final strait and I am so very tired. I'm always tired Jimmy. Maybe soon something will have to give? My back is not getting any better. My legs they,' I stop. I always feel guilty moaning about my ailments from the crash. Jean always says I was blessed to survive, that my faith saved me. Most of my boys never had the chance to moan so I like to believe I was lucky. Though there have been nights, many nights when I have not felt lucky. Never mind blessed. The memories never leave.

'Do you still have the dreams?' asks Jimmy

For a moment I am stunned. How does he know about my nightmares? My returning to that damned runway. I never told Jimmy, I never told anyone. Except Jean. My Jean… and then I realise.

'Agnes mentioned this to you right. She heard off Jean?'

Jimmy nods, 'Jean wanted to know if I had them too.'

'And do you?' I ask. Praying he says no.

He smiles and takes a drink. 'The same, always the same. I am at The Cliff on the pitch and facing me I can see the boys who were killed. They are kicking a ball around. I try going over to them but no matter how hard I can't get there. I either fall over or my legs won't move. I am shouting their names but none hear me. I see Duncan. I pray for him to turn around and say for one last time, "Alright Jimmy". But it never happens. Then they start to fade away. And then I wake up.' Jimmy wipes his eyes and takes a huge breath. 'But happily not anymore, not since last May.' He smiles.

'I am the same,' I admit. 'Since we won the bloody thing the nightmares have ceased thank God.'

Jimmy looks at me. 'You are back on the runway?'

I nod slowly. 'Always. What is strange, is when I wake up I can feel the cold. I swear there is snow melting in the bed sheets.'

Jimmy puts his hand on mine. 'Let us have a toast Matt.' He clinks our plastic cups-still half filled with whisky. 'To a bunch of bouncing Busby babes,' he says.

'To our finest red apples' I reply. We drink and both go silent for a while. But it is a good silence. A peaceful silence.

And yet still things remain unsaid.

★

From London to Paris to Madrid then a torturous ten hour overnight flight to Rio de Janeiro. Before finally a last three hour haul to Buenos Aires. And then we arrive.

'Welcome to Buenos Aires Señor Busby,' remarks the smiling young army officer as he offers me his hand to shake. A handsome fellow with a film star pencil thin moustache. He removes his cap and snaps to attention. 'It is a huge honour to have the great Manchester United on our soil.' But there is something in his eyes that suggests he does not really mean it.

I look around and the huge swathes of people who have turned out to greet us is staggering.

'If this is a lynch mob we are truly buggered,' jokes Jimmy. Our English World Cup winning duo of Nobby and Bobby are a little wary as we make our way into the terminal to greet the baying hordes.

'This lot hate you more than we Scots do lads, so good luck,' remarks Paddy. The fall out from England's infamous quarter final clash with Argentina when an incensed Alf Ramsey labelled the Argentines 'animals' still cuts deep. I worry what awaits my boys.

The Argentine welcoming committee are brandishing placards: 'Bobby Charlton, El Campione.' 'Denis Law, El Rei.' 'George Best, El Beatle,' and finally young Norbert's banner reads 'Nobby Stiles, El Bandido!'

'Bloody charming,' quips poor Nobby. He points across, 'I come all this way and look at that.' I put my arm around Nobby. He will be fine, though I did notice one particular chap make a throat cutting gesture in his direction. Nobby does not see this and I say nothing for there is no point causing him more angst.

Behind a wall of police, hundreds crowd around as we walk through the airport. They appear a friendly lot overall. Loud and passionate but no real signs of what Jock talked about. The hatred and the bile Celtic experienced has not yet shown itself. Nobby's placard and throat cutting gesture apart.

The same army officer approaches this time with soldiers on each side of him. They are armed with rifles slung over their shoulders. He motions for us to follow him. 'Come Señor, your coach is waiting.'

As we board there are boos and catcalls from the gathered locals and all are aimed at an increasingly perturbed Nobby.

'Blimey Nob, I'm not sitting next to you,' jokes Paddy.

'Why?' asks Nobby.

'Because if the sniper misses you he gets me!'

'Oh thanks Pat' he sighs. 'I really needed that.'

The journey itself is a hair raising experience as we set off with an army and police escort that would do justice to a visiting Pope. At one point the driver swerves suddenly to avoid a dead horse in the middle of the road.

'Blimey you don't see that in Manchester,' jokes Kiddo.

'You do in Collyhurst,' replies Nobby.'

After a short thirty minute drive we arrive at what

will be our base for the duration of the stay. The Hindu Golf club. A grand old rambling country manor. The staff are all lined up outside to greet us, even at this late hour. As we disembark they all start to applaud. A nice touch.

I tell Jack and Wilf to ensure the lads get their sleeping pills and go straight to bed. The Argentines have lined up a busy schedule. Whether this is designed to tire us before Wednesday's match or not I am not sure. There are invitations galore: a polo match, a golf tournament, a barbecue with the Buenos Aires mayor. And tomorrow we are meeting the Estudiantes delegation, including their President Mariano Mangano, and players for a banquet at the stadium. Hopefully that should break the ice and a few drinks together will ensure the game passes without incident.

Later that night I am stood with Jack and Wilf at the hotel bar. We are discussing, over a nightcap, the events of our first day on a foreign continent, when Jimmy enters the room. Wilf immediately points across to a grand white piano. 'That has your name on it Jimmy mate.'

Jimmy smiles. 'I am dog tired, Wilf but bugger me if I am not going to wrap my fingers around that beauty.'

I order Jimmy a beer and the barman takes it over. He places it on a small coaster on top of the piano.

Jimmy thanks him. He lifts the piano lid. He practices the keys, he smiles wide and gives us a double thumbs up.

'Go on Jimmy,' shouts Jack. 'Give us a song.'

Jimmy begins:

> *Pack up all my care and woe,*
> *Here I go, Singing low,*

John Ludden

Bye bye blackbird,
Where somebody waits for me,
Sugar's sweet, so is she,
Bye bye Blackbird!

No one here can love or understand me,
Oh, what hard luck stories they all hand me,
Make my bed and light the light,
I'll be home late tonight,
Blackbird bye bye.

Pack up all my cares and woe,
Here I go,
Singing low,
Bye (bye) bye (bye) blackbird.
Where somebody waits for me,
Sugar's sweet, so is she,
Bye (bye) bye (bye) blackbird.

No one here can love or understand me,
Oh, what hard luck stories they all hand me,
Make my bed, light that light,
I'll be home late tonight,
Blackbird…

Make my bed and light the light,
I'll be home late tonight,
Leave you bird jet in the sky
Toodle oo! Farewell! bye bye!

Blackbird
(Blackbird, Blackbird)
We'll take the flying little blackbird bye!'

By the last line Jimmy has tears falling down his cheeks. Why does he do this to himself?

★

Next Evening. So this is how it is going to be? Jock was right after all and from now on my guard is up. After an hour's journey to get here it appears our supposed hosts for this grand occasion, our opponents, are not turning up for the pre match banquet.

So much for the hand of friendship? One who has bothered is Estudiantes President Manoga. He greets me warmly with an all embracing bear hug of a long lost brother. 'Mr Busby, an honour and a privilege to meet you in person. You are a legend in my country.'

'Thank you Mr President' I reply. 'Now can you tell me, where is your team?'

He goes on to inform me that his coach Osvaldo Zubeldia approached him this afternoon and was uncomfortable with tonight's arrangements. He claimed it is not the 'done thing to dine with your enemy on the eve of battle. This is a game for men.' And he sees no point in the teams 'kissing each other?'

I would have given anything to see one of their players attempt to kiss Paddy or Nobby. 'So why invite us in the first place then?' I ask, smiling to hide my disgust.

Manoga shrugs his shoulders. I ask the president to excuse me and I walk across to Jimmy. I whisper in his ear, 'Tell the boys we stay on for twenty minutes. We sign autographs, shake a few hands and pose for a few autographs and then we are out of here. This is a set up.'

I make my way back over to a flustered Manoga. 'Well Mr President,' I take his arm, 'I did not get dressed up for nothing. Shall we go and say hello to a few of your guests who have had the good grace to show up.' His face is a fixed smile. He nods but knows what I am thinking. He does not know what to say. I get a tap on the shoulder and turn around. It is Jack Crompton.

'Excuse me boss, can I have a quick word?'

I smile, 'of course Jack,' I turn to Manoga, 'excuse me.'

Jack appears pensive. He points across to the players who are getting stuck into the buffet. 'Boss do you think it is a good idea for the boys to touch the food and drink?'

Jack is right, at this moment in time I would not put anything past the Argentines. I can see Manoga staring over. 'Change of plan' I say to Jack. 'Pass the word that we are going.' I walk back across to Manoga. 'You will have to excuse me Mr President but I am taking my boys back to the club. I think we have already stomached enough for one night.'

'Mr Busby, I must insist you remain a while longer. It is the essence of bad manners to leave so early.'

'Sir,' I reply, 'it is the essence of bad manners not to turn up at all. I bid you goodnight.'

With that we are away. Two can play at these silly mind games. They will never catch on.

Boca stadium: Wednesday 25th September 1968
Estudiantes 1 Manchester United 0

Thru the blurry mist of an exploding red smoke bomb that makes the stadium shudder, walk my boys into a footballing Armageddon. This is not a football match, it an ambush. A mugging in a dark alley. Never have I been more sickened by events on a soccer field.

Estudiantes are a disgrace: spitting, biting, pulling hair, simply nothing is beneath them. I hold them in contempt. I hold myself in contempt for putting my boys, my club, through this debacle.

We have lost 1-0 and to be honest I care little. I just wish to get home and away from this fiasco. It was a scandalous display of bad sportsmanship, the like of which I have never witnessed before. This lot make Leeds United look like choir boys. Many times I am off our bench to complain. I glare across to their bench but Zubeldia will never meet my eyes. How can they lower themselves to play like this?

George is under constant attack whilst Bobby is caught by a tackle so high it would have been frowned upon at throwing out time on Sauciehall Street in Glasgow. A fuming Denis in the changing rooms afterwards describes it as 'like playing against Apaches.'

To nobody's surprise, least of all his, Nobby was stitched up and sent off. Head butted off the ball in the opening moments by one of their best but most brutal players Carlos Bilardo, who I was informed beforehand is training to be a doctor. Judging by this performance a career in butchery might be more apt.

After a first half booking for what I can only assume was for standing to close to his opponent, he was inevitably dismissed in the second half. Nobby had beaten their offside trap to race clean through. The linesman's flag stayed down, only then for the referee to blow his whistle. It was a scandalous decision. I was on the touchline going mad when I saw Bobby go over to Nob who said to him: 'We have got no chance tonight Bob, the referee is blind.'

As the referee, a Mr Miranda from Paraguay,

approached them he shouts over: 'What did you say Stiles?'

'He is fucking deaf as well,' Nobby replies.

Then out comes a red card. Ridiculous! This is not football. Welcome to Buenos Aires? You must be joking. Now I am determined to win this trophy. I care nothing that it is deemed unofficial by the football hierarchy. For some things matter more than what is written. These people, Zubeldia and his thugs, have spat on everything I have ever believed in. Now it has become a matter of honour. Make no mistake, there is an evil creeping into our game. It has been around for a few years now. Whether it has been brought about by greater financial rewards or the greater desire for victory it's tainting soccer from top to bottom. Beating Estudiantes at Old Trafford might not turn back the tide but it will give me satisfaction for what has gone on here tonight. I find it impossible to believe the country that gave us the wonderful Alfredo di Stefano, the finest footballer I have ever seen and a gentleman to match, can lower itself to put up with the likes of Estudiantes and their desperadoes.

So let them come to Manchester. Let them bring their vile tactics, their thuggery and their gamesmanship. Their spitting and their bile. Let them come for we will be waiting. Given a fair wind a decent referee and an on fire Bobby, Denis and George we can give them a good hiding.

Bring it on.

4 - KIND HEARTS & CORNER KICKS

On the same evening we put seven past a spirited Waterford team at Old Trafford to continue our defence of the European Cup, our friends across the city are knocked out by the unfancied Turks of Fenerbahce. Malcolm Allison's brave if foolhardy words that Manchester City would 'terrify Europe' now sound so hollow. I feel for Joe but like our supporters I cannot help but find it all mildly amusing. Malcolm is always quick in the newspapers to point out our misfortunes, maybe he will learn to keep his powder dry if they ever make it back into the European Cup again?

Whilst our form in Europe remains fine, performances in the league leave much to be desired. Four wins in fourteen games and we find ourselves in mid table and heading the wrong way.

Now that is not Manchester United. Since joining us Willie has yet to reach the level I know he is capable of. Only George, always George, is operating at full tilt. Full of tricks, elusive as the wind. So brave, a truly marvellous footballer.

I sense amongst the older players no lack of effort; we are simply not playing well. In finally winning the European Cup, after striving so long and finally reaching the top of the mountain, I fear there is an apprehension amongst them. None dare whisper or ever think it. But like me after years of chasing the dream, now it has been realised the question has to be asked: what next?

Also hearing the same voice for so long may no longer be such a good thing. Bobby, Denis, Paddy, Nobby – they have kind hearts and may not admit such but it is only natural. It is human nature. The younger ones I can still influence but in my head the fires too are waning. They also may nod their heads and say 'yes boss, will do boss,' but on the pitch it appears as if a light, though not fully diminished, has definitely dimmed. Nothing lasts forever. Me more than anyone realises this. I have learned life is nothing more than periods of brief snatches in which you take what you can, while you can. For any moment it could all end. And so I think it might be time. I think it may almost be over.

But first I will attempt to put right the events of Buenos Aires and settle a score with Estudiantes.

Saturday October 12th 1968 Anfield
Liverpool 2 Manchester United 0

Another defeat. Four days before the return leg with the Argentines we travel to my good friend Bill Shankly's Liverpool with a much under-strength team and duly find ourselves well beaten. Hampered by injuries and with one eye firmly focused on Wednesday night, the two goal defeat should have been more and leaves us only four points off the bottom of the table. I take responsibility because I took a huge risk by playing so many of my younger players. They gave everything but it was not enough.

John Fitzpatrick, Jim Ryan, Steve James, Frank Kopel, Carlo Sartori and Alan Gowling. All good boys but I fear not a vintage harvest of red apples. The game against Estudiantes features high in my priorities and

I was chancing we may get a bloody nose in front of a roaring Kop with this side. And that is exactly what we got. An early headed goal past Alex from Ian St John signalled Liverpool's attacking intention and from that moment on it was wave after wave of red shirts. We held on until eight minutes from time when Allun Evans side-footed Ian Callaghan's cross home to send the 51,000 crowd wild.

A mismatch.

After the game I am sat in Bill's office. Just me and him and a pot of tea. Bill is in fine spirits and so he should be for he has built something special at this place. Two league titles already won, Bill walks on water around these parts. His team are an extension of him on the pitch: raging with fire and passion. They don't just attack you, they overwhelm and destroy you. The scousers adore him and he they. Bill has no other hobbies. His every waking moment is dedicated to football and Liverpool. The game to him is everything. He is similar to Jimmy, they could be blood brothers. They see the game as a poet sees the world. They can find beauty amid the flying tackles on a mud swamp of a pitch. They wax lyrical about sweating blood for the cause. They are football men.

Before Munich I was like them. Football was more important than life or death. But I witnessed and suffered too much. I paid my dues with winning the European Cup, now a sense of perspective exists in my life, one I never thought possible in years gone by. That there are more things important in life than the game. Though for the life of me I would never argue that point with my friend here today.

'So you're going back to war with the Argies then?'

asks Bill, as he pours me a cup of tea.

I smile. 'A few of the lads have scores to settle but I have stressed the need not to get involved with these people Bill. Some of the tricks they pulled over there were beyond belief.'

Bill laughs. 'But who is going to keep you and Jimmy calm?'

'Jimmy is a lot calmer around the dressing room these days. As for me. Ah, I am tired Bill. Always so damned tired.'

Bill looks at me concerned. 'Are you thinking of calling it a day, Matt?'

I shrug my shoulders. 'Maybe. I think twenty-four years in the hot-seat is more than enough for anyone old friend.'

Bill shakes his head 'The thought of retirement scares me to death, Matt. I could not live without all this. This city, these Liverpudlians, have got under my skin. They have adopted me as one of their own. I live now only to bring them untold pleasure and joy. They call me the Messiah and I will not rest until I bring the European Cup to Liverpool. And then I would want to do it again. And again. I have had two goes but the second time I ran into a young Dutch lad called Johann Cruyff at Ajax. What a player! A ghost on the pitch. You cannot get near him. Magnificent!'

I nod in agreement. 'A wonderful talent Bill.'

He continues: 'Ah we would have beaten them at Anfield if it was not for the fog. We could not see him.' I laugh. 'Don't do anything on impulse Matt,' Bill urges. 'Think long and hard. Maybe take a break for a while. Take Lady Jean on a world cruise. Let the sun seep into your bones.'

Bill is a wonderful man and a real friend. He is generous and kind and his advice is heartfelt. There are times I worry for him because I know that this game of ours has a horrible habit of spitting you out like garbage when your time is up. At the moment Bill is riding the crest of a red tidal wave. But things change and for someone like Bill, without football there is no tomorrow.

★

They have come to Manchester bearing gifts, smiling and shaking hands and ruffling the heads of schoolboys waiting for their autographs at the airport. Estudiantes have landed on our doorsteps and are on a goodwill blitz the likes I have never witnessed. Everyone who moves around them are showered with gifts or given a team pennant or a scarf. The President is coming across as an Argentine Father Christmas. 'Manchester is a wonderful city,' I hear him say on the television news, 'and I cannot wait to meet up again with my good friend Sir Matt Busby.' Good friend? Señor Manoga has obviously forgotten our last brief encounter.

The Argentine party are staying near where Bobby lives in Lymm. He was telling me how the locals all find them so charming and gracious. Indeed one said to Bobby 'What is all this rubbish about the Argies being thugs and animals? They are lovely!'

A delegation of their players including one of the major villains of the first leg Carlos Bilardo turned up at Bobby's front door carrying flowers for his wife and toys for his children. It ended with Bobby, Norma and the girls having their photograph taken with the Argentines in the back garden. It is all a little unnerving.

Wednesday 16th October 1968
Old Trafford – Manchester United v Estudiantes.

That same afternoon the Argentines lay flowers on the Munich memorial. President Manoga spoke well and I feel from the heart. 'Let us forget our little differences in Buenos Aires, Señor Busby and enjoy a wonderful game of football this evening.' I shake his hand: maybe leopards can change their spots. Maybe?

Nobby apart, who is suspended, we are at full strength. The team: Stepney, Brennan, Dunne, Crerand, Foulkes, Sadler, Morgan, Kidd, Charlton, Law, Best and Sartori. I have selected young Carlo to play wide and to hand George a free role. To let him wreak havoc across their front line. Find the Argentine weakness and expose it. The flame haired Collyhurst born Carlo, of Italian extraction, whose father owns a knife sharpening business, has earned this opportunity. In no way cut from the same cloth as a George or even Willie Morgan, Sartori will give me everything and I cannot ask for more.

Old Trafford feels on fire tonight, there is a tension in the air. It is electric. 60,000 are in here ready to proclaim Manchester United as champions of the world. I enter the dressing room and it goes deathly quiet. The rattle of studs the only sound. The players are sat waiting for my final words. I tell them 'This is not Argentina. This is Manchester. Our patch. So keep yours heads and hurt them with your skill. But most importantly relax and enjoy yourself. Play football. Play your game as you have been taught. The Manchester United way. Good luck boys.' I turn to go but stand at the door and leave the last words to be delivered by

Jimmy. I want to watch this.

All eyes fall upon him. With hands in pockets he approaches the boys and you can hear a pin drop. He looks around at their attentive stares. It is like they are hypnotised. He begins. 'Well boys this is it. I have always insisted, always told you, Manchester United is the greatest club in the world. Tonight you have the opportunity to prove it. To make it happen. So don't waste it. This lot you are up against?' Jimmy raises his fist. 'Bloody Estudiantes.' His grizzled Welsh accent suddenly taking on a menacing tone. 'They don't belong on the same pitch as you. They are nothing but a bunch of cheats and cowards.'

He points out Bobby with his finger. 'Now Bobby Charlton here has won a World Cup and a European Cup, haven't you Bobby Lad?'

Bobby offers a shy grin. 'Yes Jimmy,' he replies.

Jimmy singles out Denis Law. 'Denis here has played for the Rest of the World, haven't you Lawman?' Denis smiles and nods whilst tying his boots 'And I scored.' he replies.

'And he scored,' laughs Jimmy. They all do.

Jimmy looks over to George. He is enjoying this command performance.

'Aah Georgie Best,' sighs Jimmy. He walks over to a grinning George and puts a hand on his shoulders. 'See this boy here, this mere slip of a kid from Belfast. Well God did not fool around when he made George. The Almighty must have been in a good mood that day because he sprinkled on our George here more than his fair share of angel dust. And he also gave him a name, just so no one could ever doubt. The Best.'

Jimmy moves on, past Willie Morgan, who appears

disappointed to have been ignored. Instead he stops at an extremely nervous looking young Carlo Sartori. Jimmy sports a huge grin and sits down next to Carlo. He puts an arm around his shoulders.

'One of my red apples here is Carlo, aren't you boy?' Carlo nods; he is fidgeting with his hands and looking toward the floor. Clearly uneasy. Jimmy senses this. He says quietly so only Carlo can hear. 'Now listen son, you would not be in this room if me and Matt did not think you were ready. Now I want you to go out on that pitch tonight and prove us right okay!' Jimmy grabs hold of Carlos' shirt. 'This shirt you are wearing here means you are privileged. You are special. Because this means you now walk with giants. Now you go show those Argies how a nice Italian boy from Collyhurst can play football like a Red Devil.'

Carlo looks at Jimmy. He is ready. 'I won't let you down Jimmy,' he says.

'Impossible lad. Impossible,' replies Jimmy as he ruffles Carlos's hair, before returning to the centre of the dressing room. He again faces the players. For a second he says nothing. Before raising his fist once more and yelling, 'Are you ready?'

They scream in unison. I feel my own fist tightening and wishing I was going out there with them. I was wrong about Jimmy. So wrong. The fire in his soul burns brighter than ever. It is mine that has waned. And as the chant of 'animals' is aimed towards our opponents from the Stretford End, on a rain lashed pitch we begin.

Then, thirteen minutes in a free kick into our penalty area and their number eleven known as 'the witch' Ramon Veron, soars high at the far post and heads the ball downwards past Alex and into the net. Two down on aggregate and now we are chasing a miracle. Veron is a player blessed with talent, but whose arrows come dipped in poison when required. Like his compadres, he is a born assassin.

We are rocked, suddenly Estudiantes are knocking the ball around with an air of Real Madrid in their pomp. We cannot get near them. No more so than Veron. So this is why they call him The Witch? A beguiling footballer, a conjuror. And yet you just know they have a black heart. Soon it again shows itself as Veron takes out Paddy with a waist high lunge. My boys are showing huge restraint but I fear no matter what I say this won't last. The time wasting and niggly fouls mount. The frustration amongst the crowd and the players rising equally. George has a wonderful effort that goes narrowly over the bar. Denis goes down. It is only a minute before half time but he signals it is serious. The king is waning.

In the second half the antics of the Estudiantes players grow worse. They hit us low, high and use tricks that would embarrass a street mugger. It is diabolically clever, it is ultra-professional, but in my opinion an absolute disgrace. Ten minutes from time George finally snaps. His marker Medina has pulled, niggled and hacked at him all evening. This boy seemed determined to cripple my George and I have to say it was no surprise when, after one too many sly digs, and off the ball, but in clear view of the lineman and only ten yards from me, he hits Medina, with what I can only describe as a perfect right hook. When I call George in tomorrow, I can tell him with a clear conscience, 'Don't worry son, he was asking for it. You should have finished him with a left.'

We finally manage an equaliser through Willie Morgan that for a few moments gives us false hopes, but this was never meant to be our night. I cannot say I am too heartbroken. As Lo Bello blows to end this fiasco, Kiddo puts the ball in their net, but it is to no avail. A 1-1 draw and 2-1 defeat on aggregate. The thought of having to go toe to toe again with this gang of thugs in four days' time in a play-off match in Amsterdam fills me with dread. So good riddance. I look across to Jimmy and he shrugs his shoulders as if to suggest he too does not think it is worth the hassle. For if this performance of Estudiantes' tonight is what it takes to be world champions, then we are better off without. Tonight when in the mood the Argentines have electrified the old place with some wonderful football. And at times I will admit we could not get near them. But when they turn? It is with the fury and stealth of a cornered alley cat. I refuse to lower Manchester United to the kind of depravity we have just witnessed. We have given everything. I could ask for nothing more from my boys.

The Estudiantes players and staff are celebrating like dervishes on the pitch. Crying and falling to their knees in sheer ecstasy. The President and coach amongst them, thanking God for their victory. I hope the almighty had nothing to do with this for tonight in my opinion football has died a little. One of their back room boys hands me a v sign as he runs past, but I care not. These angels in white with dirty intentions have revealed their true colours. They have no class.

'Boss, it's going off in the tunnel!' cries out Wilf. I rush down and see the Estudiantes goalkeeper Poletti heading straight for our George. The two have enjoyed a simmering feud on the pitch after clashing during the second half at a corner, and obviously this idiot has not yet had his fill. However just as I arrive, from our dressing room emerges Paddy Crerand, George's unofficial minder, who with one almighty punch staggers the towering Poletti, like a tree blowing heavy in a strong wind.

Just to ensure the Argentine gets the message, Pat cracks him again and this time Poletti hits the floor. I move in to stop this version of Glaswegian street justice.

'Now, now Pat' I exclaim. 'We are Manchester United. I think this fellow has had enough don't you?'

Paddy nods. 'Yes boss.'

Together with Wilf we escort him back into the dressing room before the officials get wind of what has occurred. As Poletti lies distraught and groaning and clearly regretting his actions, George stands over him. 'Congratulations pal. You have just met Pat Crerand.'

And so ended our quest to be champions of the world.

5 - GENTLEMEN OF THE BOARD

The sport of kings? Aye well too many sure things have come second for me to say I am a rich man. 'The great Sir Matt' they say. I looked in my bathroom mirror this morning and I saw the craggy features of a fifty-nine year-old man who is honest enough to admit he has neither the energy nor will of force left to continue as manager of the most famous club in the planet and all that involves.

The Estudiantes game made my mind up. It is time to step away, so here we are. There comes a moment in life and a place in your head when you need to be honest with the one person you cannot fool - yourself. Therefore I will retire but I will not relinquish power over the kingdom I have built. There will be a new face at the training ground, the dressing room and the dugout but I will pull the strings. I am not going away. I am not going anywhere. I have decided on my successor and I will put the chosen one's name to the board this morning. My board, therefore my decision. He is one of the family. Local lad, a rough diamond. He is not me but I will keep him close. He bares resemblance to Jimmy. He loves Jimmy, but I can mould him. He can be controlled. He is a good lad is Wilf McGuinness. Wilf is one of our own.

Wilf is the chosen one.

As I turn right off Chester Road down to the ground I prepare to meet my board. Today is my time to face reality. The sky is dark on this wet and miserable mid-December morning. It is bitterly cold and there is a hard drizzle that soaks through to the bones. The city is at work. It has just gone 9-30 as I pull onto the forecourt. Trucks roar past making their way in and out of Trafford Park. One blows his horn and waves. I wave back.

The billowing chimneys spew their filth high into the Mancunian heavens. I hear the hum of traffic, the rattle of the rain on my umbrella as I head inside. A grey horizon, a grey city but my city. My Manchester. My Manchester United.

But for how much longer?

'Come in and sit down Matt,' says a beaming red faced Louis. They all stand to shake my hand. 'Would you like a wee dram?'

'Och it is not yet ten in the morning,' I smile whilst jokingly looking at my watch.

'For medicinal purposes' insists Louis. He has no idea. My Louis has no idea what is about to occur. A haze of cigar smoke has gathered over the long oak table where powerful self-made men gather. Good Mancunian men who I have approved and whom worship and respect me. They all smile and nod and want to be me. And now I them. And more.

I raise my glass.

'To Manchester United' I toast. We clink our glasses.

'To Manchester United' they repeat. All of them.

Louis' brother Douglas, his brother-in-law Denzil Haroun, Vice-chairman Alan Gibson and club Secretary Les Olive. I look at their faces. I know deep down I can never truly be like them or they me. I dabble in their world of high finance and business. But I see behind their eyes, despite the love I am but an employee. They pay me a wage. A good wage, £10,000 a year but I need and want more. I have no desire to relinquish control. Power must be maintained. I cannot let that go. I must keep hold of the reins.

'So Matt,' asks Louis, 'what is going on. Why have you called us here together at this ungodly hour?'

I light my pipe. I take my time. I let them wait a moment. I have twenty-four years of credit. They owe me that much. I feel their eyes upon me. I know they are expecting me to say I wish to buy a player. To make them put their hands in their pockets and dig out money. Money that I put there.

They are impatient. Louis' smile is fading. He coughs. He is nervous now, anxious. Behind Louis' head I catch sight on the wall of a photograph of my boys from Munich. I remember it well, taken on the pitch at Belgrade moments before kick off. In melting snow they stand proud. Young men who believed they would live forever. They are looking down at me. So talented, so courageous, so full of life and so damn young – I close my eyes, I wince. Then I am dragged back and shaken to reality to 1969.

'Come on then Matt,' asks Haroun. Always smart, a dandy and a good pal. 'Put us out of our bloody misery. Don't be shy, who is it? Joe Royle? Geoff Hurst? Or is it a centre half? God knows after Saturday we could do with one.'

I find myself smiling. 'Gentlemen of the board, my good friends.' I look at their faces. I smile; I take a sip. 'I would like to announce that it is with great sadness I have taken the decision to step down from my position as team manager from the end of this season.'

A silence descends on the room, spluttered coughs

and looks of incredulity are etched on their faces. A shocked Louis has tears forming in his eyes. Louis the butcher who, despite the immense wealth earned through his meat empire, always struggled to earn the respect he felt was due from his peers. 'Cheap meat is his fortune' they claimed, 'Not for us. Not for us' they wailed.

So the Cheshire millionaires with their huge houses in Bowdon and Alderley Edge who Louis aspired to be like, rejected him. Well I brought him in. He was my friend, I introduced him and that was enough. Louis was allowed through a door that had always been closed to him. From that moment on he would do anything for me.

'I owe you everything Matt,' he cried with joy, 'anything you want' he said, 'anything.'

My Louis – who bankrolled our return from the abyss. Now Louis must truly prove his loyalty and give me what I need. Now I need him. He has to keep his promise if this is to succeed. Together we have talked long into the Cheshire night over Cuban cigars and fine whisky of this moment now occurring. Of how our sons, my Sandy and his Martin, would come onto the United board and with our guiding hands take United forward into the seventies and beyond. He always ended such talks with: 'But this is a long way off Matt. Let us not think about it.' Then he would refill and chink my glass. 'To friendship.' And under the Cheshire stars we would raise a toast.

'I have just given you a ten-year contract and a bloody new Mercedes,' blurts out Louis. 'Why did you not talk to me about this?'

He is obviously hurting and I chose to ignore his

tone. 'We have never needed you more Matt. Never needed you more.'

The others nod in acknowledgment of Louis' words. They stare at me in furious agreement.

'Gentlemen,' I take another small sip of whisky. 'Old pals, my abdication is not something I have taken lightly.'

'Abdicating?' I am immediately interrupted by a red-faced Louis. He has built up a head of steam. 'You are not a fucking king Matt; you are a bloody football manager. You owed it to me...' He looks around at his fellow directors, 'you owed it to all of us to have talked this over before making a decision.' They all nod but it is Louis doing the talking.

'There is nothing to talk over,' I say. 'My mind is made up. Both my body and mind are worn out. This is a young man's game. What, did you think that I would go on forever?'

Still the others say nothing. I stare only at Louis. He fills his glass and drinks it in one gulp then slams it down on the table. The others jump whilst I don't move. He wipes his mouth on his sleeve.

'Well' he shouts. 'Who is it to be then? Stein, Revie, Sexton?'

'It is Wilf,' I say.

'Wilf! Fucking Wilf! Have you lost your senses?' screams Louis

'But he has no experience!' Haroun pipes up 'In doing this we would be made to look foolish. Putting McGuinness in charge of Manchester United is akin to running Steptoe's horse in the Derby. It is a non-starter old pal. What on earth are you thinking?'

'Who else have you in mind?' asks Alan Gibson in

a rather disrespectful tone. Now I am angry. My board, my men, questioning me. I glare at Gibson. He is not his father. He is not even a pale imitation of James. A great man. A grand old charming man who after a rough beginning to our relationship realised it was best to leave all footballing matters to me.

'Your father once questioned me about why I had selected a player. He did it once and never done it again.'

'I am not my Father,' he snaps.

'That is true' I reply quietly, but letting Alan Gibson know he is on rocky ground. For this is still my club. My Manchester United.

'Look,' I exclaim to all. 'For twenty-four years I have done right by this club. Before the crash I could have gone to Madrid but I chose to stay here in Manchester. Bernabeu offered me gold and riches beyond any man's dreams. He was giving me the opportunity to manage the greatest players in the world. But I said no. He asked me again after Munich. I turned him down again. With good grace he accepted because he knew deep down my first love is and always would be Manchester United.

'I felt I owed this club and the city. And so after the crash I gave everything to bring the trophy back to Manchester. Through pain and torment I suffered to repay this debt that was my every waking thought. But I believe I am justified in saying the events of last May finally saw my slate wiped clean. And in winning the European Cup it gives me the right to decide who, when and why. Not you Louis, not you Alan, not you Denzil and not you Douglas. My choice. I went through purgatory. I brought us through the nightmare.

I soothed tortured brows, I took the slings and arrows of those who always and still claim I could have done more for those who survived. Maybe so but I did what I thought was right at the time. I did what was right for this club. Through troubled waters I called the shots and now I believe I deserve nothing less than your respect for doing so.'

They all go quiet.

I take a breath. I compose myself and I continue.

'I will become General Manager. I will look after contracts, buying players and all other club interests. I will even continue my column in the program. No need for Wilf to be bothering with such minor distractions. Let him concentrate on the matters in hand. But let me assure you, fine gentlemen of the board, I am going nowhere. I keep the same office, I oversee everything and everyone.' I smile. 'I will be the gatekeeper.'

'Then what exactly does McGuinness do?' asks Haroun.

'Everything Matt bloody tells him,' laughs a now smiling Louis. They are now relaxed and are smiling but I am not. Inside I am angry. Inside I feel betrayed.

'Wilf looks after training and he picks the team.'

'What you are implying Matt, if I may be so bold,' speaks up Gibson, 'is that Wilf will be his own man only to the extent that you allow him to be…'

I nod, 'I push the buttons, I pull the strings. I take away the unnecessary angst involved in Wilf's day-to-day tasks. I let him get on with the job of putting us back where we belong. At the top of the league.'

'Here here,' bellows Douglas Edwards as he bangs the table with his hand.

'They are not going to like it,' says Haroun.

'Who?' replies Edwards.

'The senior players, Louis. We are going to have trouble with Bobby, Denis and the others. They won't be happy taking orders from Wilf. They have grown up with him. Their families socialised together. They drink with him… play cards…'

I put my hand up to stop Haroun in mid flow. Will they ever learn? 'The players will do and think as I tell them. They will want what I want. Like what I like. They are my lads, Denzil. Trust me, in time they will be okay with this.'

'And Best?' asks Louis. 'What is to be done about George Best? The only person on this earth who he listens to is you Matt. You are the only one who has a modicum of control over him. He will run circles around Wilf and you know it.' Again the others nod their heads in annoying lapdog manner.

'George is a good boy at heart,' I insist, 'he is maturing'. I notice the raised eyebrows and looks of incredulity at my last remark. 'Of course he likes the finer things in life. We all do,' I look around at the gentlemen of *my* board with their fat cigars and good whisky in hand, 'but I have noticed a mild change in George. Slight but I believe he is beginning to grow up. To honour his responsibilities both to himself and this club.'

Louis scratches his head and has a smile on his lips. To think they believe George listens to me? So many times I have had him in my office ready to rip his head off, only to end up putting my arm around consoling him. I have fined and threatened; begged and pleaded. I even considered hanging George out of my office window feet first on occasions. What worries me with

George is not so much the drinking and the ladies. They are young men's fallings that time and maturity can heal, but it is the gambling that gives me sleepless nights. I know because I understand how close to the line enjoying a flutter can take you. I have been there. The sport of kings turns rich men into paupers at the blink of a photo finish.

I know everything going on in this city that concerns Manchester United. George especially. People cannot wait to pick up the phone and tell me of his latest dalliance. More importantly my good friend Paddy McGrath, who operates at times in a world beyond my understanding, tells me George is placing bets that cause even underground bookies to flinch. This apart, no matter what, I can never stay angry long enough with him to make a difference. But I will not stop trying.

'George will support Wilf,' I tell Louis at last, 'what he needs. What they all need. Is a new voice and I believe one hundred per cent that Wilf will be that voice.'

'And Jimmy,' asks Gibson. 'What about Jimmy Murphy?'

'Does Jimmy know about your decision Matt?' asks Louis.

I shake my head. 'I will speak to Jimmy,' I reply almost in a whisper. I can feel their eyes upon me. They sense it. They sense the unease in my stance, in my manner. In my words. I take another sip of whisky. They have always thought of me and Jimmy as kindred spirits, united in red blood at Munich. Together forever more. As the reds go marching on. But it was never like that. It couldn't be. Not since the crash.

'Blood brothers are Jimmy and Matt,' they said. Well we are not. We are, were, good pals but not friends. Never close friends. Jimmy kept me at a distance after Munich. Or maybe me him? He could never ask the questions that I could not bear to give answers to. So in time it grew to unfathomable depths. We never meant to, we just drifted apart. That was the way it was. Our way of dealing with the pain. Of blocking out the memories of those killed. For the good of Manchester United. For the sake of our sanity we just looked forward. It became an obsession with no time to look back.

'Are you absolutely sure about this Matt?' says Louis in desperation. 'Jimmy will be devastated. This job is his life. If you like I can speak to him and break it…'

I cut Louis short; I speak to Louis in a manner he has never heard. In a tone I rarely use. 'Keep out! I will deal with it. Jimmy is finished. Our time at the helm is done. The club needs fresh blood and new ideas. We will both step down. Gentlemen of the board this is how it is going to be. Now, are there any other questions?'

They stare at each other, they nod and finally Louis looks towards me.

'I think you have said all that needed to be said Matt. A sad day I think we all agree. But one that had to arrive sooner or later.'

Louis picks up his glass. He raises it high.

'To Matt,' he toasts, 'and to Manchester United.' They all do similar. I smile in gracious thanks.

But I won't forget today.

6 - WHAT BECOMES OF THE BROKEN HEARTED?

It is time to tell the world. It is 14th January 1969 and the day of my official announcement that I am to step down as manager of Manchester United. Just to say these words makes my heart ache. A news conference has been scheduled for Old Trafford later this morning. I am pretty certain the press boys have no inkling of what is set to occur. There have been no leaks from the board, of which I am extremely grateful. They remain extremely dubious of my plan for Wilf to take over as team coach and at various times they have tried to dissuade me. But it is to be Wilf, although I will not name him today. Not whist our league position, sixth from bottom, remains precarious. Let us get safe and then we will drop the bomb.

I have told the players earlier this morning at The Cliff. 'I am getting too old to do this. I have been here for over twenty years and it is time to give somebody else a go. But I don't want this to detract from the rest of the season. We have still got a lot of work to do.' I kept it brief. There was shock and I also saw sadness on faces. Bobby is away with England, so I will make a point of having a word when he returns to Manchester. Paddy is upset, as are George and Denis. There were a few tears but they will be okay. I have been a player, I know the mindset. The original sadness over my going will soon disappear and all thought will swiftly turn to who is taking over. And will he rate them.

And so to a packed room of reporters with notebooks, television lights and cameras flashing, a jaw dropping audience go silent as I announce my decision to leave. I explain it is for the best.

'It's time to make way for a younger man, a track suited manager. United is no longer just a football club, it is an institution. I feel the demands are beyond one human being.'

Then come the questions:

'Who is to be your successor Matt? Is it Bobby Charlton, Jock Stein, Don Revie, Malcolm Allison, Dave Sexton, Jimmy Adamson, Noel Cantwell?' The names fly at me like bullets. I smile and look at Louis sat next to me. He has tears in his eyes. Whether it is through my determination to have Wilf or my going I am not sure.

'Of course we knew this had to come, but it does not mean that Sir Matt will be any less involved with Manchester United. In fact the post of General Manager carries even wider responsibilities, and my board are well content to think that in future they can call upon his unique football experience.

'As for a new team coach?' Louis stops for dramatic effect. 'We will take our time and make sure we get the right man for Manchester United.'

'What about Jimmy?' a voice bellows out from the press boys.

'Jimmy steps down with me.' I reply. I have yet to inform him I am leaving. I look around. He is not in the room but by now he will know. And I know where to find him.

I walk out of the tunnel into the empty stadium

and see Jimmy sat high in the stand above the dugout. I go to sit down next to him. He says nothing. Just continues to smoke his cigarette whilst staring into space. Finally, thank God, he speaks.

'So that is it then?'

'Aye' I reply. 'I have nothing left to give Jimmy. I have neither the will nor energy to carry on.'

'And what about me!' he suddenly snaps. 'Don't you think you owed me at least the decency to have told me before you informed the entire world?'

'It was just never the right time Jimmy. I am sorry.' He turns to look straight at me. He has tears in his eyes, but I fear tears of frustration.

'Don't lie to me Matt. You said nothing because you never had the courage to face me and say it was over. Tell me I am wrong. Go on tell me?'

Jimmy is right. He knows me better than my own family. 'You are right, I could not face you.'

He looks at me and shakes his head and lights another cigarette. Jimmy stares again across the deserted stadium. He smiles. 'I remember when you first asked me to come here. We were in Italy. Down in the south in Bari. Do you remember? '

I nod.

'I was screaming my bloody head off at a bunch of squaddies all because they were not putting their all into what was nothing more than a kick about. They were looking at me like I was some crazed Welshman. And then you appeared. And your exact words, I remember them like they were yesterday. "Jimmy old pal, how would you like to come to Manchester and help me build the biggest football club in the world?" I agreed and when we got there United did not even have a bloody ground! The Germans had flattened it in forty-one. It was a burnt out shell. We had nowhere to play, no money and not enough players. But I didn't care because I believed in you. I saw something. "He is just like me" I told myself. A kindred spirit. Someone who loves this beautiful game of ours. Who stares at the night sky and dreams of not just going to the stars but past them. And we did.

'Matt and Jimmy - together we built something truly special. We took Manchester United beyond the stars until that damn plane fell from the sky. And though we have achieved things since, wonderful deeds. It was never the same. How could it be?' Jimmy is in tears. 'We lost our boys Matt. And we never got it back. It was impossible; there was too much sadness and memories around here. "What became of the broken hearted" the song goes. That was me and you.'

We sit there for a moment or two in silence.

'I am not ready to go.' Jimmy lights another cigarette. He inhales. 'And neither are you if you are totally honest with yourself.'

'I am staying on as General Manager. Wilf will take over as team coach when we get safe in the league. And you are not going anywhere old pal. You have a scouting job for life.'

'Does Wilf know?' I shake my head. 'He is a good choice but is going to need a lot of support. Why not put me alongside him for a season or so?'

'He will have me Jimmy. I will still be in the office every day, but the players need to hear a new voice. Our day has gone. Can you not see?'

'My day has gone you mean.'

I stand to go. 'We could go on all day Jimmy. Like I

said, the job is yours for keeps. Let me know.'

I walk off but I can feel Jimmy's eyes burning into the back of my head all the way down to the tunnel. They tell me he was sat there for three hours.

Do I feel guilty?

I don't feel anything anymore.

News of Sir Matt Busby's retirement reverberates around the footballing world, and nowhere more than Manchester United's training ground at the Cliff, on Broughton Road in Salford. Wilf McGuinness is sat with players Denis Law and Shay Brennan in the canteen.

Shay is writing out his bets from a newspaper in his lap. It has gone one o'clock and the rest of the player have gone home. Over a pot of tea there is only one topic of conversation.

Denis smiles towards Wilf. 'So what do you think Wilf? Am I going to have to call you boss soon?'

'Fat chance of that Denis' laughs Wilf, 'I am sure he will go for a big name. Someone like Big Jock at Celtic. They are good pals. He trusts him. I will be way down the list.'

'Don't be so sure Wilf' adds Shay, 'Do you really think the old man will trust an outsider? Stein is a good man and a great manager but you are forgetting one thing.'

'Go on…' replies Wilf.

Shay takes a sip of tea before answering. 'He is not United. Right then,' Shay stands to go, folding his newspaper under his arm, 'got a certainty in the 2-30 at Kempton.'

Law laughs. 'Shay, you have more donkeys on your track record then Blackpool beach. Keep your money in your pocket man.'

'Ah but Denis, there is a world of difference old son between me, a son of Ireland, a free spirit happy to chance my arm in the sport of kings and spread my hard earned money amongst this fair city's bookies. Whilst you, a tight ham-fisted Scottish bastard would rob a blind beggars' bowl of a penny if the chance arose.'

'True but harsh' smiles Law.

'What about Bobby?' Wilf asks the two men.

'One day Wilf,' replies Shay, 'but not just yet. He still loves to play. Besides, imagine George's face if Bob gets made up. He will be off in a shot.'

Wilf nods in agreement. 'Well Paddy then? The old man adores him, we all do'

'You must be joking, Wilf' replies an incredulous Law, 'you know what I think of Pat, you could not have a finer friend. But as manager of this club? Forget it. He is a mad Glaswegian who would pick a fight with every manager or supporter who ever swore at him on the touchline. But don't tell him I said that!'

'I'm going to tell him,' Shay winks at Law.

'Right I'm off. I'll see you two tomorrow. Oh by the way?' Wilf looks up. 'You are fourth favourite with the bookies pal. 6/1. I might have a bit of that. Be lucky lads.' With that a grinning Shay makes his way out of the canteen. Wilf watches him leave. The men have been close since Munich. He was Shay's best man and vice versa. Wilf so wants to believe him, for it would be beyond his wildest dreams. And so to help fend off the disappointment when somebody else gets the keys of the kingdom, he is tending to laugh or simply dismiss the question whenever it arises. The heir to the crown will have his total loyalty, but deep in Wilf's red heart he will hate the new man's guts. Though until Busby names his successor, Wilf will continue to dream.

Six to one...

7- THE FAIRYTALE OF DIRTY OLD TOWN

Here in the Brown Bull, this run down Salfordian Victorian watering hole, sat on what Mancunians love to call 'the wrong side of the Irwell' at the corner of Chapel Street, everybody loves George.

They come in their droves to pay homage: television stars from the nearby Granada Television studios, presenters, movie stars, actors, actress… wannabees, starlets desperate to catch George's eye and get the keys to his kingdom. An invitation to the private bedroom he keeps forever unlocked and in constant use upstairs. Fellow footballers, journalists, musicians, writers, poets, politicians and the Mancunian underworld – all have taken George to their hearts. They love him. They love his lifestyle. He is one of their own, a kid from the streets. Belfast maybe and not Moston, Ancoats or Collyhurst but to them this matters little. For this kid is quality.

Manchester's Quality Street gang have pitched their tent at the Brown Bull. A dump but their dump. And George's dump. The rattle of freight and passenger trains makes the place shake whenever they pass on the nearby railway bridge, but who cares and who notices? For the beer flows endlessly, the company is good and everybody loves a lock-in.

And everybody loves George.

This fairytale of the Dirty Old Town began the

previous year when late one midweek evening, in the midst of a typical Mancunian thunderstorm, George and Malcolm Wagner called in the Brown Bull to shelter from the lashing rain.

The sudden arrival into their midst of arguably the most famous face in the world caused hardly a murmur from the nine or ten regulars present. Just shouts of 'Shut the bloody door!' and 'Still raining lads!' as the pair stood there soaked wet through. For this was Salford. If Elvis had entered the building few would have raised an eyebrow.

When the no nonsense, charismatic American landlord Billy Barr, a former GI with a Texas drawl, emerged to get the lads a drink, he equally made no fuss. Simply asking the two drenched gents what beverage they required, a light went on in George's head. This was his kind of place. His kind of people. Far from the madding crowd. A spot to have a drink and be left well alone. A back street palace with the smell of stale alcohol, tattered and sparse unpainted walls with beer stained carpets, overfilled ash trays littered with cigarette dimps.

One half ripped poster, no more, was tacked to the wall of the Manchester United team in a pre-season parade with the European Cup. Billy Barr's drinking hostel had been blessed and sprinkled with gold dust in the shape of an irascible Irish waif, whose capacity for booze and ladies is matched only by his ability to make opposing defenders appear like drunken tramps in their last moment of consciousness, before collapsing in a heap.

★

I hated it. What annoyed me more was that I could never get the damned name right. The Black Bull, Bulls Head, Running Bull? So many times George was off the rails and this place came up in telephone conversations from fans that claimed to have seen George totally out of it. How many were truly United supporters is debatable. But my information was good enough to know what that place, whatever its damned name, did for George Best. It killed him as the boy to truly go on and conquer the world. He was special, so very special, but I knew and I think deep down he understood also there could, and should have been even so much more.

But if you decide to drink and drink till the sun comes up and still chase a livener you call time on your dreams because the booze wins. So sad but what I could do? It was his time. The boy had this magical charisma that drew both women and men towards him.

Everybody loved George.

★

George is holding court in the Brown Bull with friends Malcolm Wagner (Waggy), television presenter Michael Parkinson, Sunday Times journalist Hugh McIlvanney and team mate Paddy Crerand. It is the evening following Sir Matt's announcement that he is to step down as manager and this is the sole topic of conversation.

The bar is full: but nobody bothers George. Billy the landlord keeps an eye out for strangers. He has a third eye for trouble makers. His clientele are not of the type these days to throw a chair through a window, now trouble comes in different guises: a prying journalist or photographer. A husband or boyfriend with a grudge looking to nail George. But no one ever gets passed Billy at the door. The beer is flowing as George and his crowd sit in a smoke filled corner of the Bull and dissect Sir Matt's decision.

'Did he ever give you an inkling he was going Pat?' asks McIlvanney of Crerand.

'It has been on the cards for a long time Hugh' replies Paddy. 'I talked him out of retiring two years ago after Partizan knocked us out in the semi finals. The old man is dog tired. His back is giving him hell and he has simply had enough.'

'We should have won it that year Pat,' says George wistfully, 'we were the best team in it and would have murdered Madrid in the final.' Totally relaxed in the company of men he can trust and who are truly interested in his opinion for who he is. And not what he is.

'In my humble opinion George' say McIlvanney, 'United were a better team then.'

'No you are right Hugh,' replies Paddy, 'the boss would agree with you.'

'I am curious Paddy' asks Parkinson, 'what did you say to Sir Matt to talk him out of quitting?'

Paddy laughs 'I told him to hang on because it was our destiny to win the bloody thing one day.'

Parkinson smiles. 'And did you honestly believe that?'

'I did for a long time Michael, but when Eusebio went through one-on-one against Alex in the final with eight minutes to go, I must admit to a few doubts!'

They all laugh.

Waggy, a lifelong United fan addresses the table.

'So who takes over chaps?'

'Jock Stein' answers Paddy. Without any hint of hesitation. 'Jock would be perfect for Manchester United.'

'I am not so sure' replies McIlvanney, 'Jock would come down here and demand full control over every aspect of the club. You know, as I do, that he is the mirror image of Matt. Nothing happens in Glasgow regarding Celtic that he does not know or find out about. But he is his own man Pat. Could he work under Matt?' McIlvanney shrugs his shoulders. 'I am not so sure. Personally I think he will look closer to home. What do you think George?'

'Well if Bobby Charlton gets it I am going to Chelsea!' Laughter erupts around the table but George is serious. He and Bobby have never seen eye to eye either on the pitch or off. George knows that Bobby thinks he is a greedy bastard with the ball. How many times has he heard those immortal words from Mr Clean? From Mr Manchester United. 'Pass George Pass!' A glory boy. Whilst off the field the manner in which he conducts his life is the antithesis to everything Bobby stands and believes in. The shaking of his head, the rolling of his eyes. A muted comment under his breath. But does George care?

A twenty-two year old man with the world at his bewildering feet – newly crowned European Footballer of the Year. Adored and revered. The birds and the booze and the boys around this table... George can live with Bobby's disdain. Sadly it appears not everybody loves George.

'No chance Bobby will be made up' says Paddy, 'we still need him on the pitch.'

'What about Wilf McGuinness?' asks Waggy.

'Do me a favour!' retorts Paddy again. 'If Wilf gets the job he will cause World War Three around the place.'

'A good lad though,' adds George.

Paddy nods. 'Aye a good lad with a big heart and good as gold George, but he would not go down well with a lot of the lads. Especially the older ones.'

McIlvanney smiles and shakes his head at the mere suggestion. 'I agree, putting Wilf in charge would be like putting Popeye in charge of the Titanic after it has hit the iceberg. Matt maybe loyal and want to keep the position in house. But he is not mad.'

8 - PAINTED SMILES

'This is your time Bobby. Now straighten your tie and go and do me proud.' Norma Charlton kisses her husband at the door of their home in Lymm as he prepares to travel to training at The Cliff. It is a day on from Sir Matt Busby's announcement that he is to step down and Norma thinks Bobby is set to be the chosen one.

Bobby drives off in a state of shock. After being away on international duty for England, during which he captained his nation to a 1-1 draw with Romania at Wembley, he has returned to Manchester to find himself in a strange kind of revolution. United, his United, stand on the brink of monumental change and their most famous son feels uneasy.

Inside Bobby is hurting that the news of the old man stepping down reached him through pressmen. He had hoped the boss would have given him the nod before he travelled to London earlier in the week. He feels let down. But as ever Bobby understands deep in his heart that Sir Matt Busby had his reasons, all of course good, for not doing so.

After informing him of the changing of the guard in Manchester, the reporters' questions flew at Bobby; 'do you want the job Bobby?', 'is it yours Bobby?', 'are you the King in waiting Bobby?', 'how would you deal with George, Bobby?', 'who are you going to buy Bobby?' And on and on...

Well Bobby Charlton does not want the job. He is

just thirty years old, not forty, and could not bear the thought of giving up. He loves the game, the feel of the grass, the smell of the liniment, the roar of the crowd as they emerge onto the Old Trafford pitch. Like Jimmy Murphy, Bobby feels the passion. The poets are the players and the audience clamour to hear their verses. But then there is a dark side. One that has suddenly crept up and become like an open sore.

The world is changing. People are changing, his club is changing and he feels not for the best. He does not take kindly to the barbed comments from certain team mates made behind his back. But he is Bobby Charlton. Captain of England, Manchester United and role model to thousands of schoolboys. He has won the World Cup and raised the Holy Grail of the European Cup for the team of his dreams. So he will rise above such behaviour.

The old man rang him at home last night. He said they would have a chat this morning. 'Yes boss,' he replied, 'I understand boss'. All the time he is thinking 'All those years and you could not be bothered to tell me before I left.' Bobby is disappointed, but feels bad even to even think that way. For his respect and fear of Busby remains as powerful as ever. He is dreading being alone with the boss in his office. He does not want the job. No way. Not yet. But he fears he is going to be asked. He already knows the script. 'Come in Bobby sit down, take a seat. How are Norma and the kids? And how are you?' And then Sir Matt will hit him with it. 'You are the one Bobby. You are the chosen one.' And how can he ever refuse? 'The shoes of the red fisherman Bobby. You are the one, son. The only one I trust.'

Bobby is daydreaming. Suddenly his mind clears. Norma wants him to get the job so bad it hurts her. The previous evening she gave him both barrels. 'You deserve it, Bob. You almost gave your life for this club. You are head and shoulders above the other candidates. You are better than the rest. You are Manchester United.'

He smiled and nodded for she is formidable when in this mood. But he knows she is wrong. So very wrong. For George Best is Manchester United now. The fans love George, they respect Bobby but they adore George. Would he rather be loved or respected? Bobby would rather be both. But this is the price he pays for the life of a dedicated footballer who in both body and spirit belongs to Manchester United. Not as the song goes in the chart, which was written for George, 'A Dedicated Follower of Fashion.'

He knows what people say. He is glum and sour. You could not wrestle a smile out of Bobby Charlton. He is not one of the lads. He hears the whispering in the canteen. 'A miserable bastard' they say. A loner they call him. A loner! He stops the car and starts to think aloud.

Well being thrown fifty yards from an aeroplane while still strapped in your chair and watching your best friends dead and dying before your eyes tends to leave a lasting imprint on your mind. So excuse me if I am not some laughing joker at training every day. What would they have me do? Smile through the tears of a clown! Smile and the world smiles with you! Will that bring my friends back? Outsiders tend to have fixed ideas towards me. But those who really know, my family and true friends. Shay Brennan, Nobby

Stiles, Wilf McGuinness, Jimmy Murphy. Ask them. Ask them and they will tell you the truth! My public persona is a charade. A masquerade. Painted faces and painted smiles. I don't do that, I cannot do that. I miss my old friends. I miss Duncan and Eddie. Tommy, Roger, David, Mark, Liam and Geoff. They were my friends and they were wiped out amid fire and flames. We did not ask for that. We were footballers. No one signed on to be dragged into the midst of a raging inferno. It is a long way from Old Trafford to southern Germany and death and chaos. There was no small print. Sometimes, even now in quiet moments, I feel the cold of that Munich runway. It may be a sunny day but still I feel the snowflakes dropping on my face. It has never gone away. What would I give to be back in the days before? Anything. We should never have got back on that damned plane. Somebody should have spoken up…

Somebody should have said we are not getting back on that plane.

Bobby arrives at The Cliff amid an excited gaggle of schoolboys gather around to grab a prized autograph. Pens are thrust into his face as he attempts to get out of the car.

'Let me out lads' he exclaims. Like the parting of the sea the schoolboys allow Bobby room. He takes his boots and kitbag and places them on the car roof.

'Right then' orders Bobby. 'Orderly fashion, now who is first?'

One by one autograph books are signed. Suddenly into the car park roars George in his sparkling white E Type Jaguar. Immediately the schoolboys' attention switches across to United's charismatic young Irish superstar. Even those who had not yet had their books signed rush over to swamp 'Georgie boy.'

A sad faced Bobby watches them go. A grinning George waves over to his teammate as he holds court in the midst of an ever increasing but good hearted mob. The schoolboys are joined by an over excited host of screaming teenage girls. All miniskirts and high heels, clutching pictures of George to their hearts to be signed. Their high pitch yells echo across the car park and into the annoyed ears of England and Manchester United Captain Bobby Charlton. A gloomy looking Bobby takes his stuff off the car roof and heads inside.

On entering the building, the familiar dulcet tones of Wilf McGuinness, shout over towards Bobby. 'Oi Bob, the boss would like a quick word in his office before training.'

He nods over to Wilf: 'Thanks Wilf, I will head over there now.' As Bobby moves away, a beaming Wilf calls across, 'Hey Bob, I'm 6/1 with the bookies.' Soon as he opens his mouth Wilf regrets it. He winces. So much for playing it down. The thought of Wilf getting the job had never even occurred to Bobby. It does not fill him with confidence. The opposite in fact, for he thinks the old man would be mad to even consider it. Wilf may bleed United red but to appoint a successor who is so young and who wears his heart so obviously on his sleeve seems calamitous. His old friend dances better in the shade than in the gleaming sunlight of a worldwide audience. He fears the sharks of Her Majesty's press and fellow players would eat him alive if things went wrong. But looking at Wilf's grinning, desperate features, he cannot help but smile.

'Best of luck old pal. You deserve it,' says Bob, ever

the diplomat.

★

I am sat in my office when there is a knock on the door. In comes Bobby. 'You wanted to see me boss?' he looks a little tense.

'Bobby son come in, sit down. Tell me, how are Norma and the kids?'

'Fine boss. '

'That's grand. Look, I'm sorry I never got chance to speak to you before the balloon went up. But I need you to concentrate on matters on the pitch Bobby. We can't afford to let things get any worse. I'm counting on you. Don't let me down.'

Bobby stands like a schoolboy before a headmaster. Not daring to raise his voice or in any way appear disrespectful. He is waiting for the big one. Any moment now the old man will raise the subject of offering him the job.

I look up from paperwork and Bobby is still stood there. Staring. 'Are you okay, son?' I ask.

'Yes boss' he replies. Appearing uncertain.

'Well that's all; you can go now and get ready for training. Jack and Wilf will be wondering where you are.'

'Yes boss' he repeats before turning and leaving.

Once outside Bobby takes a deep breath. So much for the shoes of the fisherman! He feels elated, relieved and he has to admit, a little disappointed. Could it be that the old man has not even thought or considered him for the job? Loved, respected but ignored – the captain of England and Manchester United shakes his head and heads off to training.

9 - NOVENA

Saturday 8th April 1969 and even though we have just been beaten at Coventry, word arrives in the dressing room that results elsewhere now mean we are safe from relegation.

There are few cheers for it is a diabolical situation for a club like ours to be in. Relief floods out but there is no celebration.

'Can't let this happen again lads' roars out Wilf McGuinness. I watch Wilf as he goes about his business with the players. I am convinced more than ever that I have made the right decision. 'It is time' I tell myself. Time for the coronation.

That same week Wilf is at Old Trafford with the reserves. At the full time whistle United scout Billy Behan shouts him over in the tunnel.

'Wilf can I have a swift word?'

'Sure Billy, always good to see you old pal' grins Wilf. The two shake hands. Wilf is really fond of the old man who discovered amongst others Johnny Carey. Behan is set to turn Wilf McGuinness's world on its head.

'I have some news for you, Wilf. You have got to keep it under your hat for now.'

'Go on Billy.'

Behan puts his arm on Wilf's shoulder. 'All I will say is that you are in with a shout.'

'Billy I don't understand. What are you on about?'

'Shoes of the fisherman, son. I have heard you are

the one.'

'Oh give over, just rumours. Even tonight I have had press men sat in the stand firing question at me. Ten of them turning up for a bloody reserve game for Christ sakes! For a reserve game!' Wilf sighs heavily and smiles. 'I hope to God you are right Billy old son but we all know what hope did.'

A smiling Behan winks at Wilf. 'He has always kept you close. All these years and he has always kept you close. There is a reason for that. Goodnight lad.'

Behan disappears down the tunnel and out of sight. Wilf watches him go. 'Bye Billy. Mind how you go.' Now he does not know what to believe.

★

The next day at The Cliff, as Wilf is coming off the pitch after training with a net full of balls over his shoulder, I head towards him.

'Wilf, when you come in tomorrow, wear a collar and tie.'

'Yes boss' replies Wilf. 'Any reason?'

To keep up appearances I act quite annoyed with Wilf's question, 'because I told you to, son.'

★

The next day is a bitterly cold April spring morning. Under a watery sun, thirty-one year-old Wilf McGuinness takes a deep breath and checks himself out in his car mirror. His hair neatly combed, he is clean shaven and looking and feeling dapper in suit and tie.

This is the day.

If only his mates killed at Munich could have been

here to witness it. Not a day goes by when Wilf does not think of them.

★

Thursday 6th February 1958. It is late afternoon in Manchester and twenty-one year-old Manchester United footballer Wilf McGuinness, and close family friend Joe Witherington, a sales rep with the *News Chronicle,* are walking up Princess Street towards Piccadilly. Wilf has been to visit an orthopaedic specialist, a Mr Poston, whose diagnosis after examining his cartilage is that he faces at least two months out on the sidelines.

Wilf is filled with joy and despair; joy at United having advanced into the European Cup semi finals stage for the second year in a row the day before, after a truly dramatic 3—3 draw away in Yugoslavia against a brilliant Red Star Belgrade team. And despair that his long term injury will hinder his attempts to cement a place in United's first team.

'Never give up Wilf. Never stop fighting.'

That was Jimmy Murphy's set phrase, with fist clenched whenever he passed Wilf in the physio's room at The Cliff. That is all very fine, he thinks, if he were just up against a mere mortal. Then Jimmy's words may hold more than a candle with Wilf. But he is up against Duncan Edwards. The greatest player Wilf has ever seen. He is up against a colossus!

Wilf and Joe's attention are struck by a paper boy ahead of them screaming loud, with a large crowd gathering around him. He is shouting out 'UNITED IN PLANE CRASH.' The two men rush over, a limping Wilf behind Joe, who reaches the paper boy first. He pays and grabs a newspaper off the stand.

'Does it say if anyone is hurt?' asks Wilf. He is not unduly worried for Wilf has flown abroad with United on several occasions. Bumpy landings and air turbulence are common and he is convinced the story is simply being over egged.

'A storm in a teacup Joe mate,' smiles a nervous Wilf. But after reading through the stop press reports, Joe is not so sure.

'Come on' he says, grabbing Wilf's arm. 'We'll go to the Chronicle's office and see what they know.' Wilf sees something in Joe's eyes. He looks scared.

'No way Joe,' he adds. Trying to assure his friend, a United supporter also, 'they'll be okay.'

As soon as they arrive at the Chronicle it is clear that a catastrophe is occurring. Everywhere people appear panic stricken. Loud voices shout down phones, one young secretary is crying as she struggles to cope with orders being barked at her by journalists suddenly finding themselves engulfed in a maelstrom of rumour and misinformation.

A Reuters news agency wire machine is spewing out streams of paper containing the latest facts and speculations of events on Southern German soil in Munich. Wilf looks on in shock.

'Give me a minute' says Joe, as he swiftly disappears amid the madness to try and find out information. He seeks out a journalist friend of his who hands him some copy. Wilf watches on as the two speak. The journalist looks across and nods towards him, his face ashen grey. Wilf raises a hand to acknowledge and smiles weakly.

'What the fucking hell is going on?' Joe returns and motions for Wilf to follow him. 'We need to talk', he sits Wilf down in a relatively quiet corner of the frenzied surroundings. 'I am afraid it is bad Wilf. First reports say there have been numerous fatalities, although we have no names.' Joe shrugs his shoulders. 'Nobody knows who is alive or dead.'

Wilf slumps back in his chair, not able to take in what he is being told. If not for his injury he would have been on the plane as cover for Duncan. The next few hours pass in feverish, haunting confusion. Wilf listens out across the newsroom floor for the mere mention of a name, but there is nothing. He prays. Wilf prays like he has never done before that the lives of his mates will be saved. But slowly the death toll rises.

'Jesus Christ, this is a bloody nightmare,' screams a journalist who has just received more reports of deaths. Seven to nine, to twelve. But no names. It is torture. Finally Wilf rings his father who tells him they too have heard nothing. Lawrence McGuinness tells his son to come home. Here is where he should be at a time like this. Wilf hangs up, he cannot take much more. He is in a daze and asks Joe to drive him home to 51 Westleigh Street in Blackley, North Manchester.

The drive back up Rochdale Road is strange for the normal busy traffic has vanished. An entire city lies in morbid wait of forthcoming radio and television announcements from Germany. Above sit black clouds and dark foreboding skies. There are no stars in the Northern heavens on this night. Mancunians brace themselves. They fear the worst. They fear the end of their world.

On reaching home Wilf collapses into the arms of his father, a veil of tears. It is too much for Joe to bear. He waves over to Lawrence and Wilf's mother, May, and heads back to the Chronicle office. Agonisingly as the night goes on news begins to emerge and on the radio some of the survivor's names are released: Bobby Charlton, Dennis Viollet, Albert Scanlon, Harry Gregg and Bill Foulkes. Duncan Edwards too, even though the BBC reporter states that he is 'grievously injured.' And then he stops. No more names.

'What about the others!' exclaims Wilf, 'Eddie, Tommy, Roger and the rest. What about them?'

'Calm down son,' his father says softly, 'nobody knows for sure. It will be chaos over there.'

May puts her arm around him, 'Wilf there is a Novena (a Catholic devotion) at church tonight. We should go. I will get our coats.' Lawrence looks at his devastated son. It feels like only two minutes ago he was making him the proudest father on earth by signing for Manchester United. He so wanted his boy not to experience what he witnessed during the war. Lawrence hoped Wilf would never live through such a day of loss as this.

Mount Carmel church is packed to the rafters. People are openly sobbing. Prayer, it appears, is the only option left to prevent the heavens falling down upon them. Wilf's entrance, flanked by his mother and father, causes a lot of head turning in the aisles. Men are wearing United rosettes or scarves.

'Hail Mary, full of grace the Lord is with thee. Blessed are the fruit...

Please let them live. Please, please… please.

1969: 'Please Please'

Wilf snaps himself back to reality and dries his eyes. 'Not a day for tears Wilf lad,' he says to himself.

'Happiest day of your life this,' he switches on the car radio and Louis Armstrong's 'It's a Wonderful World' is playing. The boss's favourite song. Wilf smiles. The car is on the final stretch of Chester Road heading towards Old Trafford. He begins to sing along.

I see friends holding hands, singing how do you do

He pulls up in the club forecourt and gets out the car. Wilf is now whistling 'It's a wonderful world' as he strides into the ground through a side entrance, marked up with a staff entrance sign above it.

'Fucking hell Wilf, are you in court today?' It is a grinning Paddy Crerand. Paddy is in collecting tickets for a forthcoming match. Wilf says nothing but gives Paddy the middle finger and saunters off. Hands in pockets and still whistling Wilf heads towards the boss's office. Could it soon be his office?

I feel no sadness or pain in today's events, just a sense of relief. I suddenly recall Sinatra's words. And now the end is near but myself, I face no such final curtain. This is still my club and will always be so until my last dying breath. There will be no last goodbye. Of course Wilf will enter centre stage today but I shall be watching his every move in the wings.

He is the Chosen One.

Wilf is United, he is family and can be trusted. And so the show will go on. But I will ensure in these uncertain times that if Wilf is in need of gentle persuasion then my door will always be open. He will listen. For he is a good lad.

I have called the press conference for later today where we shall officially announce it. I hear Wilf whistling and can see his shadow outside the door. And so this is it. I pretend to be writing and take a deep breath.

It has been a privilege and I did it my way.

I took the hits, more than any, most men could bear, and I am still standing.

Regrets?

What do you think?

'Calm down Wilf son,' Wilf says to himself. 'Calm down.' He comes to Sir Matt's office. He checks out his reflection one last time on a glass door panel. He straightens his collar and tie and hair one last time. He makes the sign of the cross and then knocks on the door.

'Come in' I shout. I look up from my pretence of writing and smile. 'You're looking smart Wilf, sit down.'

'Cheers boss.'.

'Wilf, there is no easy way of putting this, so I will come right out with it. Congratulations, son. You are the next manager of Manchester United.' Wilf remains outwardly calm, the only sign of his acknowledging the unimaginable weight of the boss's words and how much they mean comes through a simple nod of the head. Inside his heart is racing – if you are listening in Eddie and Duncan and Roger and all the angels in heaven, have a drink on me lads.

'Now you won't be known as the manager straight away because I feel the title will only add extra pressure on your shoulders. You are going to have enough on your plate, son. So I have decided you will be referred to as chief coach.'

Wilf nods sagely. I smile wide. 'The good news is Wilf, I will still be around as a General Manager. I will keep this office, you can have Jimmy's old one down the hall. He will be sharing with Joe Armstrong. In matters of discipline, transfers and such, I will keep an eye on those. Regarding wages... I look down at the sheet of paper in front of me, 'yours will rise from £38 to £80. Over double Wilf lad. So don't let me down.'

For one of the few times in his life Wilf McGuinness is speechless. No wise cracks, no jokes, just respect. He wants to cry with joy, he wants to hug the old man and open his heart on everything that has lain dormant since the late afternoon of Thursday 6th February 1958.

A cleansing of the soul – a Novena.

But now is certainly not the time, for the old man is in business like mood and certainly in no state of mind to witness his heir apparent suffer an emotional breakdown. For that is not how a Manchester United manager, sorry chief coach, behaves. These are heady times for Wilf and this is the best day of his life. All he can think about is that the great Matt Busby has chosen him to carry the torch onwards. 'I will make you proud boss. I will make you so very proud,' Wilf beams.

Official Manchester United club statement:

The board has given further consideration to the changes which will occur at the end of the season and has decided to appoint a chief coach who will be responsible for team selection, coaching, training and tactics.

Mr Wilf McGuinness has been selected for this position

and will take up his duties as from 1st June, and in these circumstances it is not necessary to advertise for applications as we first intended. Sir Matt Busby will be responsible for all other matters affecting the club and players, and will continue as club spokesman.

★

'It's a joke, a sick bloody joke. Wilf, bloody Wilf?' Willie Morgan is not happy. He is at Mere Golf club in Cheshire playing with team mate and United goalkeeper Alex Stepney. They have just heard off a fellow member of Wilf McGuinness' surprise appointment as Manchester United's chief coach. 'What is the old man thinking?' cries Willie.

It is Alex's turn to take a shot. Only five feet from the hole, he remains calm and focused. Money rides on this and Alex puts the ball in. He turns and smiles towards a frowning Morgan, who puts his hand in his pocket and hands over the cash. His day is going from bad to worse. 'So come on, what do you think Alex?'

A smiling Stepney kisses his winning pound note. 'Wilf is one of the lads, Willie. Always has been, long before you showed up. Don't worry; the boss will have him like a puppet on a string. He will still be the one calling the shots.'

'But Wilf will be picking the team. He doesn't like me, Alex. He will have me out for sure. I just can't believe it! Jock Stein, Don Revie. Don loves me. I could have gone to Leeds and been a champion but came here. Dave Sexton, Jimmy Adamson and he picks Wilf fucking McGuinness?'

Stepney shakes his head as Willie's rant continues. 'Bobby will be steaming. What hair he has got left will be falling out double quick when he fucking hears this. And the other lads, no one will be happy. Nobody.'

Willie does not need this. Not now. He cannot understand that for some reason Wilf can't see that Willie is special. That Willie is better than George. Did Busby himself not give him George's number seven shirt when he signed? Everybody likes Willie. Everybody except Wilf. The reality being Wilf regards Willie as a good player, but simply not as great as Willie thinks he is. Wilf thinks Willie is no George Best. He does not even think Willie is fit to lace George's drinks..

Alex brings Willie back to earth. 'Wilf will dig his own hole Willie. He is one of us you see. He has drunk and laughed and gambled. He has the dirt and knows where the bodies are buried. It is a delicate balancing act and Wilf is not delicate. He is loud and honest and loyal, one of the boys. A good mate, yes. But a boss? He just needs enough rope and trust me Willie, he will hang himself.'

Alex points toward the next hole. 'Now can we get on with our game?' He tees up his ball but miscues wildly, He watches on grim faced as it goes hopelessly off course. 'Looks like you have got your pound back old son,' Alex quips. But Willie is not listening. He is worried and fretting about Wilf.

He just doesn't rate him.

10 - UN ULTIMA VOLTA (ONE LAST TIME)

By no means do I think that I have a sense of the theatrical, but before I leave the stage I feel it is only right to perform one last great feat and what better manner could I leave the crowds shouting for more and demanding an encore, than to rise to the top of the mountain one final time and retain the European Cup.

Bad memories, his eyes glazed over with fury, the Welsh fires awake. We are sat in my office. Myself, Jimmy, Wilf and Jack discussing the upcoming European Cup semi final first leg away against AC Milan. Without prompting Jimmy finishes his coffee and places it on my desk.

'I remember those bastards the first time round!' Jimmy looks over to me as if asking permission to continue but who am I to deny the man who saved this club. 'Mr Manchester United' they call me, well if I am the public face then Jimmy is, was, the heart and soul that kept it alive. When others deemed it more reasonable to call time and close shop, he fought like a demon to keep us going. Never mind that we are no longer what we were - he still thinks to look towards me to ask permission…

'Of course Jimmy,' I reply with ridiculous normality. If only people knew the truth that Jimmy is the one, not me. I was lucky; I was dead to the world. Jimmy went to the funerals, he looked into the eyes of the broken hearted. He wiped away the tears of the mothers, fathers, sons, daughters, wives...

I was spared that horror.

Jimmy continues: 'I can tell you the date – 14th May 1958. It was only three months after the crash. We beat them 2-1 at Old Trafford but it was never going to be enough. Off the field in Milan they were class personified. They gave us flowers, they commiserated us on our tragic loss but on it they acted like thugs. And I could not understand why because they were simply so much better than us. The magnificent Uruguayan, Juan Schiaffino, a truly wonderful footballer. The guile and craft of the Swede Nils Liedholm. But they kicked and spat and mauled and over acted. All this was suitably ignored by a German referee who to this day is probably still wearing the same gold watch he undoubtedly earned that day. That and a fistful of Lira. It was bullying and I hate bullies for we had been decimated for God's sake! I had a team full of kids and veterans and crash survivors. The Football Association had forbidden Bobby to play because he had a nothing friendly with England. They never even raised a finger to help us out in those times. Never!

'I always thought in time my anger would pass towards those people, but when you attend eight funerals of boys whom you thought of as your own, such grief tends to linger. I hope those bastards rot in hell. When we came out of the tunnel into full sight of the crowd, 80,000 Italians went mad! They threw rotten fruit, bottles of piss and heaven knows what else. Milan hammered us 4-0 but there was no class in their victory. When Madrid beat them in the final I raised a glass of whisky to Don Santiago's boys. Trust me lads, we owe this lot, we really do.'

The three men sit in silence. He doesn't speak much these days. Tending to keep his own company. A constant presence around Old Trafford and The Cliff but rarely heard. Just another ghost in a place already inhabited by spirits and echoes of lost souls but Jimmy has returned from his self imposed exile and is clearly fired up for the two games against Milan. He looks towards me.

'We have to beat them Matt. We really do.' I can't help but feel more confident now I have Jimmy back in the fray. We have not really spoken since the day I announced to the world I was going. There have been respectful nods of acknowledgement as we both went about our way but nothing more. The magic, if there was ever such a thing between us, has long faded and died. Though now I sense and hope for one last time against Milan we can stand together and plot a path past the wily Italians. He seems keen.

'What do you say Jimmy. One last time?' Jimmy lights a cigarette, he inhales then smiles.

'One last time Matt.'

**Wednesday 23rd April 1969
AC Milan v Manchester United.**

United: Rimmer, Brennan, Fitzpatrick, Crerand, Foulkes, Stiles, Morgan, Kidd, Charlton, Law and Best.

Manchester United are ready. Everybody knows what jobs they have to do and I am confident they will do them well. In the league we have been bitterly disappointing and heaven knows what the Italian scouts have made of us recently but I sense the boys will rise to the big occasion. AC Milan have an abundance of professional, rather than ultra-clever, players and compare well with Gornik, Benfica and Real Madrid. I am glad we are playing the first leg away from Old Trafford and I would like to come away from the San Siro winning, but if we survive unbeaten then I am convinced we can finish the job back in Manchester.

Yet with record receipts of 206 million Lira, 80,000 watching in the stadium and 23,000 more back at Old Trafford on close circuit television, we suffer a bad night. Our hopes of retaining the European Cup look increasingly faint after being beaten 2-0. Goals either side of half time have done for us. The first, a clear handball by striker Angelo Sormani after Paddy's attempted clearance was handled by the Brazilian and, as our boys waited for the referee to give a free kick, he flashed one into the far corner to beat a startled twenty-one year-old Jimmy Rimmer from the edge of the box.

Losing Nobby Stiles, who was carried off with a locked knee, saw our best made plans crumble. These days Nobby has horrible luck with injuries. A career of sweating blood for both United's and England's cause is catching up with him. His best days are behind him. He was upset at being forced out of the action. This boy from Collyhurst, a warrior, no one I have ever met has a bigger heart and for what it is worth, a much undervalued footballer outside our red walls. Norrie senses danger, he faces giants and he hunts them down. He does so with a measure of fine play and an instinctive knowledge of the dark arts. When to hit and not - a style not designed to hurt but to null and destroy. It's a long way from Monsall Rec on the red shale to Wembley Stadium on Saturday 6th July 1966 but Nobby learned and listened. He listened to Jimmy and conquered the world on that never to be forgotten day for the English. Nobby is a footballers' footballer. Reviled by those unwilling to accept him but here amongst brothers he is loved and admired. The players call him 'Happy' for Norrie loves a moan. He deserves better luck. He deserves more.

Prompted by the slim figure of the beguiling genius of this son of Milan, Gianni Rivera and sensing Mancunian blood, the Italians turned up the heat. Their second goal came five minutes after the break when, with our defenders sleeping, the clever Swedish playmaker Kurt Hamrin steered his shot past Jimmy Rimmer from eight yards. I feel for Jimmy. He has been doing well recently after coming in for an out of form Alex Stepney. The five games Jimmy has played he has done splendidly and has not let us down in the torrid atmosphere of the San Siro.

The scoreline could have been much worse without him for two close range saves from Sormani early on defied belief. But it was a bad goal to lose and matters grew increasingly worse when ten minutes from time young John Fitzpatrick got himself stupidly sent off for kicking a teasing Hamrin off the ball. It smacked of a boy out of his depth here in both terms of talent and temperament, he's fallen for the play-acting of the cunning Swede. With Willie and George shackled brilliantly by their man marking duo of Anquilletti and the brilliant German Karl-Heinz Schnellinger, and with Bobby having an off night, we were outgunned, and ultimately, well beaten.

Still the two goals did not appear sufficient for the Italian fans whom pelted my boys with rotten fruit as we left the pitch and more worryingly unleashed a barrage of fireworks upon them. Luckily nobody was hurt.

Jimmy Murphy was fuming afterwards, he raged at the referee and linesmen, who luckily failed to grasp Anglo-Saxon cursing in a strong South Welsh accent. His epithets were also aimed at Milan officials, supporters, indeed anyone who crossed his path.

'On our turf, in front of our people, we shall see what happens in Manchester' exclaimed an angry Jimmy to a bemused Milanese policeman.

'They have done us again!' he cursed back in the tunnel, 'the bastards have done us again!'

Finally we get Jimmy into the changing room before he starts World War Three. In reality I believe we got away with it for the Italians were much better. Milan missed a host of chances, any one of which would surely have put the tie beyond us. However an early goal at a packed Old Trafford and it is game on. Catenaccio will show its ugly face as they come and bolt the door. A difficult task awaits, difficult but not impossible. We are going to have to not just keep knocking on it, we are going to have to blow it open.

This is not yet over.

11 - SAY IT AIN'T SO, CHARLIE

In the Quadrant pub in Stretford, several United players are sat amid cigarette smoke and pint glasses dissecting Wilf McGuinness' appointment as team coach. Opinion is mixed and voices are being raised. The 'Quad' is a regular Sunday afternoon haunt for the boys. It is also Wilf's local, and he is unusually late. Gathered around a table are Willie Morgan, Shay Brennan, Paddy Crerand and Alex Stepney.

Willie looks at his watch. He is leading the anti Wilf brigade. 'Obviously thinks he is above us now, lads. We are not good enough for him anymore.'

'Just as well Willie,' replies Paddy, 'you have done nothing but slag him off all afternoon.'

Shay is Wilf's best friend and is becoming increasingly irked with Willie's stance. The normally laid back Shay has heard enough. 'I really don't understand you ,Willie. You have been here five minutes and all you do is moan. Maybe the old man should have left you in Burnley.'

'Steady on Shay' interrupts Alex, 'Willie is entitled to his opinion. He is one of us now.' Alex's comments only infuriate Shay more.

'One of us? Alex come on. Have you been listening? He thinks he is better than George for God's sake.'

Paddy laughs out loud. 'Oh Willie please tell me this isn't true. Bestie is on another planet.'

All eyes fall upon Willie. 'Go on Willie boy,' smiles Shay, knowing he has rattled Willie, 'tell the boys what you told me. That you think you are better than George.'

Willie takes a drink of his pint. He decides not to rise to the bait of the Irishman for he knows the truth. 'Wee' Willie Morgan, adored by the Stretford End. Already the fans have a song for him. Busby gave him George Best's shirt. What does that say? He is earning £120 a week plus bonuses. Willie is the future. 'Wee' Willie Morgan on the wing. Not George. George is old news. Willie will take care of that.

'Why not give Wilf a chance?' repeats Shay. 'He's earned it. He knows us, he knows the club, and how it works. Imagine if Don Revie came in or that lunatic at Derby County, Brian Clough? They would turn United upside down. Bring in their own players. People like me and Nobby and Paddy will be thrown out with the garbage.'

'Hey speak for yourself you cheeky bastard,' laughs Paddy.

'All I am saying,' replies Willie, 'is that George is a genius I agree, but he is unreliable. A disaster waiting to happen.'

Shay rolls his eyes and smiles. 'Keep digging lad,' he says as Willie continues.

'Someone with his lifestyle. The birds, the booze, the gambling, it has to slow you down. Take away your edge. He will let you all down believe me, he will let United down. '

'He never let us down last May against Benfica Willie son.' says Paddy. 'Now George is a good friend of mine. Let it be now. Change the subject.'

'But Pat 'implores Willie. 'I was just…'

'I am serious Willie, leave it!' Paddy is losing

patience fast. Suddenly a familiar voice interrupts Willie and Paddy's argument.

'Now boys, we are all United here, what are you two old ladies going on about?' Wilf has arrived. 'Sorry I'm late lads, I have been down at the ground with the boss. I couldn't get away. Now what are you all drinking?'

'Mine is a pint please Wilf,' says Willie bold as brass. Shay and Paddy stare on in amazement. Paddy shakes his head in disbelief. Wilf points towards the others' glasses.

'Same again lads?' They all nod their heads.

'Cheers Wilf' almost in unison.

'Willie you have more front than Blackpool,' says Shay, as Wilf disappears out of earshot at the bar.

'I hope you still come in here when you are managing United next season Wilf?' Ex-railwayman Charlie Baxter is seventy-five years old and a lifelong United fan. He has two homes. 23 Kings Road and the barstool at the Quadrant pub. Charlie minds his own business, but also misses nothing. He hears and sees all whilst sat on his throne by the bitter pump.

Wilf has known Charlie for years. The day following the air crash he had reported at Old Trafford and was told the full extent of the dreadful death toll. On leaving the ground a broken-hearted Wilf headed straight for the Quad. At the bar he ordered a large whisky. Stood next to him was Charlie. Before Wilf had a chance to touch his drink, Charlie took it from him and poured it on the floor.

'Go home son, be with those you love most. Stay by the phone. God knows it will ring and you are going to need a clear head today.'

At first a shocked Wilf contemplated whether to punch Charlie, but thought better of it when he saw the tears falling down Charlie's face. For when it came to loss Charlie Baxter knew what he was talking about. He lost his younger brother, eighteen year-old Ronald, fighting alongside him at the Somme. Mown down by a German machine gun, Ronald bled to death whilst entangled on barbed wire. In trying to cut him free Charlie himself was badly injured, but survived, just, and was shipped back to England. His war was over.

Then, twenty years later the Germans came looking for him again during the 1941 Christmas blitz. Volunteering as a fire fighter Charlie found himself in central Manchester fighting a huge warehouse blaze. It was only on returning home to Stretford the following morning that he was informed by a waiting warden that his wife and two young children had been killed in a direct hit on an air raid shelter. The cruel hand of fate had intervened for a second time, tearing Charlie Baxter's world apart.

'What can I get you Charlie?' asks Wilf.

'Very generous of you Wilf' he replies, 'a pint of bitter please.'

Wilf orders the round, with Charlie watching him closely.

'A bit of free advice from an old man. Take or leave it…'

Wilf turns to face the old man. 'What is on your mind Charlie mate?'

'Watch your back son.' With that Charlie glares over towards an unsuspecting Willie Morgan. Wilf's eyes follow.

'Thanks Charlie.' Wilf understands, he knows

things have and will be said behind his back about the appointment. It hurts him to think such for beneath the brash and loud persona, Wilf is a sensitive soul. He cares about others and what they think. But this job is his dream and when the time is right Wilf McGuinness is determined not to be anyone's fool. He will fight fire with fire and sort out those who need sorting out. When appropriate he hopes to remain 'Good old Wilf,' who plays cards on the team coach and is good for a laugh and a joke. No favourites though, no matter how hard and how difficult it becomes, old friendships such as Bobby, Paddy and Shay must be cast aside and will count for nothing. Even Jimmy, he reveres Jimmy Murphy, A second Father for Wilf. His hero. He will resist bending Jimmy's ear for as hard as it sounds, it is him and Sir Matt now. Who better to call on than the great man who will still be sat just twenty yards away down the Old Trafford corridor? Besides the game is changing. "Give the ball to a red shirt" and "Go out and express yourself" is no longer sufficient in this modern era when winning by any means is what matters. Tactics and minor details now decide games and win trophies.

The beauty is close to being slaughtered by the beast. Wilf has new ideas; he was part of Sir Alf Ramsey's coaching set up that conquered the word without a winger in sight. He watched and listened and learned. Armed with the vision and passion of Busby and Murphy and the pragmatism of Ramsey, Wilf is determined to ensure the reds go marching on and on. At whatever cost. But Wilf knows there will be heartache ahead. He also wishes Charlie had not heard and told him Willie had been having a dig.

'Say it ain't so Charlie?' But Charlie nods his head. So be it, now Wilf knows he will sort it.

Wilf will sort everything.

12 - PARADISE

Ten miles south of the Quadrant pub, in Lymm, Cheshire, Bobby Charlton is opening a church fête with wife Norma by his side. To polite applause from a large gaggle of excitable well off Cheshire ladies and their star struck husbands Bobby cuts the ribbon.

Norma herself joins in the clapping with much enthusiasm. She is hiding the disappointment well at not seeing her husband appointed the next Manchester United manager. Bobby is busy shaking hands and signing autographs. He is on auto-pilot. He is being Bobby Charlton.

'It should have been you Bobby', 'You deserved it Bobby', 'You are Manchester United Bobby', 'You are more deserving than Wilf'.

'Wilf is a good lad,' he replies, 'he is United through and through and all the team are behind him.' His audience breathe a collective sigh and relax – if Bobby says everything is going to be okay, it'll be ok. And even though Bobby wants to scream out loud and declare he thinks the old man has lost his mind in appointing Wilf McGuinness, he instead smiles politely at all. 'Let us all trust Sir Matt.'

'Three cheers for Bobby' somebody shouts.

'Hip hip horray!'

Here is Bobby surrounded by grown men who adore him. Who remain in awe of the boy who survived the Munich inferno and went on to lead United back from the abyss. A young man broken almost in mind and spirit by seeing his friends wiped out around him who somehow found the courage and strength of will to go on. This is the man they crowd around and want to touch. A man they wish to thank.

But Bobby misses the person he was before the darkness. The Bobby Charlton who emerged from the smoke and flames of that wrecked aircraft was vastly different to the happy, ebullient young lad who before that dark day was convinced life at Old Trafford with his team-mates, especially best friend Duncan Edwards, was simply paradise.

★

Chamartin Stadium, Madrid – Thursday 11th April 1957: With thirty minutes to kick off in the Real Madrid-Manchester United-European Cup semi final first leg, and unable to get a minute to themselves amid the madness and nervous tension of the dressing room, Matt Busby and Jimmy Murphy decide to head for the only sane place in the stadium. The centre circle!

There before a screaming 135,000 crowd, the two men who had dreamed of this moment for over ten years can have a last chat to compose themselves before battle begins in this magnificent, awe-inspiring arena.

Jimmy gazes around at the vast imperious surroundings of the Chamartin. The towering stands that reach up towards the heavens. Almost touching the crystal blue Madrid sky. Seething and bursting to the rafters with a passionate crowd. A Madrilène support blazing with a ferocity and curiosity to see with their own eyes this team of boys from England, of whom so much has been said and written. How will they cope against their beloved Alfredo di Stefano and his collection of wizards and magicians? Di Stefano is the conductor. He waves his baton and Raymonde Kopa and Francisco Gento race like the wind. For they know with all the certainty of night following day, Alfredo will find them with a ball that arrives at the feet with their names on it.

'Why do I feel like we are the bull up against a bullfighter armed with a shotgun?' says Jimmy.

'Our bull has sharp horns, Jimmy' laughs Matt. 'We can hurt them and they are nervous.' Matt points towards the terraces. 'I can feel it in the air. They have no idea what is coming their way.'

The noise is deafening, a crescendo. Jimmy has to shout loudly to make himself heard. Seen from on high these two slight figures stood alone in the centre circle, amid an ever rising hysteria approaching kick off, plot the downfall of the white knights – the Kings of Europe. 'We have come a long way Matt from that burnt out rust hut at Old Trafford. This is what you have dreamt and worked so hard for.'

Matt leans close to Jimmy to talk loud into his ear. 'You deserve this equally so Jimmy. I could not have done any of this without you. Time is on our side old pal.'

Jimmy smiles and puts out his hand. 'To the Busby Babes.'

'To Murphy's Red apples' replies Busby.

The two men shake and then make their way back off the pitch and head down to the Manchester United changing room.

Final Score: Real Madrid 3 Manchester United 1:

'It was a splendid match Señor Busby and your boys have done you and Manchester proud. it has truly been an honour to have you and Manchester United in our city.' A smiling Don Santiago Bernabeu, President of Real Madrid, shakes hands with Matt Busby, amid the magnificent splendour of the Spaniard's board room.

Only the two men are present. It is an hour after the full time whistle has blown on the European cup semi-final first leg. Real, with the great Alfredo di Stefano outstanding, win 3-1 but the Babes have acquitted themselves well and Bernabeu knows they still face a hellish return game in Manchester. He has requested to meet the United manager.

This larger than life character, a man who exudes power from every pore, is wary of this young team from northern England who from nowhere have emerged to challenge Real Madrid's early dominance of the European Cup. He has an idea to stop them in their tracks.

'Thank you Mr President,' smiles Busby. 'You have wonderful players and I feel my boys learned some valuable lessons today.'

'Please, may I call you Matt?'

'Of course' he replies.

Bernabeu hands Busby a cigar, which has the Madrid symbol branded upon it. 'Thank you.' Class personified, thinks the United manager.

'Matt, I wish to speak to you on matter of extreme importance before tonight's banquet. I have a proposition for you.'

'Go on Mr President.'

'I will give you heaven on earth, whatever your heart desires to come to Madrid and coach my team. Name your price my friend.' Busby is stunned. He did not see this coming. A smiling Bernabeu feels he already has his man. 'There is no need for an answer straight away. Go back to England and speak to your family. I promise you I am not going away. I will never stop asking!'

Busby looks shocked.

'Mr President I am stunned and extremely flattered. And humbled by your offer. Let us speak again on this matter.'

'Of course Matt,' Bernabeu moves towards Busby and embraces him, 'when I come to Manchester we will discuss this more.'

That same night Real Madrid, with Bernabeu as host, put on a wonderful banquet for the visiting Mancunians. Each player is presented with a solid gold watch by the president. None more than Duncan Edwards are dazzled by the Spaniards gifts and generosity.

'Bloody hell Bobby this is priceless,' he confides to his friend Bobby Charlton. 'Have you ever seen anything like this?' Big Duncan holds it lovingly in his hands.

'They'll probably take it back if we knock them out at Old Trafford,' quips Eddie Colman, who is listening in.

Bobby notices the boss in deep conversation with Alfredo di Stefano. 'What do you think they are talking about Dunc?' he asks. Edwards looks up from his watch towards the two men. He laughs and pats Bobby on the knee.

'Don't worry, chief. Why would the old man want to sign the great Alfredo when he has you waiting in the wings?'

As the evening goes on Bobby is stood alone when he feels a tap on his shoulder. He turns around and it is a smiling Matt Busby with drink in hand. 'What do you think of all this Bobby lad?'

'Unbelievable boss' he replies.

'This club, this stadium, this city is marvellous don't you think?'

'Yes boss' replies Bobby. Then Busby puts an arm around him. 'But it is not Manchester is it Bobby?' He smiles: 'That is our paradise is it not?'

'It is boss' repeats a grinning Bobby. 'It is paradise.'

Busby, though flattered, has already decided he is never going to accept Bernabeu's offer. For paradise is where the heart is and his along with Bobby Charlton's belong to Manchester.

★

'Paradise' Bobby says out loud as Norma appears alongside him at the church fête.

'Are you okay Bobby?'

'Yes dear' he replies.

'Honestly Bob, sometimes you just go off into a world of your own.' Norma links Bobby's arm. 'Come on my love let's go and mingle.'

To a hub of excitement the Charltons' return to the party and soon Bobby is once more surrounded on this Sunday afternoon in Lymm.

'Tell me Bobby' a voice rings out loud, Bobby can't see the face. He looks over the crowd to make eye contact but there are simply too many people. He finally gives up, only to hear it once more.

'What was Duncan Edwards really like?' Bobby thinks of Duncan looking at his watch given to him by

President Bernabeu.

'Priceless,' he replies, fighting once more to hold back the tears.

13 - THE LAST BATTLE CRY

Encore: Wednesday 15th May 1969: If this is to be my last encore in the European Cup, then I am glad Jimmy is going to stand beside me. Once upon a time we shared a dream. We were going to build the greatest team in the world and we were going to do it by using our own boys. Our ripe apples. Reared from a Mancunian tree, taught by Jimmy, the finest red.

And I believe we succeeded, only for our dreams to be torn from the sky. Tonight we are facing a fine AC Milan team that are two goals up and I am convinced already feel they are in the final. We shall see.

This competition in time I have learned to love, loathe, fear and adore. It has broken me both physically and mentally, only then to raise me back up again. And so to my last game. If there is one thing I have learned in managing this magnificent club of ours for twenty-four years it is that nothing is impossible. For we came from nothing to the stars.

My team for the last encore: Rimmer, Brennan, Burns, Crerand, Foulkes, Stiles, Morgan, Kidd, Charlton, Law and Best.

The Italians are not just confident of going through; they are a little cocky with it, I believe. Their coach Nereo Rocco declared yesterday: 'When we knocked out Celtic last year in Glasgow after drawing 0-0 at home we had nothing to lose and were hoping for a miracle. This match against Manchester United is very different. The Italian public and press expect us to go through. And if we resist for twenty minutes at Old Trafford, I am sure that here in Manchester, you will witness a great Milan.'

Fifteen minutes before the game begins I address the players. It feels strange as they sit there in an all white strip. A rule stipulated by UEFA after we played in red in Milan. I look around at the faces.

They look ready.

'Now lads we know what we have to do so let's get after them from the first whistle. Play hard, let the ball do the work. But keep your cool, don't let them rattle you. George and Willie, I think you owe your markers a game after the first leg. Don't you?'

'Yes boss' they both reply.

'Their coach Rocco seems to feel they are already in the final. So let's ruin his night shall we? Let's send the Italians home crying.'

With that I step away. I have always been a support act to what is to follow. I nod to Jimmy and he steps forward. You can hear a pin drop, not a rattle of a stud, even the crowd noise outside seems to diminish. I imagine a huge hush settling over the terraces, as if even they wish to listen in. He says nothing for a moment. The calm before a raging storm. Jimmy simply smiles and stands with his hands in his suit trouser pockets facing the players. He loves them all. For a second their faces disappear and he sees instead Duncan Edwards, Eddie Colman, David Pegg, Roger Byrne, Tommy Taylor, Liam Whelan, Mark Jones and Geoff Bent.

He looks to his left and sees the beloved Tom Curry and Bert Whalley. His dear departed friends and fellow trainers killed at Munich stand at his side. They are smiling. Jimmy rubs his eyes. He looks again and they are all gone. He composes himself. He takes a deep breath and begins – the last battle cry.

'I want to tell you all a quick story. We have time. Now you all know me, I am a man who likes the simple things in life. A quiet pint, a sing song in the midnight hour. I have even been known to twinkle on a piano or two.'

The players smile, their love and respect for Jimmy obvious.

'I want to tell you a tale about a rainbow. It is a magical rainbow. It does not need sunshine and showers to light up the skies because it only exists in our world. You see boys it is a Manchester United rainbow and its colours are red, white and black. And it is filled with miracles and wonder and awe. Now the great thing about our rainbow is that if you don't believe you cannot see it. Now this lot we are playing tonight. They cannot see our rainbow and do you know why? Anyone?'

A laughing George Best puts his hand in the air. 'They don't believe in it Jimmy.'

'That's right George' smiles Jimmy. 'And do you know what lads? For me that is a sin. And so we are going to have make these non-believers pay. And how do we do that?'

'We knock the bastards out Jimmy'! replies Brian Kidd.

'Exactly Brian' says Jimmy. 'Tonight we have to ensure our rainbow is glowing over Collyhurst to make sure your Mum and Dad can see it, okay?'

Brian nods.

'Now for me the story is almost over lads. Soon I retire to my piano and I sing songs of past deeds.

Of glorious heroes who have gone before you. Boys who performed as men, who were taken before their time and who form that rainbow which we treasure as our own. I love three things in this word. My family, my God and this club. Now let's get out there and do this lot and ensure our rainbow is shining over Madrid when we go there for the final. For they love us there, boys. This tonight is the one, we get to the Bernabeu and I promise you a glory night under Spanish stars.' Jimmy clenches his fist and roars out: 'Now come on!'

The players jump to their feet. There are roars and screams of encouragement. Jimmy Murphy has done his part. He can do no more. With such passion and fire he departs the stage. Without this man there would not be a Manchester United as we know today.

As kick off draws near, 63,000 file inside Old Trafford, and the ground heaves with both excitement and trepidation. The Stretford End rocks and sways and then explodes in a cascade of red and white as the two teams come out of the tunnel into full view. And so it begins and for seventy minutes we huff and puff and at times bang loud, but Milan, these supreme masters of the defensive arts, remain unyielding. They are defiant.

None more than Angelo Anquilletti, once more, whose man-marking of George has been ferocious but fair. His has been a dark shadow, one George has struggled all night to escape from. But George keeps going. As does Willie Morgan, who has been equally sedated by the German stopper, Karl-Heinz Schnellinger.

In all honesty Rocco's men could have finished the tie off in the first half as they broke twice from defence with the ever dangerous Sormani and Prati to give us heart attacks. Luckily we survived but as the clock ticks down the European Cup is surely slipping from our grasps. We desperately need divine intervention, a slice of luck. A moment of inspiration.

A thirty-yard Bobby Charlton thunderbolt to rip through the sky and the Italian net. A Denis Law blistering scissor kick through a heap of bodies. A drop of the shoulders and a rasping drive into the goal from my magic man, George. Come on George, one last time. For me George.

For me.

Still we charge as George beats one, two. I am off my seat.

'Go on Bestie' screams Wilf. George flies into the box, he lays off the ball for an incoming Bobby Charlton who lashes a shot past the keeper Fabio Cudicini into the net. Old Trafford explodes, it ignites!

Jimmy punches the air. We need one more to force extra time. The Italians are rocked. The ground is shaking. We have a corner. Please just one more time! One more time. Brian Kidd's header is cleared off the line. Torture, sheer unmitigated torture.

Time ticks away, seconds turn agonisingly to minutes. I so wish I could stop the clock. I glance over to the Milan bench and the coach Rocco appears a man close to jumping off a mountain. Still my boys attack, the crowd are near exhaustion. Voices hoarse, nerves shattered and done for. We all are. The ball is once more in the Milan penalty area. Paddy crosses it into the six yard box to Denis who scores! We've done it! Wilf is hugging me and Jimmy's smile is wider than the Irwell. But wait, what is happening?

No, no, no! The French referee Roger Marchin has

deemed the ball did not go over the line. A diabolical decision. Anquilletti fished the ball out but it was clearly four yards over the line! Paddy comes to the touchline and shouts: 'It is a bloody disgrace. Willie was stood on the line. He did not even bother to follow it in he was so certain.'

I tell him to forget it. 'Keep going Pat. They are on the rack. It is just a matter of time.'

Time, time, time stops for no man and time has run out for Manchester United. And then the darkness. The final whistle.

We are out.

I look across to Jimmy, he is sat head down, slumped. His rainbow has gone now. A last goodbye. I feel it is only right for us to form a tunnel and applaud the jubilant Milan players off the pitch.

Rocco appears. 'A long night Mr Busby. I think another five minutes and you would have scored again. In defeating your great team I feel we have already won the final.'

He offers me his hand and we shake. 'Congratulations on your victory my friend. I wish you luck in the final.'

I go to commiserate with Jimmy but he has disappeared. Then another hand is thrust upon my shoulder. I turn around and it is Denis. The referee Marchin strolls past but will not meet my eyes. Denis goes to confront the Frenchman but I pull him back.

'That ball was over the line boss. We have been robbed.'

I put my arm around him.

'Nothing we can do now Denis lad. It is over. It is all over.'

★

In the Manchester United dressing room before the last league game of the season against Leicester City, I say a few words.

'Gentlemen, it has been a privilege to call myself manager of this great club for the last twenty-four years. Of course there have been periods when it has not been so good. Tragic even. There was a period just after Munich when I did not think I could do this job any more. But ultimately I decided I had to come back and give it a go. Sometimes I think I was given a push by angels. I think you know who I am talking about.

'Last year winning the European Cup was, I have to admit, a final chapter of a book I should have closed after the final. Anyway,' I smile, 'I am here now. And today I pass the baton on to a man who has my complete trust and backing. To Wilf here.'

Wilf steps forward to stand alongside me. I continue. 'A red to the core. A United man and babe. My final words to you all is to show him the same loyalty and passion you have me over the years…

'I ask you now to stand by your new manager.'

14 - A NEW DAY

It is a beautiful, sunlit, June morning in Manchester and Wilf McGuinness is first to arrive at United's training ground, The Cliff. He is nervous but equally excited. It his first official day as team coach. Wilf wants an early start. Later, he will get everybody together and lay down a few house rules. No one is going to fool around with Wilf. A new brush… nail them before they do for him.

Wilf is sat at his office desk going over his speech notes when suddenly a familiar voice makes him look up.

'You look good, Wilf. It suits you.'

Wilf stands. 'Sit down, boss.' I smile and shake my head.

'It is your desk here now lad. Are you ready?'

'Just a few welcoming words,' Wilf points to his notes, at least four pages deep.

'Keep it short and to the point, son. No need for War and Peace,' I smile, 'most importantly be yourself, that is why you got the job. Don't change, be straight with the boys and they will do right by you. They are good lads. They just need a new voice telling them the right things to do. That voice is yours Wilf. Always remember you have the tools to do the job. Handle them firmly but with respect and everything will be fine. Okay?' Wilf smiles. I pat him on the arm. 'Good lad. Right I will leave you to it. Oh one last thing.'

'What's that boss?'

'Forget about Colin Todd, Mick Mills and Malcolm Macdonald. We don't need them. We are okay with what we have. Let's keep it the same for now.'

A part of Wilf crumbles, it is worryingly soon to feel such disappointment. But the best of days remain relatively untouched. Still plenty of time for dreams.

Wilf gazes out of his office window at The Cliff. He makes the sign of the cross and says a swift prayer. And a quick aside to Eddie, Duncan and the boys. 'Help me out lads. This is a big day.' The players are all gathering together, waiting for his speech. The grand oratory. Wilf's opening message as team coach of Manchester United Football Club.

He knows they will be watching for weaknesses. Some may try and take the piss. He will remember faces that are looking at him, whose eyes are on the ground. Who is smiling, who is laughing. Who is saying with their eyes, 'not for me McGuinness. You are not for me.'

Jack Crompton and John Aston senior, his mates and now his staff, have rounded them all up before training starts. George, Bobby, Bill, Denis, Paddy, Alex, Shay, Nobby and Willie. The entire squad. They will be judging. Watching and listening to his every move and word. Life will be strange for a while, especially with the senior players. Men he has laughed, fought, cried, drunk and played cards with. Bobby and Bill who survived the hell of Munich. Bobby and Bill who walked out of the flames. What will they be thinking today? But ultimately Wilf knows, for he is the boss. Now he will decide careers and pick the team. He will be the judge. Wilf has a speech and he has rehearsed it well. Churchillian! The old man will be proud. Things will change; training, tactics. United will join the real world.

'All right lads, listen up' says Jack, 'the boss is going to say a few words.' There are a few grunts and awkward coughs, but nobody speaks.

Nobody.

Wilf looks across to Bobby Charlton who is staring at his boots and appearing to wish he could be anywhere but here today.

'Thanks Bobby' thinks Wilf. 'Thanks for your fucking support.' Jack moves aside and Wilf steps forward.

'You all know me' begins Wilf, 'I like to think I am a fair man. I have had fall outs with many of you. Whether it be on the training ground, in the dressing room or in the pub or on the coach. But I have always ended up shaking hands. I have never held a grudge. So I am not going to change.'

Wilf points at the crowd of players.

'You are going to change. You. Not all but some. And I think you know who you are. Don't you? This club stops for no one. The old man may have stepped down but I will ensure United go on to even greater things. You are either with me or...' Wilf smiles, 'Well I am sure I don't have to draw you pictures.'

Wilf meets no one's eyes but is aware of many boring a hole through his head.

'Don't balls this up Wilf' thinks Paddy.

'Little man in big shoes' thinks Denis.

'He better not be talking about me' thinks Bobby.

'Just try it Wilf and see how you get on without me' thinks George.

'Steady on Wilf' thinks Nobby.

'You are not going to last lad' thinks Alex.

'Taxi for Willie' thinks Willie.

'There is going to be more emphasis on tactics. Everyone will be made more aware of their jobs. All aspects of the team will be improved. In so many areas of our game we have slipped behind sides such as Leeds, City, Liverpool and Everton. I will change that. We have to become more professional, we have become sloppy and soft in our ways. Our attitude is not good enough. Well I will change that. The word out there is that we do not have the heart for a fight anymore. That we can be bullied and just cave in. Believe me, so long as there is a sun in the sky, I will change that.

'People are looking at Manchester United as a fallen giant. A busted flush. I am sick and tired of that big mouth, Malcolm bloody Allison saying they rule this city. It is a blue city. Well this is a United city and I want that title back. I want to shut that idiot up. Boys' smiles Wilf, 'United, us,' he puts his hand on heart. 'We are now seen as a bunch of players living on their past. Others are not good enough, or simply not bothered and more interested in the birds and the booze. Well I promise you, this is a red fucking dawn and take it from me I was there at the beginning of this rainbow and I will be fucked if I will be there at the end. For United are going to go on and on. And anyone not wanting to come with me, speak up now. For this is a new day. This is my time – now'

'Calm down son,' thinks Jack Crompton. Jack catches John Aston's eye, he shakes his head. Both men feeling Wilf has begun like a hammer smashing apart a wedding cake. The grand speech goes on.

'Now my door is always going to be open, so any

of you whom feel they are not getting a fair crack come and see me. Don't go bothering Sir Matt, he has far too much on his hands now. You will not be doing him or yourselves any favours. All first team affairs are down to me and if anyone does go running telling tales, well, no one likes a sneak.'

Wilf claps his hands together. 'Right speech over; let's get down to some hard graft.' If the new United team coach was expecting a standing ovation he is sadly mistaken, as a cold silence cuts across The Cliff training pitch.

Wilf's frenzied excitement and eagerness to get his point across has seen him get carried away. Jack whispers quietly to Aston as the players scatter in small groups with looks of incredulity on their faces.

'He's just a little hyped up, John. Give him a week or so and he will calm down.'

'I hope you are right Jack' replies Aston, 'otherwise we are going to have a bloody revolution on our hands.'

'Blimey mate' says Nobby Stiles to Paddy Crerand, as all the players begin running together around the training field. 'Wilf thinks he is going to war.'

'Aye that he is Nob' answers Paddy, 'and it is one he will never win.'

George jogs up alongside Nobby and Paddy. He is smiling. 'I wonder who Wilf's comment about birds and booze was aimed at?' Both men laugh.

'Where did you end up last night then?' asks Paddy.

'I cannot remember where, but she was an air hostess. Scandinavian type, blond haired, long legged, blue eyes. She dropped me off here this morning.'

Nobby shakes his head. 'Lucky sod, are you seeing her again?'

George smiles like only George can. 'You are kidding aren't you Nob?' George is genuinely amused by Nobby's question. 'I asked her to marry me but sadly she is flying out today. So I am just going to have to find another bird tonight. You can come and watch if you like?'

Nobby attempts a playful slap on George's head but he ducks and sprint away just in time. 'Cheeky bastard ' smiles Nobby.

'Where does he get the energy Pat?'

Paddy is still staring at George now twenty yards away. 'I don't know but I can smell the booze on him from here.'

Willie Morgan sidles up next to Alex Stepney. Willie is worried. 'Well that went well don't you think. Not exactly the old man is he, Alex?' The United keeper is breathing heavily and does not really need to hear Willie's woes at this time.

'Give me a break Willie, I'm dying here!'

Watching the players closely, Wilf spots Stepney and Morgan chatting.

'Oi Willie, Alex, this is not the fucking golf course. This is work, put some effort in.'

Stood next to Wilf is Jack, who rolls his eyes at the new coach's comments.

'I am going to get some more balls from inside Wilf,' says Jack. Desperately needing to get away for a moment to compose his thoughts. As Jack walks off the training pitch he hears Wilf shout out:

'All right lads gather round. I am going to educate you now. Listen hard because this is a whole new bible. I am going to tell you about restarts.'

★

I never listened to Wilf's speech, I chose not to – thinking all eyes would be on me and not him. No, my time is over on the training pitch. It is Wilf now. Instead I will venture out when the press lads turn up later for the photo shoot. One big happy family. I did watch through the window and Wilf appeared animated. Hopefully he has managed to keep his emotions in check. If not I am sure I will be hearing about it sooner rather than later. I see Jack walk past my open door.

'How did it go old son?'

'Like the Saint Valentine's Day massacre boss. Wilf got a little carried away. Maybe you could have a word?'

'No Jack, I cannot interfere. He has only been in the job five minutes. You and John will have to keep an eye. Wilf will be fine. Trust me, things will settle down.'

Jack sighs and does not seem convinced. 'Okay boss.' He goes to leave but suddenly turns around. 'Oh by the way, have you ever heard of restarts?'

I shake my head. 'No why?'

'Something Wilf is keen on.'

Jack smiles ruefully. 'A new day.'

15 - MAN ON THE MOON

Run by the mother of soon to be rock legend Phil Lynott, Phyllis's unlicensed drinking den lies south of the city in Whalley Range, Chorlton. It is a private house, set downstairs in a large Victorian building. A lounge with a bar. Almost like a living room, no more, with thick red velvet curtains forever closed to the outside world and prying eyes. There are no clocks – night or day does not exist at Phyllis's. Just the race to the bottom of the glass. And another and a...

They never go home, they never sleep. Invitation comes through word of mouth. Once in, never out. A private club with no airs or graces. All backgrounds bound together by the promise of just one more. For the lost souls who don't want to close their eyes. The home of those who live in the darkness – the night owls, alcoholics, gangsters, club workers, croupiers, bouncers, taxi drivers. Dark shades of the law; policemen, barristers, High court judges, the nightshift... and famous footballers.

All are welcome so long as you behave and show class and respect to fellow drinkers.

Phyllis serves you with a warm smile, a wink and open arms. 'How is it going love?' The promise of an Irish stew mixed with vodka at breakfast awaits those who make it through till morning. And then the party goes on.

To such a place a man comes when all his friends and companions have had enough. As the lights on the dance floor are switched off, glasses cleared off the table and the DJ has gone home. When eyes have grown weary. Conversations are tired, littered with yawns. When Manchester's throwing out time is long past and mere mortals yearn for a taxi home and bed.

George goes on. One more drink, then one more. No beers just shorts, vodka sweetened by lemonade. Through the darkened deserted streets of the city, George's black cab makes it way.

'Have you had a good night George?' asks the driver. George is deep in thought, staring out the window. He likes the night. For him it acts as a magic cloak giving him invisibility from the madding crowds. At least temporarily. Waggy has gone home; David Sadler and Mike Summerbee, his recent partners in lust and life have recently married. Two friends who tended to have George's ear when it came to deciding enough. 'Let's go home George.' Few say that now. Those that do he tends to ignore. Now all alone in the back of a cab he cuts a lonely figure, as it winds its way ever closer to Phyllis's.

'Good thanks' smiles George, back in the land of the living and replying to the driver who looks in his mirror and thinks George does not look drunk. He just looks sad.

It has just gone three in the morning when the cab pulls up outside Phyllis's. George gets out and pays the driver. 'Any chance of an autograph for my little lad please George?'

'Of course' he obliges. The driver passes him a pen and piece of paper.

'Could you sign it to Tommy?' George smiles like only George can and signs: 'To Tommy from George

Best.' He hands it back over.

'Thanks George.' The driver puts his hand out and the two shake.

'What's your name?' asks George.

'Tommy.'

'Just like your lad eh?' grins George.

'To be honest,' replies Tommy, 'I've got two daughters! You take care. Stay safe George.'

'Thanks Tommy.' George watches as the black cab drives off. He is on his own again.

On entering, George is greeted by Phyllis. An attractive Southern Irish lady in her mid forties. Once a stunner, once beautiful, she is still a looker. But formidable with it. She's not someone to take liberties with. Her boyfriend Dennis acts as lookout and bouncer by keeping constant watch from an upstairs window for unwanted visitors. On the odd occasion an undesignated visit from the a nosey panda car did arrive, most times such occasions were simply handled by the officers being plied with a bottle of vodka to take away and a handful of bank notes. The word was out across the city. This was a classy joint. Leave well alone.

Especially when amongst the clientele were high ranking policemen and respected judges and lawyers. Their only vice an unquenchable thirst for the demon drink. A gentle whisper in the right ear goes a long way in this northern outpost. This cottonopolis of intrigue and drama… Manchester: A living and breathing organism. A city of rogues and rascals. Of singers, writers and poets, drunken and unknown – many of whom remain silent and invisible until the clock strikes midnight.

On a theatre stage, on a table they climb. In Phyllis's they are given their moment and the magic words fall in a cascade, like raindrops in a summer shower. An audience enraptured, fellows and ladies, themselves lost in a haze. Lost in a bottle. Their tears and laughter in this world apart.

Phyllis loves George. She gives him a hug and a kiss. 'How is my favourite Irishman doing?' She fills his glass. Around him faces, some he knows, and some he doesn't but they all know him. Everybody knows George. All are friendly. George acknowledges those staring at him. Through a haze of cigarette and cigar smoke come the replies. 'Evening George.' 'Hope you are well George?' 'How is your luck George?' After the initial bevy of greetings a lone voice calls out: 'Did you see the moon landing George?'

Approaching George, with no hint of malice, comes a well-dressed man in suited attire. A smart middle-aged plump gent with a pleasant round, red face. A whisky in hand, he has long since stopped counting...

'May I introduce myself? My name is Robert Myers, I am an investment banker and I have had a particularly rough day. My wife has decided to leave me for another, of much younger years. And to hurl further fuel on the flames already burning in my heart, I told my boss to fuck off earlier this afternoon in a fit of self-pity and he sacked me.'

Such is the look of tragi farce sadness that is etched across Robert's face that George feels like giving him a hug, just to let him know he is amongst good people. But Robert already seems to know! 'Thus I find myself in this wonderful lady's abode. With these equally generous and beautiful people.' Myers bows dramatically to his drinking partners across the room. He appears to have made a decent impression on the varied and colourful clientele.

'You're a good lad Robert', comes a reply from a darkened corner where sits Manchester's Quality Street gang. From whom one raises a glass in the pair's direction. 'Nice to see you George. You need anything let us know.' George acknowledges the offer from the Mancunian underworld by lifting his glass and smiling.

'Would you like a top up Robert?' asks Phyllis.

'You are too kind my love,' Robert takes Phyllis's hand and kisses it much to Georges' amusement.

'Mr Best, I would be honoured if you would sit with me for a brief chat. I would dearly like to speak to you about the moon landing. Only you who have lived among the stars can possibly give me an answer to a question that I cannot rid my mind of.' Robert gesticulates to a corner of the room. He smiles: 'I have reserved you a chair with a wonderful view of the bar and this beautiful lady.' He motions to Phyllis who laughs and is clearly fond of this funny but broken-hearted character who desperately needs a shoulder to lean on and a gentle soul to listen. Luckily he has come to the right place.

'Of course Robert,' smiles George. 'No problem.'

The two men make their way and sit down. Phyllis watches them go. George is someone she is always happy to see but there remain a small part of her that wishes he had no need of her services. There is something in his eyes... a pleading. Eyes so big that are screaming out for help but it is already too late. Phyllis knows George has started out on a path that will lead to his undoing. She has seen the type before. It is a fate already written and it never fails to break her heart.

'George, may I call you George?' asks Robert as he takes another large gulp of whisky to finish his glass. Like magic Phyllis appears with a bottle.

'On the house,' she smiles.

'Thank you my dear, dear lady,' sighs Robert, almost in tears at Phyllis' generosity. She walks away. Other equally tortured souls require her assistance elsewhere in the room, Robert turns his attention back to George. 'Mr Best.'

'Please Robert, call me George. All my friends call me George. What would you like to ask me?'

Robert tops his drink up. 'You remind me George of the astronauts, Neil Armstrong and Buzz Aldrin. I have followed your career. I am not a great football fan but I am a George Best fan. You fascinate me George. You intrigue me. Last May you reached the heavens by winning the European Cup. You have achieved all that is possible for a son of Belfast. Likewise what do Armstrong and Aldrin do now? What was going through their mind the other night when they looked at the earth from the moon? How insignificant must life feel to them now? When those men return home how can they possibly live with the knowledge that whatever they achieve or attempt, their greatest moment, their crowning glory, has gone forever. Everything else is irrelevant. It is the same for you George. I have to ask. You are my man on the moon. My man from the stars. How are you going to cope?'

George has not taken his eyes off Robert all the time he has been speaking.

'Robert, it is no problem whatsoever,' George downs his large vodka and lemonade in one and slams the glass down hard on the table. He wipes his mouth and smiles.

'I am going to stay pissed.'

16 - MY WAY

Saturday 15th August 1969:   Manchester United 1 Southampton 4.

It has not begun well. An opening 2-2 draw at Crystal Palace was acceptable with Willie grabbing a second half equaliser in South London. But then four days later we were well beaten at home 2-0 by Everton. An Alan Ball inspired side outclassed and overran us with worrying ease; Ball again scoring and aiming a little glance in my direction. Bad as that was, events today at Old Trafford against Southampton have proved disastrous. I decide to stay out of the dressing room and give Wilf time with the players to get his point across. Let them know what went on out there was unacceptable. Meanwhile I need to make a phone call to my old pal Bertie Mee at Arsenal.

This can't go on.

★

An irate, red faced Wilf rolls a hand through his hair in the dressing room as he faces his seated players. Jack Crompton and John Aston stand behind him.

'So this is how it is going to be is it? Everything we have said and talked about you have ignored it. Our man marking, restarts, I might as well have been talking in fucking Chinese! Four fucking one: Jesus Christ, the Titanic had more of a result when it left that place than you lot have had today.'

Wilf locks his stare onto an exhausted Bill Foulkes,

who was responsible for the majority of the goals. Foulkes was only playing because of injuries and serious doubts over homegrown talents as Steve James and Paul Edwards. Bill is a former miner from St. Helens, a Munich survivor, the hero of the Bernabeu and a no nonsense character. He goes to take off his shirt, only to stop halfway when Wilf shouts across.

'You'll get changed when I say so Bill.' Suddenly a cold chill fills the dressing room. Bill glares at Wilf. His face ashen. His blood slowly boiling. He is not going to stand for this. 'You heard me' screams Wilf, 'I'm talking here. The centre forward Ron Davies scored all their goals and you were supposed to be marking him. You made him look like fucking Eusebio.'

Bill snaps back. 'You are making yourself look stupid, Wilf. I only played because you asked me to. You know very well I wanted to retire. Now calm down and stop ranting at me and you just might keep your teeth.'

Knowing he may have pushed Bill too far, Wilf looks around and notices Shay Brennan has a wry grin on his face. 'You too Shay. You looked and played like a carthorse out there. Every goal came from your side. You were made to look like a dummy by their winger John Sydenham. And why the fuck are you smiling?'

'Losing a football match is not the end of the world, Wilf. Besides my horse came in at Kempton. I won fifty quid!' Laughter erupts from the other players.

All except Bobby, who is simply staring at the floor. In the last two games Bobby's form has been badly off, his passing has been woeful and against Everton, players in blue shirts were running past and swarming all over him. Bobby could neither catch or shake them off. It scared him. 'Is this it?' he wondered, 'Is this what it feels like when players talk about their legs going?' Not him! Not now! Bobby has his head in hands.

Not him! Not now!

Wilf is shaking his head in disbelief. He is upset and furious at his team's showing. He is also embarrassed. This is not how it was supposed to be. He addresses Shay. 'Let me get one thing straight. Your contract is up at the end of the season right. And you think performances and comments like that are going to see you be handed another one?'

Shay's smile disappears. 'Not so smug now eh Shay?'

The Irishman stares angrily towards Wilf. Shay can't believe that this man before him is, and was, among his oldest and best friends.

'What the hell is that supposed to mean?' he barks. Wilf smiles but it is not a facial expression Shay recognises.

'Things have changed Shay. United are changing. Believe me, you do not want to get on my bad side.'

Denis 'The Lawman' sits quietly watching Wilf go mad. He, like Bobby, knows he has not played well and hopes Wilf does not have a go at him because he could not hold his tongue…

'And you Lawman, what the fuck was wrong with you? You were a yard off all afternoon.'

'Oh here we go,' thinks Denis.

'Where is your fire and passion. I did not recognise you out there.'

Denis snaps. 'Get someone to pass me the fucking ball and I will score and don't you dare talk to me like that!'

'Wilf leave it for God's sake' says Paddy.

'Come on Wilf' adds George, 'We have had a bad day, it happens.' An exasperated Wilf looks close to tears.

'Bad days happen in factories and warehouses George. We are Manchester United. We can't afford to have bad fucking days.' Hearing enough Jack Crompton intercedes before fists fly. He claps and shouts loud.

'Right lads into the bath. Come on.'

Wilf backs off and tempers calm.

★

Later, when the players have gone their separate ways, Wilf is sat in his office with Jack. Between them they are finishing off a bottle of whisky and dissecting the day's events. Whilst also planning for the following game against Everton once more.

Both are worried.

'I have got to change it Jack. God knows it is going to rattle a few cages but I have to do something. Everton killed us in the middle last week. We need more legs, more pace and mobility. I am going to drop Bobby and Denis. I am going to do this my way.'

Jack finishes his glass and stares almost in disbelief at Wilf. 'A big call, Wilf. Denis has a slight groin strain so we can swing that. But Bobby? To get away with this one thing will have to happen at Goodison Park.'

'What's that Jack?'

'We better win.'

★

'Bobby can I have a minute before you get changed mate?'

It is Monday morning at The Cliff. Training has just finished and Wilf is about to tell his long time friend and Manchester United legend that his star is waning and he is dropped. Wilf has not slept. Over and over again he has rehearsed this speech but now his throat has gone dry and he feels physically sick. The dream now real, everything his heart desires has been given to him. So why does he feel like a complete and utter bastard?

Bobby comes across. He smiles. 'Hi Wilf.'

'Look Bobby old pal, I am going to make some changes for the Everton game. I am going to give you a rest.'

Bobby looks confused. He scratches his forehead and cannot believe what he has just heard. 'You're dropping me?'

'Rested Bob, give you a chance to recharge your batteries.'

A shattered Bobby is struggling to take it in. 'Have you spoken to the boss about this?'

Wilf visibly bridles at the question, 'I am team coach Bob, my call, my decision. It is not just you being left out, I am revamping the whole side. There will be four or five changes. We cannot afford to get hammered again. The press will kill me.'

'Fair enough' says Bobby, looking at his boots. Not wanting to catch Wilf's eye. 'If that is what you want?'

Wilf pats Bob's arm. 'That's how it is going to be mate. Now go and get changed.'

Bobby walks off with hands on hips, deep in thought. He is in a strange place. Why him? Why now? Is Wilf trying to lay down a marker? It is the first time in nine years at United that he has been dropped. Angry, but more upset, Bobby will keep his own counsel, for now.

Wilf watches him go. A part of him so wants to shout over and ask him if he fancies a coffee and a catch up but he knows it's best to leave Bobby alone for a while. Next on Wilf's agenda is the boss to inform him of the team changes. Though under no pressure to do so, Wilf feels such drastic measures deserve his attention. Besides, he does not want him finding out second hand. Either within the club or god forbid on the fifteenth fucking hole at Davyhulme golf course.

Paddy, Alex and Willie are now the boss's regular golfing partners. Paddy he is not concerned about but the other two?

He remembers the Quadrant pub and the conversation with his old pal, Charlie Baxter.

'Watch your back Wilf' he warned.

'Watch your back.'

★

I don't know whether he is brave or foolish. Maybe both and a brave fool disturbs me. Wilf's decision to drop so many players, Denis and Bobby in particularly, could rebound badly if a result is not forthcoming at Everton. I don't need panic. Sat here before me, Wilf is explaining his plan. 'Flood the midfield, block them out and squeeze them?' These are terms alien to me.

'Bring George and Willie into the centre, play young Don Givens up front as a lone spearhead. Suck them in, kill the space?'

This is not Manchester United. This is not my United I should add. I simply nod as Wilf talks me through. Finally he finishes.

'So what do you think boss,' he asks nervously, desperately in need of my blessing.

I smile.

'You're the boss now Wilf. Good luck lad.'

Inside I think we are in big trouble.

★

Tuesday 19th August 1969: Everton 3 Manchester United 0

It is no contest as we are put to the sword by a rampant Everton who rip apart Wilf's new United with consummate ease. I watch through haunted eyes as we are humiliated. Alan Ball, again ably abetted by Howard Kendall, are simply too good. Their clever movement, sublime passing and speed making us appear second rate in comparison.

At the full time whistle Wilf looks up towards us in the director's box. He wears the look of a schoolboy caught in the act of sticking chewing gum on his desk. Louis Edwards is sat next to me and whispers in my ear. 'You need to have a word Matt, and now. This is not good enough.'

I nod, we need to get someone in and I have just the man. But Wilf needs to feel he is not being undermined. I need to handle this with care. Already there are United fans near me screaming 'Sort it out Matt,' 'Come back boss', 'Get rid of this idiot.' Early days I tell myself. Teething troubles... but this is truly a bad day. I will ensure Bobby and Denis are put back in straight away. I will insist on it. Wilf has free reign, sufficient rope I feel to get the job done but I have to ensure not enough to hang himself with.

★

A disconsolate Wilf can't face the players straight away.

He feels it best to leave it until Monday. To let him calm down a little, Jack puts an arm around his shoulder outside the United dressing room.

'I will talk to them. Harry Catterick is asking after you. Go and have a drink with him in his office.'

'Cheers Jack' say Wilf. His shoulders slumped. His eyes are heavy and his voice hoarse. He turns around and looks close to tears.

'I tried doing it my way. I am sorry old pal I let you down.'

'Don't be bloody daft Wilf. We'll be alright son. We will get it right.' Jack waits until Wilf has disappeared then enters the dressing room. What he sees and hears disturbs him. There are no arguments amongst the players. Almost a resignation at being well beaten. Only Willie, as ever, mouthing off.

'I am a winger not a midfielder. What the bloody hell is he playing at? The amateur.'

Jack hears and snaps. 'An amateur. Who? Wilf? Let me tell you something Morgan. Wilf has got United blood running through his veins. He does not deserve those comments from the likes of you. What gives you the right to call a man who has sweated blood, sweat and tears for this club?'

An awkward silence fills the air. The players are not used to seeing Jack lose his temper to this extent. They watch spellbound, but also slightly unnerved. Jack continues tearing a strip off a speechless open-mouthed Willie. 'Wilf was fighting to keep this club alive after Munich when you were still in short trousers holding your mother's hand. He saw his best friends killed in the crash. It broke his heart but he knuckled down and played his part in helping United come back.

He was a coach under Sir Alf of an England team that just so happened to win the World Cup three years ago.

'And then there is you… a self-styled big shot from Burnley. A small town in the hills of Lancashire, who we took a punt on. You are good but you are not there yet son. Being a United player requires a lot more than just talent. You need to have a little class. You have yet to do anything in the game or at this club to even have an opinion on a man such as Wilf. Never mind have the temerity to slag him off. Now this conversation stays in the dressing room. No further. My lips are sealed. I pray you do me the pleasure of doing similar. Do we have a deal?'

A shamefaced Willie nods his head.

'Good lad' says Jack. 'Here endeth your first lesson. There is hope for you yet son.'

Monday morning in my office at Old Trafford. Myself and Wilf are talking over players to bring in. Notably defenders.

'How about Colin Todd?' he asks, 'the best young English defender I have seen for ten years' claims Wilf.

I shake my head. 'Too expensive, son. Derby want near £400,000. The board would not sanction such a sum for a defender.

'How about Arsenal's Ian Ure?' I add. Wilf does not look too sure. But I am. I have already done the deal. 'He has a good presence, a good lad strong in the air. Just what we need.'

'He has had a few battles with Denis over the years boss. Remember two years ago they nearly killed each other?'

'Denis won't mind Wilf. Besides it is nothing to do with him. Bill's legs have gone now, we are not being fair asking him to delay the inevitable. It is like making a classic but ageing mare drag a heavy rag and bone cart around. Ure is the man for us. Let me speak to Bertie Mee. See if we can sort something out.'

Wilf nods and I reach for the phone, Bertie answers. , 'Hi Bertie it is Matt again. How are you old pal?'

Again?

A worrying penny drops. So this is how it is going to be? Busby replaces the receiver. He turns to Wilf. 'Looks like we have a deal Wilf lad' smiles Busby, 'We will travel down to London tonight and speak to Ure, but all is settled. We have got ourselves a new centre half.'

We?

★

Despite Wilf's initial doubts Ian Ure proves an inspired signing and United embark on a ten-match unbeaten run. Suddenly the smile is back on Wilf's face. 'You are a genus boss,' he has said to me recently on several occasions. But there is only one man at this club worthy of such a description. And while I would be first to admit Ure has undoubtedly helped to tighten us up at the back, it is my George who has been the catalyst for this sudden dramatic turn of form.

I sense he really likes Wilf and not enjoying his friend, a decent man, being hammered from every direction, he has decided to do something about it. George Best has been magnificent. I know well away from my prying eyes, mine mostly, what he gets up to would turn my already receding hair even greyer but when I see this boy on top of his game, he continues to makes my heart soar.

Quite simply George has won games on his own. Between 30th August and 20th October he hit thirteen goals in fourteen games. But there was so much more. Inspiration and wonder. When we were in need of a miracle and all seemed lost, there was the jinking run, the sleight of foot, the bewildering burst of pace between defenders and a game was saved or won.

'Thank God for George'

No more so than at Elland Road when he scored a brace in a dramatic and ultimately disappointing 2-2 draw. George's second, a stunning drive ten minutes from time that crashed against both posts before flashing into a helpless Gary Sprake's goal, gave us a 2-1 lead against the best team in the country. We were mere seconds from claiming victory and handing Don Revie's men their first home defeat for over a year, only for Billy Bremner to hit a brilliant overhead scissors kick in injury time past Alex Stepney, right into the top corner. It left us reeling and Wilf on his knees. We deserved better. I have respect for Leeds and Revie but I don't like them. I believe the feeling is quite mutual. For me the games are a clash of styles. And we have it.

But then once more the wheels came off in spectacular fashion at the most inopportune venue – Maine Road. Whilst remaining rather unpredictable we appeared in decent health for the first Manchester derby of the season, but a depressing 4-0 mauling left the blues dancing with joy and our supporters despairing. Colin Bell was outstanding. The scorer of two goals, he tormented us throughout and ran the boys ragged. The boy nicknamed 'Nijinsky' is a hell of a footballer. The result was no fluke and we were well beaten and Wilf cut a sorry figure post-match. Myself and Wilf are stood outside the city boardroom. I look at Wilf's face and he is clearly angry and upset at the performance of our team. It will not take much to ignite his short fuse, so I attempt to offer some advice.

'Before we go in Wilf, remember Malcolm will be at his annoying worst. Don't fall for it. He will be gloating. Rise above it. Remember who you are and who you represent. Stay away from him and if he does start mouthing off, you ignore. Do you understand?'

'Yes boss,' says Wilf, still utterly reeling from the 4-0 scoreline. From behind the door I hear loud voices and much laughter – most, if not all, I am certain is at our expense.

In we go.

'Here come the reds' shouts out Malcolm as we enter. As ever with a glass of champagne in hand and a cigar in his mouth. His big mouth.

'Remember my words, Wilf,' I say as he stares with murderous intent towards the City coach, who is sporting a huge grin. 'Thanks for turning up boys, more than your team did.'

That is it all it takes and Wilf goes nuts 'We have Derby in the League Cup quarter final at home next Wednesday, you mouthy bastard. Once we beat them I pray our paths cross again the semi final.'

So much for my advice?

★

Manchester United did indeed overcome Derby four days later with a lone Brian Kidd goal, and the scene was set for an almighty showdown against their neighbours in a two-legged tie. Both occasions were set to go down in Mancunian folklore. As for Wilf McGuinness, an opportunity had arisen to finally make his mark by overcoming their closest rivals and get his beloved United to Wembley.

17 - LOOSE CANNON

Wednesday 3rd December 1969:
Manchester City v Manchester United
League Cup Semi Final First Leg.

Big Mal has got Wilf's number. He throws a little bait, a sarcastic comment, even a mocking wink is enough to send his opposite number from across the city into meltdown. Big Mal likes Wilf, it is nothing personal but this is war. The battle for Manchester's football soul. And one that City are winning.

When Busby put Wilf in charge of the team he thought Christmas had come early. For along with Joe Mercer, Big Mal has made this a blue city. The trophies are mounting up and they, the reds, have had their day. The old man let things slide. They needed new blood believes Big Mal, but Busby remained loyal to those whom had taken him to the top of the mountain.

United had achieved their goal. The European Cup, now they are hurtling down the same mountain at the speed of a landslide. Their best players, George apart, are getting old. Bobby, Paddy, Nobby and Denis. Willie Morgan is decent but he is no George. He is no Summerbee, Bell or Lee either. Only George, who is beyond comparison when the mood takes him, remains a potent threat to trouble Big Mal's reign as clown prince of this rainy city. To whom the blue half have taken this opinionated, cocky, brash, arrogant, controversial but brilliant Londoner to their hearts.

They love him. They love his ability as a coach and his showmanship but above all they love him because they think he has put United in their place. Big Mal knows victory in the forthcoming two legged league cup semi final against United could well finish them off as a serious rival for years. And so he lets fly in the newspapers, he agitates, he irritates, and he drives the red half to distraction.

Meanwhile Wilf watches, reads and listens and grows increasingly incandescent, his face going a nasty shade of purple. 'You just fucking wait Malcolm…' he seethes, 'just fucking wait.'

In the Maine Road dressing room, with the crowd noise resonating loudly through the walls, Wilf prepares to give his final team talk before kick off. He stands with arms folded, slightly in front of Jack Crompton and John Aston Senior. He claps his hands together.

'All right listen up lads. Malcolm Allison does not rate anyone here. Nobody, not me or any of you. No one. He thinks I am a fucking nobody.' Wilf points around the room. 'As for you lot, he considers you lower than dog shit on the street. We are yesterday's men, a music hall joke.' Wilf's eyes settle on Bobby. 'He called you a glory boy Bob. He thinks you are stealing a living now.' Bobby appears bewildered. Wilf then seeks out Nobby Stiles. 'Nobby, he says you are creaking mate. Good for a kick about on the Red Rec but on a proper football pitch, a liability. That is Malcolm for you Nob.' Nobby is granite faced.

'George,' Wilf grins wide, 'The Belfast boy.'

'Go on Wilf,' smiles George. 'What has motor mouth been saying about me?'

'Again I plead not guilty George, I am simply

the messenger. Malcolm says you are nothing but a waster. Now that the old man has retired, you are only interested in the birds, booze and bookies. Washed up and a degenerate, not a footballer. His words George, not mine.'

A shocked George sees Big Mal regularly on his nightshift sorties around the city's clubs and drinking holes. They always get on well and have shared many a bottle. He is surprised these comments have come from his mouth.

'Are you sure about this Wilf?'

Wilf nods. 'So I have been reliably informed.' Wilf addresses the entire room. 'I am only telling you this because tonight we have a perfect opportunity to stick these comments right back down Allison's throat. He claims this is a blue city now. Well I am not fucking having that. There are 40,000 blues out there who hate you and our lot screaming in defiance. I was embarrassed the way we got turned over 4-0 last time we were here. "Put in our place" Allison said. Well I want you to go out there and show him our place, as he fucking calls it, is to be the number one team in this city. We are still by far a superior team. Who would you rather have Best, Law and Charlton or Bell, Summerbee and Francis fucking Lee? No Contest. Right then, end of speech, it is your time now. Come on and up the reds!'

Wilf's face is contorted with excitement and rage. He feels like he is off to war. Amongst the United players there is a mixed response. The younger ones, Brian Kidd especially, appear ready to run through a brick wall for their manager. Others are more distant in their reaction. On the way out of the dressing room,

George sidles up to Nobby.

'Do you really think Malcolm said that about us?'

Nobby laughs. 'Don't be soft George. Wilf is just trying to get us fired up.'

'So where did those comments come from?' asks George.

'Wilf's imagination,' laughs Nobby, 'you know what he is like for getting carried away.'

Bobby is listening in but says nothing. He feels different. Bobby feels Wilf was simply expressing his own feelings. He will not forget this.

Manchester City 2 Manchester United 1

'That bloody Lee has done us! He is a disgrace, a fucking disgrace!' A late penalty two minutes from time scored by Manchester City striker Francis Lee, after a mischievous overreaction to a clumsy tackle from Ian Ure, has earned City a hard earned, first leg win.

A Bobby Charlton equaliser looked to have given us a deserved draw only for Lee's theatricals to seal the game. Wilf is close to hysterical in the Maine Road tunnel. I have come from the director's box to try and calm him down. If that is not bad enough George was sent off at the end and is now going mad and banging on the official's room. He is seething after being dismissed for stupidly knocking the ball out of the referee's hands. I shout for Jack to grab him back inside our dressing room before it escalates further. George is aggrieved because of a late penalty shout he felt should have been given. Jack Taylor, the referee, has confirmed he is not happy with George and is going to mention it in his match report, which will definitely bring about a suspension. Anyone else and I am quite certain Taylor, a butcher by trade, would have just let it go. But this is George, and I fear the next few week's headlines have already been written. He is going to be crucified.

'We've been robbed,' exclaims Wilf, 'That fucking Lee has stitched us up.'

'Come on' I say, putting my arm around his shoulder. 'Nothing we can do about it now. We'll put matters right at Old Trafford.'

'I thought the lads did us proud tonight boss,' says Wilf, his eyes moistening over, 'they gave us everything.'

'Aye son, that they did,' I lead him by the arm over to our dressing room door, 'Now you get in there and you tell them just what you said to me. Okay?'

Wilf nods. He turns to me, 'I will get even with that bastard Allison, boss. If it is the last thing I do.'

He goes inside. I stand alone in the tunnel with my thoughts and wonder for the first time. Have I done the right thing? If it is possible for someone to care too much about their job, then Wilf is at fault. His passion will prove to be his downfall if he does not learn to separate the logic from the fire and the fury at the height of battle. He is a General wanting to be with the troops on the front line whilst finding himself outflanked and outwitted by the enemy. He must learn not to bite every time Malcolm opens his mouth. He must learn and he must do so quickly for Manchester United cannot afford, I cannot afford, to have a loose cannon in charge of the team. Louis and the others are already making noises and questioning if we should make a change but I can't hold them off forever.

I can be ruthless. My public persona can be

misleading, those in the business know I am not one to cross. I believe I have a good heart but no one in any walk of business can afford not to make big decisions that may break hearts. For my ambitions now exist off the field. Politics is power they say. Well I have a plan to lead Manchester United into the seventies and take on not just domestic rivals in Leeds, Liverpool and City but abroad also. We have more unfinished business in the European Cup.

No other club has given or suffered more to win that trophy and I am not prepared to watch it disappear and be fought over by clubs without our calibre or history.

We are going back.

Wilf definitely gets this season, but next year, despite my personal feelings, if he has not sorted himself out I will have to act.

We have fallen from the stars, they say, but I cannot allow us to plummet all the way to earth.

18 - BRIDGE OVER TROUBLED WATERS

Wednesday 17th December 1969:
Manchester United v Manchester City
League Cup Semi Final Second Leg

These people never fail to shock me. Is it a long standing vendetta, bitter remnants left over from when Manchester United first took flight into the great beyond and in doing so incited the wrath of an establishment unable to see beyond their smoke filled committee meetings and double brandies before dinner. Maybe my long standing bitterness against the Football League for matters unspoken is simply a state of mind and I am over-reacting?

Nevertheless George has been handed a ridiculous four week ban, five games, for his petty actions against referee Jack Taylor at the end of the Maine Road semi final.

What is this game coming to when the modern assassins can kick, maul and scythe down our few remaining ball players and simply have a finger wagged at them by a benevolent referee? Whereas for a childish act such as this one finds themselves treated worse than a common criminal?

The newspapers have gone mad. My Irishman is public enemy number one. He is being blamed for all public ills. Sometimes I wonder if it was not for Manchester United and George in particular, just what would these scribes write about?

George is a scapegoat. A simple prisoner of fortune, fame and infamy. There has never been anyone before of his ilk and they cannot get enough. It is open season and their 'Georgie Boy' is not of the type to clip his wings and disappear into the distance. His life is now played out on the back pages and the front. He has nowhere to run, or hide. The best of times they say. I am not so sure.

Our efforts to appeal George's ludicrous ban means he will be available for the second leg. A match we just have to win. Our form is good. No better than Saturday's 4-1 thrashing of Liverpool at Anfield. When even Bill was forced to admit we deserved it.

'Bobby was magnificent Matt' he said to me afterwards, 'he could almost have been a Liverpool player.'

Bobby was indeed stunning, rolling back the years.

Wilf recalled Paddy, Denis played with a devilish glint back in his game, George was on fire and we flew with the angels. Bob's goal was outrageous. A one-two with Willie Morgan, who is playing sublimely well now, and a ferocious rising shot that flew high into the net from twenty five yards. In all my years I have never leapt to my feet watching from the director's box but when Bob's hit flashed past Tommy Lawrence, I was on my feet applauding. He deserved that.

I was touched at the reaction of the Liverpool crowd after that goal as they gave Bobby a standing ovation back to the halfway line. He has not had the easiest of times but class never goes away. Robert Charlton such in abundance. As does Liverpool Football Club – the supporters and especially their manager. Wilf and

Bill had a lovely chat afterwards in his office. I left them to it. I adore listening to him talk and this was a perfect opportunity, even after being beaten so heavily on his own patch, Bill was magnificent; honest, wise, warm and humorous.

Just Shankly.

'Wilf lad, you have taken over from the greatest manager the game has ever seen. That man over there.' Bill points and smiles at me. I drink my tea and acknowledge the compliment. Grand coming from him. 'He came back from the dead. The man upstairs twice tried to sign him. But oh no, not Matt. He had business on this earth. And last May he achieved his dream. But now you must carry that same dream Wilf. Remember results can damage managers but players can destroy them. So try and keep a distance. I know you have friends amongst the United boys. Bobby, Paddy, Denis, Nobby. Wonderful lads, but they are still players. They think, act and dream like players. You are the boss. Keep it friendly Wilf, but with a firm hand. You may be in troubled waters at the moment but there is always a way through. A path, a bridge to the other side. Find your way son. Find that bridge over troubled waters. And one last thing?'

'What is that Bill?' asks Wilf.

'Next time you come here we are going to wipe the bloody floor with you'

Wilf laughs but Bill is serious. There is class and then there is Bill Shankly.

★

It is the day before the second leg against Manchester City at Old Trafford and United are staying at the

Lymm hotel in Cheshire. Denis Law is undergoing a fitness test with Wilf and Jack and it is not looking good. He comes to a halt after a tormenting attempt at running.

'It's not happening Wilf, I'm not going to make it,' explains a pained Denis, clutching his troublesome knee. A season wrecked by injuries looks set to continue for the Scottish striker.

'All right Lawman' replies a miserable Wilf. 'Get yourself off to the physio and we'll try and get you right for the weekend. Wilf turns to Jack as Denis limps away for further treatment, 'Tell Kiddo to get himself right. He is in.'

★

It is the morning of the big game and I am told by Wilf that Denis will not be playing. This is such a vital game that I decide to have a word. Denis is a lad that has played through the pain barrier for me. He can do it for Wilf now as well. We chat alone over a cup of tea in the hotel restaurant. It is empty except for us.

'How bad is the knee Denis son?'

'Flared up pretty bad boss.' Denis knows what is coming.

'I need you for this one, lad. United need you. You have been in worse condition and played and won games for me. Tonight could be decided by one moment of magic. Will you be my magic man Denis? Can you get us to Wembley? How about you have an injection to see you through?'

'I am not so sure. It needs rest.'

I smile. 'Get through tonight and we won't play you until you are one hundred per cent.'

'But I have already told Wilf I'm not fit. I don't want to cause any problems.'

'You leave Wilf to me' I say. 'He will just be pleased you are going to help us out. You are a good lad Denis.'

I pat his knee. 'I won't forget this.'

Denis can't believe it. The old man has talked him into playing tonight without him ever even agreeing.

I go to find Wilf who is sat reading a newspaper in the foyer. He looks up on seeing me coming and points to the headlines. 'Malcolm is at it again boss. I can't wait to shut him up tonight.'

I sit down next to him. 'I have good news Wilf. I have just spoken to Denis and he is going to play tonight'

A shocked Wilf struggles to take it in. 'But yesterday he said there was no chance. And I have already got Kiddo wired up and ready. It won't be fair to…'

I cut Wilf short. I am terse and to the point. 'I am not going to make a habit of this. But it has to be done. Who would you rather have a chance falling to in front of their goal to win the tie? Denis or Brian? No. Denis plays. No arguments, Wilf. This one time I have to insist.'

Wilf goes quiet. He starts to read his paper once more. He turns a page and without looking up replies: 'If that is what you want boss.'

I decide to best leave him to it.

'It is son' I say before walking off. Wilf watches the old man stride away. For the first time in his life he is not in awe of the boss.

Instead Wilf wants to throttle him.

★

Eight minutes remain of an emotionally draining night at Old Trafford. In front of a roaring 63,000 crowd, this battle for Manchester's pride hangs by a thread for United have levelled the first leg deficit to lead 2-1 on the night.

In a gruelling, hard fought but spellbinding contest, it was City who struck first on seventeen minutes, midfielder Ian Bowyer, shooting home past Alex Stepney from eight yards after Ian Ure had cleared Neil Young's goal bound effort off the line.

With a two-goal lead it appeared City were home and dry but United hit back from an unlikely source when just six minutes later Old Trafford exploded as twenty-two year-old right full-back Paul Edwards lashed a crashing twenty yard drive high past Joe Corrigan, after a sublime defence splitting Paddy Crerand pass. After an even first half United turned the screw and went in desperate search for the goal to level this gripping semi final.

On the hour bedlam broke out on the terraces when George Best swept brilliantly down the right wing, leaving City defenders training in his beguiling wake. George has been up for this game like no other. His impending suspension meaning he wanted to give the fans something to remember whilst he was out banned. With time and space George unleashed a fierce low shot that Corrigan failed to hold and who else but the Lawman was on hand to pounce and lash home from six yards out.

Now it was 2-1 United and despite struggling all evening Denis had produced what Busby asked for. A piece of magic. At 3-3 on aggregate all is to play for. Old Trafford is ablaze with noise and colour as United now in the ascendancy, look to finish this tie without the need of extra time. George and Bobby both go close and City are wilting under the pressure.

The away supporters are silent, whilst the Stretford End roars out in expectation of that killer third. Malcolm, for once, is quiet on the city bench. Almost as if resigned to defeat. But not Wilf, he is up and down and screaming like a madman. He can sense glory.

Revenge.

It is all United, all is red and it appears under these black Mancunian skies, littered with stars, just a matter of time before they score again. Under ever increasing pressure the City defence are given a moment's respite, when for once the ball is up the other end of the field. Ian Bowyer find himself knocked to the floor after being clumsily tackled by Willie Morgan on the edge of the Manchester United penalty area. The referee immediately awards an indirect free kick.

A hush descends over the terraces. Eight minutes remain. Bobby, Paddy and Nobby rush to form a wall as Francis Lee stands over the ball. Expecting a cross or short pass Lee surprises all by blasting it straight at an unsuspecting Alex Stepney who fumbles the ball badly. As Old Trafford watches on in horror, an alert Mike Summerbee races in to smash the rebound from Stepney into the net. Whether genius or pure chance or on instinct, Francis Lee's decision to shoot has resulted in silencing the home crowd and sending the travelling blue hordes wild with delight.

It is a sickening blow for Wilf and his team and the final whistle brings only more sadness and despair. It is the blues who will be competing in the League Cup final against West Bromwich Albion. Manchester City are going to Wembley. Malcolm comes across to shake Wilf's hand.

'Good game Wilf. Hard luck.' All said with a wry smile.

Wilf keeps his composure. 'In triumph or defeat the boss told him beforehand, be the better man.' But inside his heart is breaking.

Later Wilf is alone in his office. Just him and a bottle of whisky. All official duties are done. Now it is time to drown the memories of Alex's aberration away. No blame could be apportioned in the dressing room. Everyone was simply too disappointed. There were tears among the younger ones. That upset him. His desire to want to rip Willie Morgan's fucking head off for the stupid challenge on Bowyer which led to the free kick, was more, he feels, an excuse to hit back at the rumours flying around that he has been bad mouthing him.

No, even Willie gave everything this evening. For tonight, thinks Wilf, they played and felt like his team. He knows Denis was thrust back upon him, but how can he complain when the Lawman scores? If he is going to be over ruled at times on team selection, who better to do so than Sir Matt?

Wilf can just about live with that. For what's the alternative? Normally this office would have been a lively and full place post match, but Wilf feels there is an air around him. One that people are wary of breathing. Nobody knocks, no one comes.

So he sits alone and has no intention of going home just yet. Instead he will now aim for the bottom of the whisky bottle. He will listen to ghostly far off voices and footsteps in a practically deserted Old Trafford.

19 - TESTAMENT

Mad as it may sound, I once believed George Best was gifted to us by the almighty because of a guilty conscience over Munich. It is not a notion I have ever aired publicly, but one when I first saw George in full cry; swift as a summer breeze, will o' the wisp, such beauty and grace. He reminded me of a lightning bolt illuminating the horizon on a night time ocean. Simply magical. But not anymore.

Not now.

For the old adage 'with every wish comes a curse' appears to have been proved true in George's case. For every drink, there is a beautifully hit pass, for every bet or punt made, either won or lost, there is a defender left in a crumpled heap and bewildered. For every girl there is a flashing goal, an unworldly moment of skill that causes crowds to rise, eyes to blink and souls to soar.

Come 1970, twenty-four year-old George is entering what should be his most expressive stage for the outrageous talent he possesses. At Manchester United he is providing salvation not witnessed since biblical times. Dragging his team, kicking and screaming to victories thought impossible and snatching draws from the jaws of certain defeat.

He is supplying win bonuses, he is saving and prolonging careers. He is George Best and drinking pints of vodka and lemonade thinking it is all still just a game.

Saturday 24th January 1970
FA Cup Fourth Round: Old Trafford.
Manchester United 3 Manchester City 0

'That was for you Wilf!' shouts Brian Kidd as he falls into his coach's arms at the final whistle of a glorious victory for Wilf McGuinness and Manchester United. A much-needed three goal win over their rivals with two scored by Kiddo has sent the vast majority of the 63,417 Old Trafford crowd delirious. It is such sweet revenge for the heartaches of last month's league cup semi final defeat.

'Kiddo, you are a beauty my son,' exclaims a beaming Wilf as he leads the young United star, born within a stone's throw of his parent's home in Collyhurst. 'Keep this up and they will build a statue of you outside Saint Pats.'

An ecstatic crowd wave them off. For Wilf it is undoubtedly his finest moment since handed the job. He glances around at the massed terraces, rejoicing and finally able to hold their heads up high against their blue neighbours. And it was all achieved without a suspended George Best.

'Look at that lot Brian' says Wilf, pointing to the joyous supporters. All singing Kiddo's name. 'This is what it's all about at our club. Winning. I love it!' Wilf waves to the crowd. The rare taste of victory fresh in his nostrils. Now for Malcolm.

The packed United boardroom heaves with bodies, half hidden amid cigar and cigarette smoke. The drink is flowing. Bottles opened and glasses refilled. Talk is loud, boisterous and good hearted. The City representatives are somewhat quieter – here out of courtesy no more, the crushing loss has hurt. Now, as their dear neighbours discovered in previous defeats, these moment have to be endured and dealt with in a gentlemanly style.

I am stood with Joe Mercer. Both of us at an age where defeat may hurt but does not spear the soul. We can deal with one another with good grace. Others not so.

'All right Malcolm, old son. Where are you then?' The loud booming voice announces Wilf's arrival in the room. Amid the crowd, with cigar and champagne glass in hand, Malcolm Allison is in conversation with United chairman Louis Edwards. Malcolm looks up on hearing Wilf. He was expecting this and is ready.

'Over here Wilf,' he shouts, whilst smiling wide. Wilf makes his way through the crowd. He grabs a glass of red wine off the table as he goes. He takes a swift drink. Suddenly he feels a little faint. His stomach goes cold. I try and make my way over towards Wilf to intercept him before reaching Malcolm but too many are in my path. Wilf faces Malcolm. For so long he has rehearsed this speech. This was to be his Henry V. His Agincourt. But the words won't come.

'Are you okay Wilf?' grins Malcolm, 'you look a little pale.' The next moment Wilf is arching over and violently throwing up. The nerves of the day and the excitement of winning finally overcoming him. Thus he is denied his moment of glory. Instead an amused Big Mal stands above him trying hard not to laugh.

'The sweet taste of victory my son,' smiles Malcolm,

'enjoy it!'

Watching on with a look of disgust and much embarrassment Louis Edwards admonishes his team coach.

'Go and get cleaned up Wilf.'

'Yes Mr Chairman' says Wilf, wiping his mouth clean. Like the parting of the red sea the crowd moves aside and he leaves the room. I don't know whether to laugh or cry.

★

In George Best's absence due to his suspension we embark on an unbeaten run. His return coincides with a Fifth Round FA Cup tie away against Northampton Town. In some sections of the press there are calls for Wilf to keep with the same team. These people. Sometimes they make me want to weep. They are probably related to those who abused Michelangelo for refusing to rush his masterpiece at the Sistine Chapel. Or those who ruined Mozart because his talent scared them and made feel their lives were worthless. And so they out to desecrate and destroy.

In our genius's absence young John Aston, back from injury, has been outstanding in his position and is many things that George is not. The perfect professional for instance. Something George could never be accused of. The lateness and absenteeism is increasing. The drinking is getting worse, a clear sign...

When he can't get out of bed, whoever's it is, then so begins a slippery slope. This alarms me for George is one of the best trainers I have known. The stories that pass my desk about his drinking and womanising leave me in despair. I only have to read the newspapers to learn his latest exploits. The truth is probably stranger than the stuff that is made up. But he is still George and John Aston in comparison is a crowd extra to Laurence Olivier.

There is simply no argument and no contest. Despite what some think Wilf is not mad and George is immediately put back in the line up to face the Cobblers at the County ground. They are hardly surroundings fit for the comeback of the golden boy of British football but Wilf knows that the eyes of the world will be on George and he will be bursting to put on a show. His pride has been badly hurt by suggestions United are better off without him. This boy, who believes he is the best player in the world, is scared of nothing or no one. Also, as it now seems, I am finally resigned to the notion that nobody can tell him what to do. George Best is on a path to only God knows where, but one thing I am certain drives him insane. It is the thought of being ignored.

Something special will occur in Northampton, of that I have no doubt.

Northampton Town 2 Manchester United 8

On Saturday 7th February, 1970, George gave notice of his genius with six goals against Northampton Town, and a performance that will remain an everlasting epitaph to his genius. Raised voices screaming 'wasted talent' will claim there should have been so much more from him and it is difficult to raise an argument after this performance. For here at Northampton, against journeymen professionals, George has indelibly inscribed a living obituary in pure gold.

On such occasions you simply thank God for working overtime on the Sabbath and in a mood of generosity and wearing a red and white scarf, creating the eighth wonder of the world.

George Best.

20 - ALL ABOUT GEORGE

There was a time when the Busby Babes would travel to the 'Big Smoke' with all the pomp and swagger of visiting Hollywood movie stars. Their arrival would be greeted with huge excitement. They were showbusiness – glamour and glitter. Nothing of their ilk had ever been witnessed. Londoners found it hard to believe. Footballing superstars from Manchester? Whatever happened to the cloth caps and the ferrets and the chimneys poking through dark satanic skies?

These boys in their sharp suits, smiling with a wink and a handsome smile to the ladies, so full of fire and youth and talent beyond the heavens, who played with a devil on their shirts and in their play.

'It's grim up north' claimed the London 'papers. Well a dash of red sprinkled with gold dust and Matt Busby and Jimmy Murphy put paid to that.

And then Munich put paid to them. Was it all simply a mirage? The lights once more went out in the north and for Londoners the magic waned. The fairytale of those kids who had bloomed for a while under northern skies faded from memory. They reverted to type – Spurs became the glamour team, the birth right of all cockneys.

But then came George…

★

Saturday 30th September 1964
Chelsea v Manchester United – Stamford Bridge

Twisted Blood: It was a performance that reduced his father to tears and left Matt Busby and Jimmy Murphy speechless. They knew more than any other that this slip of an eighteen year–old kid was special. They knew something extraordinary existed within his thin balletic frame but what they never counted on or realised was the swagger, the courage and the sheer joy at putting on a show for the crowd.

In the capital at this time there was no better stage to introduce yourself than the glitzy surroundings of Stamford Bridge, a football club that acted like a magnet to the movie, music and theatre stars who resided in West London. An awed Chelsea crowd that came to watch Charlton, Law and Crerand take on their own exciting, vibrant team captained by a young Terry Venables, were left marvelling at the thin, red, scrawny like whippet, tearing apart their right full back, the highly regarded and experienced Ken Shellito.

It never appeared just enough to simply beat him, the kid seemed intent on turning the unfortunate Shellito into a gibbering, shaking wreck. He would turn him one way then another, the ball would go through his legs, Shellito would move to turn, only to find George was already past him. It was cruel yet beautiful to watch.

A sleight of foot, a conjuror's touch with the ball obeying his every command; it was if all present had fallen for this magical Irish waif whose smile could light up a city and in time would melt and break the hearts of millions of both sexes. George walked off at the end, head bowed and embarrassed as the entire stadium rose as one to hand him a standing ovation.

'Shellito must have twisted blood after that,' claimed Paddy Crerand in a post match interview, as the word went out and the whole world gasped at the sight of 'Georgie Boy.'

★

I remember that day so well. Later I joked that, whenever we went to Stamford Bridge, I thought I ought to phone the police and warn them a murder was about to be committed. That was the beginning of the circus. Now it appears we are entering the last act of what is turning out to be a tragic drama.

★

The Brown Bull, 1970: Fast asleep under a coat, amid broom handles, crates of ale, boxes of crisps and cigarettes, lies the great George Best. Too drunk to drive home or even to make it up the stairs to his own room given to him by the grateful landlord Billy Barr, the greatest talent in world football has been put to bed by the American landlord under a rain coat with a cushion wedged under his head.

It had been another crazy night at the Bull with the usual television and pop stars amongst the clientele but as ever all eyes, both male and female, were on George. It's all about George. Celebrities and every day punters came and went but come the end George was still going strong. Never stopping, his glass never empty. Eyes glazed, incapable of even talking. Finally, when he could drink no more and after many failed attempts to get him up the stairs, Billy made the decision to let him sleep off the booze in the back room.

The noise of early morning traffic and the rattle of freight trains making their way across the nearby rail bridge out of Manchester waking George from his slumber. He opens his eyes, and for a second has no idea where he is. Then remembers, he checks his watch. There is an outside chance he could make training but decides against it. He couldn't handle another shouting session with Wilf, a lingering stare of disdain from Bobby and a lecture off the old man. He will take the fine. It's only money. There is plenty in the bank. He checks in his pockets and pulls out a bundle of scribbled pieces of paper. Girl's phone numbers. He smiles and just wishes he could remember what they looked like.

George stands and yawns, he rubs his eyes and notices a small chink of light shining in through the dark, dank walls. He stands on an empty crate to look through and finds a gap in the brickwork, harbouring a view from a feet high up of the outside street. George peeps through, like a prisoner in a deep dungeon, staring forlornly at the outside world, as people go about their morning business. It fascinates him. He feels safe, for once it is he who is prying.

A bespectacled schoolboy, no more than twelve years old, is sat on the upper deck of a bus going past the Brown bull. It stops opposite at the traffic lights. He looks across and notices a man's eyes staring back up at him. He recognises the face. No it can't be. The schoolboy takes off his glasses and rubs his eyes. He looks again. It is. It is George Best!

The lights change and the bus drives off with the boy continuing to stare. George has caught his eye. He smiles. The schoolboy grins back. Nobody will ever believe him.

Nobody.

George climbs back down. He spots a bottle of vodka on the shelf.

What the hell...

21 - LEEDS AND LADY LUCK

After a hard fought, even brutal first FA Cup semi-final against Leeds United at Hillsborough, when the ball was often an innocent bystander, we meet them again later tonight at Villa Park. The lads are in their rooms resting.

I have decided to stay in mine and out of Wilf's way. The most important thing at this time before such a crucial game is rest. Keep everybody nice and calm. Including the excitable Wilf.

'Where is that fucking George!' Unbeknown to Busby, Wilf McGuinness is prowling the corridors of the Worcester hotel, only hours before the game, looking for his wayward Irishman, convinced he is with a girl. Wilf is mumbling under his breath. 'I will kill the little bugger!' He comes to George's hotel room. He knocks on loud.

'George are you in there. George, open this door now!'

No answer, so Wilf goes downstairs and asks for a spare key. He heads back up with a porter in tow. By this time his forehead is stained with sweat. He cannot believe that on the day of the most important match in his United career as coach, their best player, and so called friend, is fooling around!

The porter opens up the door and they are greeted by the innocent sight of George simply sat on the bed with the girl. A bookish lady, early thirties but extremely pretty. George has met her earlier in the day. They chatted a little and had decided to continue their conversation in privacy. George's idea of talk not hers. Not yet but then Wilf's barnstorming appearance has cramped George's style and ruined his plans for the afternoon. He is not happy, but one look at Wilf and he decides to stay quiet.

An irate, red faced Wilf takes a deep breath.

'Excuse me Miss, can I have a word with George alone for a moment?' Wilf steps aside as the lady walks past. She stops at the door turns to George and smiles.

'Later, George.'

George returns her smile like only George can. Wilf slams the door shut behind her. He glowers at George. 'What the hell do you think you are doing George?'

'Calm down Wilf' grins George.

'Calm fucking down! We are just hours away from playing the best side in the country and one match from the FA Cup final and I catch you with a bird. And you have the nerve to say calm down!'

'Wilf nothing happened mate. We were just talking?'

Wilf rages. 'Only because I stopped you in your tracks.'

He sits down on the bed next to George. His voice mellows. 'Why do you keep doing this George? The birds and the booze. You have a God given talent. You are one of the greatest players in the world and you are throwing it all away. You have always said to me that you would love to play in an FA Cup final. That it is your dream. We had a great chance of doing Leeds tonight with you in the side. But I can't play you now. You've just screwed everything up. Not just for United, but for yourself.'

George is not smiling now.

'You can't be serious Wilf. You have to play me?'

'I don't have to do anything, George. I need to teach you a lesson. This can't go on. You are on the bench, lad. You are dropped.'

Wilf gets up to leave. George is speechless. He never saw this coming and is close to tears, borne of anger and frustration. Feeling that if he is not going to play, why not go and find the girl to finish what he started?

Wilf has gone straight to the bar and ordered a double whisky. He needs a stiff drink before he goes and explains to the old man what has happened and that he has dropped George. He downs the whisky in one go then orders another for double Dutch courage.

There's a knock on my hotel room. I go to open and it is Wilf. He looks terrible. I can smell whisky on his breath.

'Wilf, what on earth is up? Come on in son.'

He enters and I shut the door.

'Boss I need to tell you something but I had to have a drink first.'

I am dreading this.

'Well you have had your drink.'

'I caught George with a bird in his room. I have told him I am not having it anymore. He's dropped.'

I can't believe my ears. 'You've dropped George Best?'

'What choice did I have? I had to make a stand, otherwise he is never going to learn!'

'George is our best player Wilf. I am sorry son, you are going to have to reinstate him. Bring him to me and I will give him the rollicking of his life, but he has to play.'

'You are doing it again' says Wilf. 'You promised me this was not going to happen anymore. That team selection is down to me. And now you are saying I have to start George? You can't keep undermining me like this boss. It is not fair.'

I am angry now and in no mood to argue. 'Life is not fair Wilf, nothing is fair. You are not ready to make these kind of decisions yet. It is the wrong call. We desperately need to make Wembley if just to signify to the rest of the world that we are still here. We both know George is a special case. There has not been or probably never will be another like him. He is a shooting star. His lifestyle is going to destroy him in time and we need to grasp whatever magic George has left whilst he is still around. Do you understand son?'

A crestfallen Wilf nods. He says nothing.

'Good now go and get the bastard and bring him to me.'

Wilf sets off to get George, only to find his room empty. Again he can feel the anger building up inside. On his way back to the boss he spots George coming out of another hotel room. The same girl from previously kisses him as he leaves before shutting the door.

'Oi Best' shouts out Wilf, 'get yourself over to the old man's room now.'

George smiles and winks. Wilf shakes his head.

'Sometimes George, no matter how good you think you are, and you are special George…but today you have crossed the mark. What you have done is unforgivable.'

Wilf walks away, he cannot even bear to look at him anymore.

I hear a knock, it has to be George. I shout loud, 'Get in here!'

He enters to find me standing waiting for him.

'I am going to keep this short George. Today you are the luckiest man alive. Now you owe us. You owe Wilf, you owe me and you owe your teammates. More importantly you owe our supporters who pay your wages to act like a professional and put on a great performance tonight. I am fining you one hundred pounds, but this is not about money, it is about respect. Respect for yourself and those around you. If you ever pull this trick again, you are finished. Do you hear me?'

'Yes boss' replies a seemingly repentant George. In reality he has heard it all a hundred times before and he will hear it again and again..

That night, in an immensely tight but entertaining contest we draw once more with Leeds United. The pitch is a quagmire but our football at times has Revie's lads on the back foot. We are the better team and should have won. Should have but in the late stages George has a great chance to clinch our Wembley place when he goes through with just goalkeeper Gary Sprake to beat, only to fall flat on his face in the mud. He gets little sympathy and cuts a pathetic sight as he lies disconsolate with jeers ringing in his ears.

All evening George was being wound up by the Leeds players, who had heard on the footballing grapevine of his earlier nocturnal adventures and taken great exception to it. They were seriously not amused, feeling George had let down their profession.

Johnny Giles spent the entire game whispering into his ear that he was a disgrace and seemed to take great delight in punishing George by kicking him to get his point across. Never my favourite person Johnny, we had more than our fair share of disagreements when he was here as a headstrong, opinionated youngster but he is a wonderful footballer. Even if he possessed a dark side to his game that he didn't pick up off myself and Jimmy. He can thank Don for that…

I can't help thinking that the day's events back at the Worcester had taken its toll on George and that, if just slightly fresher, he would have kept his balance to go on and beat Sprake. He has let us down hugely and our lads, in particularly Paddy Crerand, give him both barrels on the coach afterwards.

Wilf said little, probably fearful of strangling George if he so much looked at him in an annoying way. Paddy is close to George and for him to let fly like he did, hopefully it will knock some common sense into my troublesome Irishman.

Blood out of a stone comes to mind.

★

Three days later at a blustery, windswept Burnden Park, a Billy Bremner goal just eight minutes in was enough to end our Wembley dream to play Chelsea in the final. Afterwards I went into the dressing room to try and pick heads up. It has been an epic trilogy and over the three games we have more than matched without doubt the best team in England, if not Europe. We simply did not have lady luck on our side.

Wilf is devastated. His first season in charge has seen him lose two semi finals and he is hurting badly. An eighth position in the league goes in his favour but Wilf does not need to be told. Manchester United are expected to win trophies.

He is a good bloke. Wilf is family and I like him a lot but if we do not start well next season he is finished.

22 - THE LIST: DENIS

It has gone nine o'clock in the evening and Denis Law is at home when his phone rings. It is Manchester United club secretary Les Olive.

'Hi Denis, I am sorry to ring you so late but Matt would like a chat with you at The Cliff tomorrow morning around ten o'clock.'

At first Denis is taken aback and then the alarm bells start to ring. He is going on the list. Denis puts the receiver down without even replying to Olive. Loyalty? Such a word does not exist in football, thinks Denis. When you are playing well, scoring goals and winning trophies the sun shines every day and they love you. Nothing is too much for them they bend over backwards to keep you happy.

Then that dark moment, when the black clouds gather and the magic wanes. The Lawman, once so electric, thrilling and scintillating in his pomp. The devil with a flash of genius; an overhead kick, a flashing shot to win a title or save United's neck. 'The King of the Stretford End' the fans hail him.

But then the injuries mount and the legs sag. The kicks and lunges, the brutal assaults. The battles fought for the cause. For United, for Busby. When you can't rise from bed. When you need an injection to stand the pain to just walk, never mind run. When he asks you to play, even though every bone in your body, every brain cell in your head is telling you, 'Please God no.'

But you do it.

You do it because of your love of the game, your duty as a Manchester United footballer, but most of all because of your love and respect for the old man. It always came down to Busby and an utter determination not to let him down. Not to displease him. The satisfaction that came from a simple 'Well done son' or just a friendly ruffle of the hair that spoke a thousand words.

But underneath Denis has always known the old man was hard as nails. The grandfatherly persona, the gentle image of this grand old 'Father of Football' is an act. They have had more than their share of scrapes and fall outs. No more than back in 1965. Denis's star had never been higher so he demanded a pay rise. Demanded? Unheard of at Old Trafford. A few who had attempted such folly were shown the door – 'no one is bigger than the club' went the mantra and Busby could not allow his position to be undermined. It could open the door to anarchy.

It was whilst playing golf in his hometown of Aberdeen that The Lawman discovered he had been placed on the transfer list! Denis immediately returned to Manchester for he had underestimated the old man. Behind the scenes however Busby reluctantly went along with his demands, for he knew United could ill afford to lose such a magnificent footballer at the peak of his career, a player who would immediately be snapped up by a domestic rivals or return to haunt them with say Real Madrid in the European Cup.

Face had to be saved and this scenario could not be allowed to happen again. So a charade was played out with Denis agreeing to publicly apologise for rocking the boat and admitting he had backed down.

Having been taken off the list both sides won, meaning Busby's aura and Denis's weekly pay packet profited equally. However Denis was warned by Busby never to mention this, otherwise he was finished at United.

Denis agreed and the subject became taboo and the Lawman carried on illuminating many a Saturday afternoon in the devil red shirt. And even up until this troublesome season Denis had given everything and more for Busby. Even though his knee was almost wrecked he still could not say no – this season's semi final second leg against City, when only one man on this earth, the old man, could have talked him into playing. The jagged needle searing into his skin, the thrashing of the leg, the muscle spasm as the cortisone sunk deep and Denis played and Denis scored, the Lawman pouncing in typical style. But come later that night, the next day and even now six months on, the after effects of the jab, and many before it, lingers.

Well tomorrow morning, glory, glory Man United. The reds will go marching on but without him. Not Denis. Out the door he goes. The decision taken, Denis Law is past his sell by date and it's time to cash in. Time to toss him out with the garbage.

Thanks for the memories Lawman.

Now fuck off.

★

Denis knocks and enters the old man's office and is surprised to see Wilf McGuinness also present, Wilf is wearing a suit and tie. His face stern and serious. 'Hello Wilf', laughs Denis. 'Have you been to a funeral?'

Wilf smiles, inside he is hurting. So this is the dark side of the dream.

'Hello Denis mate.'

I look at Wilf and it is obvious he is upset, so I will try and get this over with quickly as possible.

'Denis son, I am sorry but we are putting you on the transfer list. The club would like to thank you for everything you have done in your time here.'

'How much?' asks Denis, interrupting.

'£60,000' I reply.

'Why not give me a free. I think I have deserved it don't you?'

'Now Denis,' I say, 'we both know you have been well paid here during your time at Manchester United.'

So that's it, Denis thought, payback time for five years ago. Well he was not going to argue. If they don't want him, Denis will get fully fit during the summer to ensure come the new season he is back firing in whatever coloured shirt. Denis has too much pride to make a scene. Even though he feels hurt and more sadly, betrayed.

'Fine' he smiles. 'Is that it?'

I am not sure what to make of Denis.

'Denis, we are sorry. I'm afraid this comes to us all.'

'For God's sake Matt, I am twenty-nine years old' Denis snaps back, 'you have not seen the last of me.' He stands to go.

Wilf has the despairing look of a man watching a good friend seeing his world turned upside down.

'Denis, you need anything give me a shout.'

Denis turns to stare at Wilf. Then at me.

'You look after yourself Wilf. Make sure it is not you stood where I am next season.'

There was no doubt who that was aimed at! Denis leaves and Wilf has his head in his hands. 'Sort yourself out Wilf' I say. 'Always remember this is not personal, but once a player cannot run any more, they become a liability. Like a lame horse that was once a Derby winner. There is nothing to do but get rid. Denis was a great player, he is no longer.

'Now who is next on the list?'

23 - THE LIST: SHAY

At first there was no sense of panic. All seemed well. He had been measured up a suit for the tour to North America later this year, everything was normal. Then the whispers began. When Wilf could not meet his eyes, when he could not answer his straight question, 'Am I safe Wilf?' When Wilf replied 'Come on Shay mate, don't ask me that' and then the look in Wilf's eye. He is not ready to leave United. This club is his life and at thirty-one years old Shay 'Bomber' Brennan knows nothing else. Shay has always been good for a laugh and joke but he is not smiling at the moment. Shay is worried.

A terrible season is all but over. It began with injuries and a lack of form but ultimately what hurts is that his supposed best mate, Wilf McGuinness, does not rate him anymore. Shay is convinced he is going on the list. Wilf is saying nothing now, a sure sign all is not well.

But then again, thank God, Shay believes it will not be Wilf's decision. Surely the old man will have the final word on who is staying or going? Wilf is just a puppet. He has made himself an outcast with the lads. Nothing much is said to his face, but behind his back they rage. They slaughter him.

'Who the fuck is he to tell me that?'

'He is not the old man.'

'He has not got a clue.' And so on.

Willie and Alex are the loudest, Bobby simply

watches and says nothing, but says everything with his silences. A disdainful shake of his head. George, well George is just out of control. Wilf simply cannot manage him. After what happened with the girl before the Leeds semi-final he cannot even look George in the eye anymore but then when George is not birding and boozing, he tends to keep his opinions to himself anyway. So far as Shay can make out, George simply does not care anymore.

The others; Paddy preaches patience but even he is starting to doubt what is going on? As for Nobby, he is far too concerned on getting himself fit again to worry about anyone else. He, like Shay, feels the breath of Father Time breathing down his neck. It is a heinous stench, one that places fear in the soul and a chill in your heart.

Denis just stares on in bemusement. The Lawman loves Wilf but he can only take so much. That wonderful, world weary smile of his has turned more into a grimace these last six months. Nothing would surprise Denis anymore.

Of the younger ones: Brian Kidd, Francis, Burns, Paul Edwards, Carlos Sartori all adore Wilf. He brought them through, they are his boys and he is given them a chance. Mostly at the older player's expense. But are they good enough?

★

Training has just finished but those unsure whether they are set to be placed on the list hang around at The Cliff with fear in the hearts and desperation in their eyes. These include Shay who is speaking to Jimmy Ryan and Don Givens.

They tell him the boss has called for them. 'Looks like we are off Shay,' says Don. He is near to tears.

'Been nice knowing you Bomber' smiles Jimmy. Laughing off a broken heart.

They set off to the boss's office. Shay shakes both their hands and ruffles their hair.

'Good luck lads' wishes Shay as they walk off. He decides to take himself off to the canteen. It is unusually quiet. Shay sits down and pulls out a copy of the Racing Post from his pocket to mark off a few more losers for later that day. Then he hears a voice. It is Jack Crompton shouting him from the canteen door.

'Shay before you leave, the boss would like to see you upstairs in about twenty minutes.'

With that Jack disappears. Shay's heart sinks.

He looks around the room and there is not a soul around. A silence so rare in a place normally vibrant with laughing and loud voices. Good friends chatting and smoking and joking. Drinking tea and putting the world and this football club to rights.

Not now, not today. For it appears Shay is being avoided. Maybe everybody knows except him?

★

With heart in mouth and his stomach churning, Shay knocks on the old man's door. 'Come in' I shout. This is going to be difficult because Wilf and Shay have been best friends for years. Best Men at each other's weddings. Brothers almost. But as a player Shay has gone. His usefulness to United over. A great servant and a good lad but there have been many good lads stood where he is now. Shay looks over towards Wilf who can't meet his eyes.

'Whatever it is boss I didn't do it!' Shay grins wide. I smile.

'Shay, son, sit down. I am afraid we have come to the end of the road.'

Still Wilf keeps his head down. I pass over the club proposal for Shay to read.

'Now we are not going to give you a free transfer because I know what will happen to the money. Your love of the horses will soon see any such sum dwindle son. So instead United are going to give you a lifetime pension of £20 a week. Believe me it is for the best.'

Shays picks up the proposal. He is glancing through it. 'For the best,' he says quietly. He puts it back down on my desk.

'So that's it then. All those years and it's over. Just like that. Mr Busby, would you mind if I called you Matt? Just this once.' I nod. Shay smiles again. 'You are too kind Matt. May I say in all our time together I have found you a wonderful and inspiring man. At times you have been like a father to me. I know you are a good man and I also know not a day goes by when you don't think about what happened all those years ago. I know you never mention it, I know your hurt goes way beyond physical pain and if I could take away that pain, believe me Matt, I would. I swear on all the angels and saints in heaven I would. But at this particularly moment in time, may God forgive me but I hate your guts.'

Shay stares across at Wilf. 'You too old pal' Wilf blinks fast to avoid tears. He is smiling once more. 'I am going to go now. But let me assure you gents. I am only laughing on the outside.'

Shay stands to go. I shout after him. 'Shay son,

come back. Please?' He turns.

'Have a good day Mr Busby. I have a certainty for the 3-20 at Chepstow if you want it?' He smiles and leaves, shutting the door behind him.

I take a deep breath. 'That is it for today Wilf. You get yourself home. '

I look across and Wilf has tears streaming down his cheeks.

★

Shay's mind is reeling. He does not want to go home, so as if by instinct he finds himself driving down Chester Road towards Old Trafford. There he goes and sits in the stand. Shay stares across the empty stadium. Suddenly he hears a voice behind him.

'Want some company?'

It is Jimmy Murphy. The Irishman smiles on seeing Jimmy. He motions to the seat next to him and Jimmy sits down.

'I heard what happened. I am sorry son. I had no idea.'

Shay shakes his head.

'When did it all change, Jimmy. How can something that was once so beautiful turn so ugly? I don't recognise this place anymore.' Shay looks at Jimmy. 'And how can they treat you like this? Don't these bastards realise all this would not be here if it was not for you? Why are you not still at the old man's side instead of...' he stops, 'well you know who...'

'Shay son, a little advice. Don't let this game come between yours and Wilf's friendship. No one will be hurting more than him now over this. Believe me, I have been in that room and I have had to tell boys a lot younger than you that they are not good enough for United. And every time when I saw the hurt in their eyes, it cut me. Please don't hold this against Wilf. Besides it would not have been his decision. Matt is still pulling the strings.'

They both go quiet. Content to just stare out across a deserted Old Trafford. Finally Shay speaks. He is grinning. 'Jimmy I have a confession to make. I figure twelve years on you might not shout at me now.'

'Don't be so sure. Go on,' smiles Jimmy.

'The Sheffield Wednesday FA Cup tie at Old Trafford. The first game after Munich when you gave me my debut?'

'What about it?'

'Well you told me I was playing on the afternoon of the game. I had no idea you were going to pick me remember?' Jimmy nods. He is not sure where Shay is going with this. 'Well we won 3-0 and I scored two goals, so I suppose it did not affect me too much?' A quizzical Jimmy simply stares non-plussed at Shay. 'I have to confess the night before I was in a bad state over the crash. And a couple of mates took me out for a few drinks. Well it turned out we had more than a few actually. I got myself stinking drunk and the next day when you pulled me into the office, and said I was in the team? Well I could hardly see straight.'

Jimmy smiles wide. 'Well that will explain your two goals then!'

They both laugh out loud and it echoes across the vast empty terraces.

'Do you mind if we just sit here for a while Jimmy?'

'Of course not' he replies. A tear rolls down Shay's cheek. 'Thanks Jimmy. Thanks for everything.'

24 - SAIL THIS SHIP ALONE

The new season dawns, 1970-71, time fades away so fast, my life played out in seasons and not years. Where does it go: the days, months, marriages, christenings, funerals and friends? And so I cannot put this off any more. I think it is time to give Wilf his extra stripe and for me to step back. Maybe I have been a little eager at times to meddle in team affairs. To give an opinion - it could be seen as sticking my oar in. And that is not fair on Wilf. So from now on it is his ship that sails alone out into the ocean. I stay ashore and he as captain will decide whether we sink or swim. With all the glory and consequences of failure that go with it.

'I won't let you down boss,' Wilf is ecstatic when I tell him.

We are watching the lads in pre-season training.

'I have an idea to replace Denis,' says Wilf. 'A young lad at Luton, he is lethal, fast and powerful and confident with it. A cocky so and so but we could knock that out of him and he is a decent price.'

'What is his name?' I ask.

'Malcolm Macdonald boss.'

'Alright Wilf, we will check it out.' But Wilf continues: 'Also a replacement for Shay at right back? There is another kid at Ipswich called Mick Mills. Not spectacular but steady as a rock. He would fit us like a glove.'

I smile. 'Okay Wilf, let us see what happens. For the moment concentrate on what we have okay?'

Wilf nods. 'We need to make a good start and cannot afford another season without a trophy. Make it happen son, make me proud. You steer this ship alone to success.'

Wilf's face is etched with nervous energy, excitement and determination to make this so. Maybe too much. I leave him alone and return to Old Trafford. Home for me this season from now on. If he needs me, Wilf can call. Wilf heads over to the training pitch. Buoyant and boosted by his new grand sounding title. Wilf McGuinness. Manager of Manchester United.

Let anyone fuck with him now!

★

It begins with defeat at home to Leeds and slowly descends into disaster. Just three wins in our opening twelve games and in the dressing room, I am reliably informed, they are gunning for Wilf's head. Some things never change in this game.

Players don't take responsibility for the bad times. They never blame themselves, it is always somebody else's' fault.

Notably the manager.

I am hearing things. I hate tell tales and gossips but the stories I am told whilst playing golf with Paddy, Willie and Alex make my blood boil.

I am told of an incident involving Bobby last week which if true, well, there really are no words.

It was a cold and murky rain-sodden Mancunian morning when Bobby's car pulled into The Cliff car park. The season is not going well and he no longer recognises his old friend Wilf. Pressure does strange things to people and Bobby feels Wilf is struggling badly to cope with the stress of management. However, being captain, Bobby feels uncomfortable with the jibes and backstabbing that are occurring. They are hurtful and personal. Bobby knows Wilf's family like they are his own. It is not right some of the things that are being uttered and by people Bobby feels ten years ago would never had been allowed a place in the club car park, never mind the Manchester United first team.

'Bad eggs' Jimmy has always called them. Sadly in Bobby's mind these bad eggs have genuine grievances. For Wilf appears to have lost the plot. Every week a different team, tactics once straight forward are now convoluted and baffling. Everything has been made complicated. Under the old man and Jimmy it was straight forward; 'Play the ball to a red shirt, pass and move and win!' How Bobby pines for those days.

He has already been approached by a delegation of senior players. Some he has known for years. A kangaroo court, more like! He's been asked to go and talk to the boss on their behalf. He refused, not because he thought the old man did not have a right to hear what was going at his club, but that Sir Matt would already know.

Nothing gets by him.

Hidden eyes and spies, golfing buddies and Saturday nights at the Cromford club. One big United family. Sir Matt and the inner circle of senior players. Bobby would never dare. He would not have the nerve. Too much respect.

Oh the old man would know what is occurring in his name. Loose lips, late nights. 'Wilf is destroying everything you have built, boss.' They would raise their glasses and toast 'Cheers,' United all as one.

Except one. One who has probably loved United longer and more than any of them – Wilf.

Bobby enters the already packed dressing room. He says little these days but this morning has to speak to Wilf about finishing training early because of a business appointment in London. He places his suit on a hanger.

'You got a hot date Bob?' quips Paddy.

Bobby attempts a grin that comes off more a grimace. Wilf comes in and Bobby shouts him over.

'Wilf can I have a quick word?'

'Course you can. What is it Bob?'

'I hope you don't mind but I need to disappear twenty minutes early. I have to catch the train to London?'

'No problem old mate' says Wilf, 'just nip off and get changed when we do the kick in, then come back whilst we have a quick team meeting.'

'Cheers Wilf,' replies a smiling Bobby.

Come that time it has begun to rain and Bobby runs off the training pitch and appears ten minutes later all suited up. Wilf is holding the meeting in the centre circle. Bobby looks at his shoes but thinks Wilf was good enough to let him go, so he walks over to join the rest. He can clean them later on.

'Here comes the captain all spruced up and handsome' calls out Nobby.

Bobby laughs. His old mate is one of the few left here he can still relate to. By now the heavens have opened and the grass is soaked and mud splattered.

Wilf begins his talk.

'Right lads listen up.' Bobby puts the collar up on the jacket to try and stay dry and places his hands in his pockets.

Suddenly Wilf shouts and points across.

'Bobby Charlton, hands in pockets! Twenty press up now.'

An in house rule states that anyone with hands in pockets has to do this on the spot.

'You know the rules.'

The other players look bemused. Some are smiling but Bobby's friends are embarrassed. 'Wilf come on,' pleads Paddy, 'Bob has got changed for Christ sake.'

'Now, now Pat. Bobby is no different to any others.'

'This is fucking out of order' mutters a fuming Nobby.

'I have my suit on' says a disbelieving Bobby. 'You can't be serious?'

A smiling, somewhat frenetic Wilf claps his hands.

'Come on now Bob, no exceptions, we can't have sloppiness here at United.'

Bobby looks around, few can meet his eyes. Some are smirking but he is not surprised at the faces. Bobby Charlton, captain of England and Manchester United, gets down on the floor and does as Wilf orders.

Twenty press ups.

'There is a deafening silence amongst all looking on. Nobby can't bear to watch. He has turned his back. When he's finished the front of Bobby's suit is wet through and caked in mud. Standing up, he stares towards Wilf then simply walks away off the pitch.

'Oi Bobby come back, we have not had the meeting yet.'

Bobby ignores him and keeps walking.

'Bobby Charlton' screams Wilf. 'You come back here right now.'

Bobby does not turn around. He walks on. If there was one final bridge to be burnt it has just gone up in flames. Wilf has lost his captain and he is heading into stormy seas alone.

★

Wilf is certainly doing himself no favours by alienating the senior players. At the moment Paddy, Willie, and Alex are all dropped and playing in the reserves. Paddy apart, who I can see is desperate for me to simply have a word with Wilf and calm matters, the others are fuming.

'We just want the best for the club boss,' says Willie, who I have grown to like and trust. It is the same state of mind in the boardroom. Never his greatest supporter, Louis Edwards is breathing fire and almost out of patience. I am here with Louis and Denzil Haroun. Both have a fat cigar in one hand and whisky glass in other.

'We should never have given it to him,' Louis declares in my direction, 'the man is an embarrassment. A walking disaster. McGuinness has had his time Matt. I understand you acted in good faith when you recommended him old pal. But he is out of his depth and something must be done. And now.'

'I agree. This can't go on' adds Denzil Haroun, 'put him out of his misery Matt, end the pain'

I have already heard enough and finally snap: 'He is not a damn horse Denzil. Do you think I am blind and cannot see what is happening? Let us at least give Wilf the League Cup semi final against Aston Villa. A two legged tie against a Third Division team? If he fails then we shall talk some more. I am sure a day out at

Wembley where you can both shake hands with the great and the good in the Royal Box, might help you think different about Wilf's position?'

Both go quiet. I don't think either are willing to take me on too much whilst I am this mood. Louis takes the whisky bottle and tops mine up. 'That kind of comment is a little uncalled for Matt don't you think?'

So it seems the worm is turning...

'I beg your pardon Louis?'

'I just think you should remember Matt that I am the chairman of this club. I pay the wages. I call the shots. The buck stops with me. And yes myself and this club would not be where we are today without you.'

'And Jimmy' adds Denzil.

A shot fired low across my bow.

Louis continues: 'But I don't like your comment about the Royal Box and feel you should apologise?'

This has left me a little taken aback and I must say shocked. I look at Louis. His stare does not leave my eyes. He does appear hurt and maybe it is right I should take back what said. If only to make right appearances.

'I am sorry Louis, and to you also Denzil. I meant no offence.'

Denzil raises his glass. 'Already forgotten Matt.'

Louis comes around the table. He puts his drink on the table and embraces me. 'Come on old pal, let us have another drink and have no more talk of this.'

I smile and accept Louis' bearhug as if we are brothers in arms. But we are nothing of the sort. Louis is no different than the rest of his type. Chairmen? Give them the merest sniff of power and they get ideas above their station. I will not be lectured to about what is to happen with Wilf. I cannot stomach that type of arrogance from men whose place is to sign the cheques.

For Manchester United belongs to me. I made it. I nearly died for it.

And I have earned it.

25 - THY WILL BE DONE

I am stood at the bar of the Cromford Club with its owner, my close friend Paddy McGrath. It is always good to speak to Paddy. He is a no nonsense fellow with a heart of gold and always comes straight to the point.

'How are things going with Wilf?'

I shake my head. 'He is headstrong, full of new ideas. The lad wants to grab the moon from the stars, he is a stubborn so and so.'

Paddy smiles and lights up a cigarette. 'Sound like someone I used to know.'

Paddy is correct of course. Wilf is me all those years ago just after the war. Back then no one or nothing was going to stand in mine and Jimmy's way of creating the greatest football club in the world. 'You have to let him breathe, give him time Matt' continues Paddy. 'Let him make his own mistakes then pray like hell he learns fast from them.'

'It is difficult Paddy because that is the problem, I do give him space. I try so hard not to interfere but I have players moaning about him on the golf course. The one place I try to forget about football. They are simply not having Wilf at any price.'

'How many?' asks Paddy, 'two or three?'

'More like six or seven' I reply. 'And senior pros. Men who have known him for years. At this rate if I don't step back in we are going to have a damn mutiny on our hands.'

A sombre-faced Paddy stubs out his cigarette in the ashtray. 'Do that and you will destroy Wilf. Why not sell the players and stand by him. He deserves your support. At least for another six months?'

I shake my head. 'Can't do it Paddy. If I don't act now we will be relegated. They are not playing for him. Oh, I'm sure they are trying but it is more out of a sense of duty to me. Old pros can stink out a club faster than a nest of rats. They infect the young ones. Ripe apples become rotten. I can't have it. I just can't have it.'

'You had something similar in '63 if I remember Matt' remarks Paddy, 'you and Jimmy came down hard as nails on the bad eggs. What's different now?'

'I'm different Pat. As for Jimmy, me and him, well… like I say things are just different.'

'It is a crying shame with what has happened to your friendship with Jimmy. You two have been to heaven and hell and back again.'

'That there is the problem Paddy. We never made it back from hell. We never spoke about Munich. Never. The boys that were killed. I have tried to mend bridges. Approach the subject, but we never get there. Never.'

Paddy says nothing. My friend knows that for me and Jimmy it is just too late.

As I fear it could be for Wilf.

Saturday 12th December 1970:
Old Trafford: Manchester Derby

Humiliation is hard to take at any time but sadly these days when we are up against the top sides, like unfortunately our near neighbours, it becomes expected. If the red devil is in the small print then this could be it, for I cannot put up with much more of this rubbish.

Manchester United 1 Manchester City 4

All week Malcolm Allison has been mouthing off in the newspapers that City would score four goals. Well as they say these days, to talk the talk you have to walk the walk and Malcolm's boys have strutted their stuff wonderfully today. The blues have been magnificent

Malcolm being Malcolm, he almost caused World War Three by coming on the pitch at the full time whistle and taunting the Stretford End by putting four fingers up at them. In doing so he only enhanced his unpopularity with our supporters, whom I feel, if they were not so depressed might have lynched him.

A sad note from today was the injury to Manchester City midfielder Glyn Pardoe, who suffered a broken leg after a hefty challenge from George. At first the City players were fuming with George. Mike Doyle, hardly our number one fan, not surprisingly calling George every name under the sun on the pitch, 'You dirty bastard Best!' But George has some good friends amongst the city team and they, like me, know he is simply not capable of purposely 'doing' Pardoe.

It was a point George was determined to make himself at the full time whistle by heading straight into the city dressing room to plead his innocence. This calmed tempers a little, only for Malcolm to then say in front of everyone present, 'only you know George if you meant it.' George came back to us sick beyond words.

A Mike Doyle header and a Francis Lee hat-trick were the cornerstones of a City performance that left us with our biggest Derby hammering for fifteen years.

This one hurt and I feel it is truly damaging. Unless I act we are on course for the Second Division.

Wilf simply cannot do it. He is a broken man. His eyes gaunt, he appears to have aged ten years. I cannot be angry with him, for he is probably the most disappointed Manchester United supporter in the stadium. Every bad pass and goal conceded cuts him like a knife. But this cannot go on. Wilf has the two legged League Cup semi final against Aston Villa to save his job. If that goes awry my hands are tied and I will be forced into something that will break my heart.

But rest assured, for the good of Manchester United, thy will be done.

Wednesday 23rd December 1970:
League Cup Semi Final second Leg
Aston Villa 2 Manchester United 1
(Villa win 3-2 on aggregate)

It could be tomorrow, it could even be tonight but I have to act fast and get this over and done with. Wilf is beyond help and consoling after the game. He looks dreadful, like a man not only with the troubles of the world on his shoulders but that are collapsing on top of him.

I enter the dressing room. No one meets my eye, except Jack.

'Wilf is in a bad way boss,' as he points him out, sat with his head in both hands staring down at the floor. The players are going about their business, totally oblivious to his pain. This annoys me, I look around.

'Has anyone got anything to say?' It is like a grenade going off as every eye turns to meet mine. 'Now maybe some of you here might need a history lesson. What

I have just watched was simply unacceptable. It was not Manchester United. I know you have all tried. But when you play we expect that to come as naturally as breathing. I felt no passion or desire. I did not see the willing and hunger to run that extra yard. Put in that tackle that maybe could hurt. I winced as the men in red gave up the ghost. Maybe some of you think it is unfashionable, old fashioned even, but here at United, where boys just like you have in the past given and sweated blood right up until their last game in that same shirt you have just shamed. They gave everything, heart and soul and more. Well how dare you perform like that? It is an honour to be chosen, to represent not just this club in the present but those who have gone before you. And rest assured if they were watching and knowing each and everyone of them they would have been. Your names would have been mud tonight and considered a disgrace to that red shirt. Now we can handle losing here but what we cannot stomach is surrender. I will not stand for what I have witnessed out there tonight. '

Wilf lifts his head.

He cannot believe what he is hearing as the old man lets fly with a passion he has not heard in years. I stop to catch breath. I catch Wilf's eye.

'This man here… he is me. He has been by my side and you must understand, even though I may not be present, Wilf is my voice. He lives and breathes this great club. So I am warning you all now.' I smile and almost laugh. Almost. 'I shudder to think what would have happened if Jimmy was stood here in my place tonight. Some of you as we speak now would be being scraped off the walls and so as you go about your way, picking up wages and thinking this is just a job, another football club. Maybe it would be wise to check out the clock in the forecourt and read about what has gone before you. Because you here, all of you stand on the shoulders of giants.

'Let me assure you gentlemen if you do not learn this matter fast you will be out the door. For this is Manchester United.'

Wilf watches in stunned awe as the old man, his point made turns and walks back out the door.

'Fuck me' he says. 'How do I follow that?

'You don't,' mutters a voice from the players. But when Wilf turns to look no one is looking at him. And he is simply too exhausted to demand who said it.

He does not want to fight anymore.

Boxing Day 1970
Derby County 4 Manchester United 4

At training on Christmas Day morning I receive a call from Wilf that George has not turned up. All attempts to contact him are rendered useless so I tell him to pick his side for tomorrow's Boxing Day clash with Derby without George in mind.

A furious Wilf is raging. 'I can't believe George would do this to me, just when I needed him most.'

'Forget him Wilf, the only thing we can rely on with George these days is that he is unreliable. I will speak to you on the coach tomorrow.'

'Okay boss. Oh and one more thing.'

'Go on,' I sigh.

'Merry Christmas boss.'

'Merry Christmas Wilf.'

The phone goes down. I have already made the decision. Wilf is going. We just have to get the Derby game over with then I am stepping back in.

The next morning a worse for wear George turns up at the coach.

'Where do you think you're going?' demands Wilf, as George and the other players are boarding.

'Come on Wilf,' smiles George. 'You need me.'

'I need you George but I don't want you. You are dropped son. Now go home.'

I am walking up behind and hear the conversation.

'Let us not be too hasty Wilf.' I turn to George. 'You, get on the coach.' A sheepish but still smiling George, smelling strongly of alcohol, with Paddy alongside him, steps on quickly.

Paddy cuffs him on the top of the head. 'You stink George, I want a fucking word with you.' Just myself and Wilf are left outside the coach.

'You can't let him play boss. You just can't?'

'I have slept on it and come to the conclusion we need the points son. I'm sorry.'

Wilf stares at me but says nothing. He gets on and I follow slowly behind.

★

It is a great match, a stunning 4-4 draw, and there are shades of the real Manchester United on view once more. On an ice and snow covered surface we fight back from 2-0 down at half time. It is one of the old boys, Denis, who appears to have a found new lease of life. He was removed from the transfer list after a lack of interest and thank goodness for that. Nothing was said on either side. It just happened. It suited both parties that Denis remain at United and I hope there is no bad feeling on his side. He is a man who I would hate to alienate for he is still capable of moments of genius.

A wonderful cross by George was headed in into the top corner by the Lawman from eight yards, suddenly it was game on. And then, divine providence or the devil's work, I cannot call it these days, George pounces from three yards to level from a Bobby Charlton corner. Almost immediately from Bobby's next corner, Denis smashes home his second headed goal! Three goals in four minutes and now we are 3-2 ahead.

I look down to the bench but Wilf has hardly moved. He appears resigned. As if he knows what is set to occur. Whereas Brian Clough is going mad on the touchline. An interesting character this one but not for us. Not for Manchester United,

Derby hit back with goals from Kevin Hector and Archie Gemmil only for Brian Kidd to save us with a strike from yet another in-swinging Bobby corner. And so we snatch a point. Struggling at the foot of the table, once more flattering to deceive, a defensive shambles and relying on relics of a golden age.

But for Wilf it should go down as a decent enough epitaph for his time in charge.

26 - LET IT BE

The Cliff: Monday 28th December 1970: I am sat at my desk. I look at the clock; it is time to see Wilf. My boy, my Wilf. There is a knock at the door.

In the corridor outside a track-suited Wilf McGuinness stands. He shuffles nervously. Pensive. He straightens his hair and is shocked to find a small strand has come off in his hand.

★

I call out, 'Come in.' Wilf enters. I smile. 'Sit down and take a chair son.'

'Cheers boss' replies Wilf. He sits but is clearly uneasy. I wonder if he senses what I am about to say.

'Wilf lad, I have got some bad news. It is not working out. The board have decided to make a change.'

'What kind of change?' he asks.

I take a breath. 'It is over, son. You are out. I... we cannot risk relegation and the board feel unless changes are made it could happen.'

'Fuck off' says Wilf. He's angry and shocked and now he lets fly. 'I cannot believe you of all people have stabbed me in the back. You, who I have worshipped since I was a kid, I thought you were different but Jesus Christ. You're just like the rest.'

'Wilf, what am I supposed to do? I have been

217

hearing stories; the players are not happy.'

Wilf goes mad. 'They are not happy. Fucking hell I am not happy Boss. I am glad they are not happy. They should be ashamed of themselves.'

This is not going well.

'The Board have insisted. My hands are tied. They are worried. I am going to step back in until the end of the season and then we shall see.'

Wilf is trying to hold back the tears. I can see he is choking. 'And what about me?' he asks.

I smile. 'Well I have had a chat with the board and they are willing to let you have your old job back with the reserves. Obviously your wages will have to change to match the new position. But you will still be one of the family Wilf.'

'One of the fucking family!' screams Wilf. 'You do this to me after everything I have given to the club and you expect me to simply tip my hat and go back to the stiffs?'

I am shocked. 'I expect you to show some respect. And maybe a thank you?'

'Thanks for what?' he shouts. 'For shafting me? Well I can't accept this. There is no chance I am going to step down and make it easy for you. Do you know something, it feels like all my life has been spent trying to please you. Well not this time, this is wrong. No way.'

I feel like crying myself.

'Wilf please, do not put me in this position. The decision has already been made. It is out of my hands.'

Wilf is not having this, 'Oh please, don't treat me as an idiot. Are you seriously trying to say that you do not agree with them? Anything you say to Edwards, him and the board just jump and ask how fucking high?

Now just be honest with me. You can do that can't you? After all these years. You can do the courtesy of telling me the truth.'

'What can I say except, you are out Wilf.'

He walks away. He stays that way for a couple of moments and then turns around to face me. I can see the hurt in his eyes. 'I have to get this off my chest,' he says quietly, 'and may God forgive me. For twelve years it has been eating me up. When you were lying in that hospital bed in Munich and I heard you had been given the last rites I spent whole nights praying you would pull through. I lost so many pals, good friends that were like brothers. But you? I honestly thought if you didn't pull through then I really could not see any future. Any hope. And when Duncan went, may he rest in peace, I so nearly lost it. It was only the thought that you would come back and make everything right that kept me going. I told myself in time life at Old Trafford would revert back to what it was like before the crash. 'Paradise' as Bobby calls it. But it never did.

'The place went stale, it lost its soul. Too many strangers, new faces who just did not get what Manchester United truly means. It wasn't just Tommy and Eddie, Roger and Duncan and the rest that we lost on that fucking runway. Somewhere along the line we lost our spirit. United lost its spirit. Nothing has been the same since. Nothing. Oh yes we carried on, kept the red flag flying fucking high and we came back and won the damn thing. But it was never the same. Bobby knew, he just never talked about it. He still won't. But I see it in his eyes. He is still on the plane. Every day I see him still looking around for Duncan and the others. Force of will and a determination not to look back kept him from going mad with grief. And me. And Jimmy. And you? My god, we can only guess what kept you sane?'

Wilf is in tears. Forgive me but I can't help myself but feel anger towards him.

'Sane. You have no idea Wilf? Do you think there has not been an hour of every day since when I have not thought about the boys that I lost? It has not been easy for any of us who came through that hell but we have had to move on. Of course things changed after the crash, we had our hearts ripped out. Something like that hardens men, lad. It makes them what they are. What they become. Manchester United must come before everything and so despite everything – this is where we are today. I am sorry son. I really am.'

Wilf sits back down. He wipes his eyes dry. He straightens his hair. My heart is breaking. Wilf is sweating, never before has he spoke to the boss like this and inexplicably, despite what has happened to him, he feels guilty. He takes a deep breath and begins to speak again.

'Now I am not going to beg. We don't do that where I am from. My Mum and Dad would disapprove but I will ask you one more time. Reconsider. Give me a few more games, I can do this. Get me a few players in and I can turn this season around. I swear I can do it. Christ you have not let me spend a bloody penny apart from Ian Ure and you bought him. Loosen the purse strings then at least I will have a fucking fighting chance!'

I stare straight at Wilf. I push a piece of paper over the desk towards him. 'I want you to sign this. Your letter of resignation. We will tell the press that you came to us and for the good of Manchester United stated you wished to go back to your old job. That is the deal.'

Wilf looks at the sheet of paper. 'And if I don't sign it?'

'Well like you have said, things have changed.'

Wilf smiles and gently pushes the sheet of paper back towards me. 'They were good days boss,' he says. 'They were the best of days.'

Wilf stands and walks out the door.

I pick up the resignation letter, screw it up and throw it in a waste paper basket. I lean back in the chair and shut my eyes.

Wilf is in a daze. He rushes past Jack Crompton in the corridor. Knocking him aside. He turns to apologise, 'I am sorry Jack mate,' then he continues on in haste

Wilf cannot get out of the training ground quick enough.

Jack takes one look at Wilf's face and he knows.

I appear.

'Bad news Jack, I have had to let Wilf go.'

Jack glowers at me.

'He was family boss.'

'I had no choice, we're on our way down. I have to step back in.'

Still Jack stares.

'Jack please'

I need him to understand. Indeed everybody to understand. What I have done is for the good of this club. Of Manchester United. Surely Jack knows I am hurting inside.

Finally he shakes his head in disgust and turns to walk off following Wilf.

★

Wilf gets in the car and is trying hard to keep his eyes dry. He switches on the radio and the Beatles 'Let it Be' is playing.

> *When I find myself in times of trouble*
> *Mother Mary comforts me*

Wilf finds himself singing along and the tears start to flow. He dare not go home. His wife Beryl, now pregnant with their third child and worried sick about her father who has cancer, doesn't need a third problem. It is not fair to saddle her with this news.

He needs a drink.

A stiff one.

Many of.

So Wilf pulls up outside the Quadrant pub. He has decided to go and have a drink with his old mate Charlie Baxter. Charlie is a good guy, honest as the day is long. Charlie is as straight as they come and he would never stab you in the back. It was Charlie who originally warned him.

'Watch your back son. And stay in touch. You make sure you in touch.'

Suddenly Wilf feels guilty. Wilf has not seen or spoken with Charlie since he got the job. There simply has not been enough time. But anyway, he will get Charlie a few drinks, apologise for being a stranger and it will just be like old times. Charlie will make him feel better.

'They are not worth it Wilf,' he will surely say, in

that wise old sage like manner. 'Fuck em Wilf!'

On reaching the bar Wilf looks around but there is no sign of him.

'Where is Charlie?' asks Wilf of the landlord.

'Hello Wilf, long time no see. I am so sorry mate, you have obviously been busy so you must not have heard. Old Charlie passed away two weeks ago. It is a shame you never saw him before he went. Charlie was always fighting your corner in here. He would not have a bad word said against you.'

A devastated Wilf sits himself down on Charlie's old barstool. 'What are you having mate?' inquires the landlord.

Wilf stands back up. 'No, I'm sorry' he says. 'I have to go.'

He has lost his job, Charlie is dead and it is not even fucking twelve in the afternoon, thinks Wilf. He leaves the pub and gets back in his car. Wilf decides to go to the ground, for there is always booze knocking around the boardroom. On arrival at Old Trafford Wilf heads straight in. His sacking is still not pubic knowledge, so those working at the stadium have no inkling of what has occurred at The Cliff that morning. Wilf goes into the empty boardroom. There is no whisky but he spots an unopened bottle of Sherry.

'This will do' he says, whilst getting himself a glass and pouring a large one. Wilf sits down at the long table. He downs the drink in one mouthful and slams it back down on the table. Then another, and another. He picks up the Sherry and stands. His eyes focused on a picture of the United team line up in Belgrade.

'Not been a good day lads' smiles Wilf. Then in utter frustration he head butts the wall. Again and again. The second time Jack enters. Seeing what state Wilf was in, he had made the decision to follow him from the Cliff.

'Wilf what the bloody hell are you doing?'

Jack races over to takes the bottle off Wilf, who collapses in his arms. He starts to sob.

'Let it out mate' whispers Jack. 'Let it all out.'

The next day all the players are gathered at The Cliff as I stand alongside Wilf to explain what has occurred. I have to ensure his dignity is maintained. I owe him that much. Wilf has decided to have his old job back to remain in the family. Although I doubt he views it like that.

'Alright listen up. As of today Wilf is to step down as first team manager and resume his responsibilities with the reserves.'

No one speaks. Not a murmur. Wilf is looking at the floor.

'Now there are some here today who will know they could have done more to help him. You will know who you are?'

A sea of blank faces meet my words.

'I will be stepping back in until the end of the season. Just until we can get somebody else permanent in the summer. Now let me make one thing clear. This is truly a dark day for the club. Wilf McGuinness here is United to the core and I feel personally responsible for what has occurred. No blame must be attached to Wilf. No toolmaker can do a job if he does not have the tools. Or indeed if the tools are faulty.'

Looking at certain faces that line strikes home as I

try to make my point without digging out those I feel should hang their heads in shame.

'Any comments or lack of respect directed towards Wilf from this day on will be dealt with by me and I promise you, whoever it may be, you will not want to feel my wrath at this moment in time. Now Wilf will say a few words.'

Wilf steps forward. He appears pensive and upset. He finally looks up to face both those who have been with him and his accusers.

'Lads, I would like to thank you for all your hard work during my time. I am just sorry it has not worked out. Anything I have said or done these past eighteen months has been only for the good of this club and improving you as players. For me it has been an absolute privilege. If only for a short time, I have lived my dream. So let us put all misunderstandings behind us and let bygones be bygones and move on to put Manchester United back up where we belong. Right at the top.'

Nobody applauds or speaks. There's just an uneasy stifling silence.

'Come on Wilf' I say. As we turn to walk away I hear a voice break rank amongst the players.

'You have let him down you lousy bastards.' It is a tearful Brian Kidd letting fly.

'Now now Brian' says Wilf. Heading back towards his fellow Mancunian. He puts an arm around Brian's shoulders. 'We are all United here, lad. Let's have no more of that.'

Inside Wilf's stomach is churning. He is so proud of young Kiddo but dare not say so out loud. The 'We are all United here' comment was meant to be ironic, not that anyone would ever notice, thinks Wilf.

In this backstabbing dysfunctional Old Trafford 'family'.

27 - THE LIST: NOBBY

Come 1971, the ageing warrior, the man who has hunted down the greats of Real Madrid and Benfica, and succeeded. Thirty-one year-old Norbert (Nobby) Peter Stiles, now knows his fourteen year career at Old Trafford is winding down fast.

Nobby is on the transfer list. He understands this present day Old Trafford is no place for sentiment. Old pros, good friends, are being shipped out and discarded like cattle to make way for new blood. Men whom have served this club with distinction and honour and courage beyond the call of duty. Men like he, who over the seasons have played on in searing pain. Kept going only by the cortisone needle and the boss's persuasive "Go on Norrie, do it for me." And Nobby did play on. And now his left knee, for want of a better word, as Nobby so grandly puts it, is knackered.

Madrid 1968: half-time at the Estadio Bernabeu, in the European Cup semi final second leg and United are going out. Being horribly outclassed by a Real Madrid team rolling back the years and giving their Mancunian friends, but on this tumultuous occasion, foes, a hideous chasing.

3-1 down on the night, 3-2 on aggregate, the overall scoreline is misleading. This is a mismatch, United are being murdered. Step forward Nobby, whose personal duel with Real's darting centre-forward Amancio in the first half has at times verged on all out war. Amancio has gone toe to toe with Nobby, no quarter given or asked by either. Off the ball it is a war but when he has it, Amancio is winning hands down as he rips apart United's wilting defence.

Matt Busby watches in despair from the touchline as Amancio lets fly a volley right on half time to surely end United's latest quest to win the European Cup. The years are moving on, the sands of time have almost run out. Madrid looks set to be Matt's last stand. Some things are just not meant to be.

In the visitors' dressing room Nobby sits pouring whisky on a leg wound caused by an Amancio lunge. The Spaniard may have pleaded self-defence as his English opponent had shown no mercy throughout a first half that seemed like a spaghetti western showdown without the guns. Blood is seeping out of Nobby's knee but nothing was going to stop him coming out for the second half. Meanwhile Busby stands speechless. For once he has no words of wisdom. No pearls to inspire. In fact he appears a broken man.

Instead Paddy Crerand, defiant to the end, stands to declare.

'Lads this is not bloody over! Come on, I am not going home tomorrow without knowing we have given these bastards one hell of a fight.'

Just as the United players are leaving to go back out for the second half, Busby finally speaks.

'Just remember boys, we are only one goal down on aggregate. So let us just have a go at them. Do it the Manchester United way.'

Now nobody loves Busby more than Paddy, but even he stands and stares at his manager like he is a madman. Have a go at them? We are getting bloody slaughtered!

As the teams emerge back onto the pitch, the experienced Italian referee Antonio Sbardella grabs both Nobby and Amancio. He bangs his fist down onto his other hand, signifying, 'No more'. Both players nod, as if it is all a big misunderstanding.

Then in the first moment of open play Amancio goes to finish Nobby off with a vicious kick out at his injured knee. Now it is kill or be killed.

Nobby knows there is little choice left. United are being overrun, the dream is dying, he has one card left to play as Señor Sbardella turns his back on him, a left hook born and bred just off Rochdale Road and cultivated in Collyhurst, lays Amancio out flat.

The crowd rage, objects fly down at the gringo assassin in red. But no action is taken as no official has witnessed what happened. Amancio staggers back to his feet, not even sure where he is anymore more. For the remainder of the match he is a passenger.

Suddenly shaken, the great Real no longer strut, they appear rocked and a miracle occurs. First David Sadler slides forward to sneak home and make it 3-3 on aggregate. And then the angels take over – Bill Foulkes takes flight.

It is eight minutes from time with Manchester United now in the ascendancy, that the ageing centre-half moves forward with a United attack. It is almost as if ethereal voices are urging him on. 'Go on Bill mate....' As George Best receives a throw in on the right and beats one and then another, Bill is ghosting, unseen, into the box. George looks up, sees a red shirt and rolls in the perfect cross. He is as astounded as everyone else in the ground to see that it is Big Bill that has stepped forward to finish off the Spanish champions.

At the full time whistle Bobby Charlton falls to his knees overcome. Matt Busby comes onto the pitch. He cries and cries.

'I can't help it' he weeps in the dressing room. As reality sweeps over the United manager that the almighty has at last glanced in their direction and given them a break. Jimmy Murphy embraces Busby. But it is only a fleeting embrace. Together they will now go on to clinch the measure of their tormented dreams. Jimmy goes looking for Nobby. He grabs him in a headlock.

'If I had to come back as any player it would be you lad.' Nobby has no words after hearing that from Jimmy. He sits down and reaches for a beer. He loves this club. He just fucking loves it!

As for the travelling Mancunians, they party in Madrid like it was the rainy city itself as Manchester red explodes onto the Spanish capital.

The Real President Santiago Bernabeu accepts defeat with typical wonderful grace and style. 'We wish our great friends from Manchester the best of luck in the final. We shall be cheering for them.'

Meanwhile as toasts are made to everlasting friendships, a drunken Amancio tries one last time to finish Nobby off with a wine bottle over his head in the post-match banquet, but fails.

As a bloodied Nobby fumes and goes looking for revenge, it is Busby who pulls him away from the fracas with the words.

'Leave it Norrie, we are in the final not them. Let us just go home. I owe you for tonight son. I won't forget what you have done for me here.'

And so the Reds went marching on.

★

But that was then, this is now. Yet despite it all, Nobby is far from bitter. His love of Manchester United and respect for Matt Busby dwarfs all other considerations. He has been amongst Busby's most loyal lieutenants. And now as the end draws near Nobby knows the boss will see him right. They are family. United as one.

392 matches and 19 goals and a body battered, bruised and almost broken. An integral part of the European Cup winning team; sent out to tame the Panther, a cocktail of Collyhurst streetwise brutality and tactical nous caged Eusebio but now those days are over and now Nobby has received a phone call.

Manchester United have him valued at £25,000. At that price he is seen as a risk to any suitors, due to injuries and age but Second Division Middlesbrough manager Stan Anderson has been in touch and is willing to take a punt. He contacted Nobby with an idea. Boro want him but not at the asking fee. Anderson has asked Nobby to go and see Busby to see if he will consider say £20,000, and if so a deal could be struck. Then Boro would be willing to give him the spare five grand.

For Nobby this is a lifeline. He has never earned big. Nor has he rocked the boat over wages. Five grand to him and his family would be a lifeline to start elsewhere. Nobby's meeting with the boss is, he feels, a mere formality.

★

The following morning Nobby knocks on my door at Old Trafford.

'Norrie come in son, how are the family. How are Kay and the kids?'

'They are great boss, thanks for asking,' says Nobby.

'And you, how are things with you Norrie?'

'Well boss, I need a favour,' he smiles.

'What can I do?'

'Well the twenty five grand you are asking for me is a little steep don't you think? I have had a call. Boro manager Stan Anderson has been in touch. He says if you are willing to drop five grand then he is willing to do a deal. What do you say? For old time's sake.'

'Why did Anderson simply not ring me?' Nobby shrugs his shoulders. He smiles.

'Maybe he thinks it is better if me and you do this between us. Man to man like, it makes sense to me.'

I shake my head. I can't have this. 'I am sorry son, but that is not how this kind of thing works. I am afraid the price is twenty five grand, no less. We are not a charity for small clubs.'

Norrie looks disappointed. 'What if I was to say you would be doing me a personal favour by accepting the twenty grand? It is clear I am no longer in your plans. My knees are gone, you know that, so why the reluctance. I don't see the problem here.'

'Cannot do Norrie,' I repeat. Now he is getting agitated.

'We are a family right. That is what you always told us. We look after each other. Both on the pitch and off. Is that not how it works? Now you have had good service, more than value for money. I played when you needed me, even when I was nowhere near fit enough. I took that jab for you. For the club.'

'You have always been well paid by us over the years

Norrie. I am sorry, I simply cannot put this proposal to the board. It is not good business for Manchester United.'

'Good business' says Nobby, as standing to leave.

'Okay. I will ring Stan and tell him twenty five it is then.' He looks up towards me. 'Thanks for your time boss.' Norrie leaves the room. He does not shake my hand.

★

Nobby cannot wait to get out of the stadium and into the forecourt. He runs through a side entrance. He feels like he cannot breathe. Nobby is saddened and angered by the old man's refusal to accept Boro's offer.

All those years.

Fourteen fucking years giving everything and more for United's cause. Blood red to the core. Heart and soul. And this is how it is to end.

Suddenly Nobby realises just how the boss came through the disaster all those years ago. How he came back to lead and finally achieve their dream ten years on against Benfica at Wembley. There is no mystique or magic about it. The truth being Busby is simply a hardnosed bastard. Nobby smiles at the thought and says quietly to himself, whilst walking away from Old Trafford.

'And they say I took no prisoners!'

28 - JIMMY: 'WHAT NOW MY LOVE?'

On 30th September 1971, Jimmy Murphy officially retired from Manchester United, but Jimmy knew his turn was up a long time before. A letter dropped through the door in his home in Whalley Range from club secretary Les Olive. Jimmy had never driven a car. The letter was to inform him that United would no longer be paying the £3 each way for the black taxi cab between his house and Old Trafford. Also, Olive went on to say that they were no longer prepared to cover the cost of his telephone bill.

Now Jimmy never cared about money but this hurt and upset him. Though it did not surprise him. Olive blamed the board, but Jimmy knew better. He knew whose last word they listened to. Being denied a cab never stopped Jimmy from travelling to the ground each day. He instead took the train and the British Rail guards would refuse to take his money and simply usher him through.

'On you go Jimmy.'

'Up the reds Jimmy!'

'God bless Jimmy.'

For they knew, as every United supporter did, that if it hadn't been for this fiery, passionate and emotional Welshman from the Rhondda valleys, with a penchant for the piano and a heart as big as a mountain, there would be no Manchester United

★

Monday 10th February 1958, Old Trafford

The boys come home. As black drapes and wreaths and heartfelt epic poems to the fallen cover houses and shop windows across the city, the coffins of the seven dead United players lie in state at the club gymnasium. They are being looked over by two policemen, whose only task appears to be handing out tissues for the tears of weeping visitors.

Manchester's heart is broken.

Jimmy has a promise to keep. And Jimmy always keeps his promises.

Before the lads set off to Belgrade he told them that if they managed to knock out Red Star and make the European Cup semi final, then on the following Friday on their return to Manchester, he would go easy on them in the gym.

In his darkest, most primitive thoughts, Jimmy could never have imagined the sight that greets his eyes, as he enters that same building to gaze upon the coffins.

The policemen step outside to give Jimmy time alone. Tears form in his eyes. He walks across to Tommy Taylor's coffin. He slowly runs his hand over the top of it. Sleek black with gold handles.

Jimmy moves slowly among all of them: David Pegg, Roger Byrne, Geoff Bent, Liam Whelan, Eddie Colman and Mark Jones.

'Well done lads,' says Jimmy. His voice almost choking with emotion. 'You did it. You got through. A little close from what I heard. Now if I remember rightly I promised you all an easy time if we won, so I won't keep you long. I will let you sleep. Just bear with me for a little longer eh you lot? I know you always thought I was hard on you. That I was a tough taskmaster but it was only because I saw greatness in you boys. I just needed to sharpen down the rough edges and then you would be ready to conquer the world. To spread your wings and fly. And you have done it, you have soared beyond the heaven boys. You have charmed the Gods, you have created a sense of wonder amongst all who saw you play.

'And even now when you have fallen from the stars, although our hearts are broken and probably will never mend, I can promise you this. From the bottom of my own broken heart. That you will never really die boys.'

Jimmy crouches down, overcome with grief. The policemen re-enter and help him up. His face etched in sorrow, his eyes weeping tears. 'Come on Jimmy mate' says one of them. 'Let's get you a cup of tea.'

★

Manchester 1971: Jimmy makes his way inside Old Trafford through the staff entrance. Greeted by a host of waves and smiles as he makes his through to a small office he shared with the recently retired chief scout Joe Armstrong. He regularly goes in every day to pick up his mail.

Today there is little so he decides to go for a pint in the nearby Quadrant Pub. The atmosphere around here is not to his liking. He is set to leave when a voice call his name.

'Alright Jimmy, how are you doing?' It is a smiling George Best.

'Hello son' replies Jimmy. 'I am well thanks. And

you? Reading the papers I see you are still intent on giving the old man a heart attack?'

'Oh don't believe all you read Jimmy.'

'Which bits should I believe George?'

'Oh just the parts about girls and the booze.' George winks. 'It is good to see you Jimmy. It reminds me of better days.'

'You too George. Take care of yourself.'

George smiles like only George can and vanishes from Jimmy's sight with a huge bag of fan mail.

The Quadrant is quiet. It is early afternoon and Jimmy has the pick of a dozen tables. Frank Sinatra is playing on a radio at the bar. 'What Now My Love'

He buys a pint and spots a corner away from the door so he does not attract any undue attention. He is thinking of George and where he could have played him in the pre Munich side. Who would he leave out? Suddenly somebody is stood above him.

'Alright Jimmy, how are you keeping?' Jimmy looks up. He has no idea who this is. He stares at this man's features. Something stirs.

'Don't worry if you cannot remember me. I don't expect you to.'

Jimmy smiles. 'I am sorry son I have no memory for faces.'

'It is okay' says the stranger. 'It was a long time ago. I was one of the policemen looking after the gym when they brought the boys home from Munich.'

Now Jimmy can see it. He remembers that night. The coffins. The breaking down and the two policemen helping him back to the office.

'Aye I remember now,' Jimmy points at him, 'you made me a cup of tea. You and your mate.'

The man grins. 'That was us. Can I just say it was an honour and a privilege to guard those lads that night. Do you mind if I sit down?'

'Not at all' says Jimmy. He pushes around so his new arrival can squeeze in.

'The name is Mike Talbot.' Mike puts his hand out and the two men shake.

'It is good to meet you again Mike Talbot.'

'I take it you are a red?' smiles Jimmy. Mike pulls out a pack of cigarettes. He offers Jimmy one who politely declines.

'I am a blue actually' says Mike, whilst inhaling, 'but they were my boys that night Jimmy. Manchester's boys. But in here I tend to keep that to myself.' He points to the mass of United regalia on the pub's walls. Jimmy laughs. 'Jimmy would you mind if I asked you a question about what happened back then. It is something I have never been able to figure out?'

'You can ask Mike but I am not sure I will be able to answer it. Over the years I have tended to block most of what happened in those first few days out of my mind.'

Mike takes a swig of the pint and inhales on his cigarette. 'Why Jimmy, why did they get back on that fucking plane?'

29 - THE LOST WEEKEND

Bobby Charlton stares into his bathroom window at home. He is tired. So very tired. He is not looking forward to training and he is so sick to the back teeth of George bloody Best.

Through painted smiles and lying eyes I have kept my own counsel but no more. I am going to see the boss and tell him what is on my mind. What has always been on my mind about George. It is always damned George. The Holy Trinity, Best, Law and Charlton. Why is his name first? Why not me or Denis? I should be first, me. Robert Charlton, Captain of England and Manchester United. World Cup and European Cup winner. Me, not him. I survived the crash. I lost my best pals. I came back and helped Jimmy. I was hurting so bad. So very bad. I could not sleep. I cried the tears no one ever saw. I saw some terrible, terrible things. We went to play football and were wiped out. It is not fair, it is not bloody fair. It should be Charlton, Law and Best. Holy trinity. Then again what does God know?

What has he done to help this club? Where was he when Billy was praying at just past three o'clock on that damn plane? Pass George Pass, how many times. How many times? And then he scores I say nothing. I clap and I applaud. For I am Bobby Charlton. Supreme sportsman. I say and do the right thing always. Jimmy told me I represent Manchester United even when I sleep. And so I have carried the flag. The red banner. I have felt the loss of mates on my shoulders for twelve years. And now I am tired, so very tired. And I am so fed up with George bloody Best.

The Stretford End sings his name, they scream and shout. They hardly notice me now, apart from to roar abuse whenever I mishit a pass. Through painted smiles and lying eyes I have played the game both on and off the field.

No more.

My heart was broken long ago. I am a shell but nobody notices. I so wish I was back in paradise. This is not my time and this is not my club anymore. Let George have it. George, George, George.

Suddenly a voice interrupts Bobby. It is his wife Norma.

'Hurry up Bob, you're going to be late for training. You are the Captain and have to set an example to George and the rest. Let them be like you.'

'Yes dear' replies Bobby. Still staring in the mirror. 'I am coming now.'

★

The boy Best is a supernova and soon will crash and burn, but never in all my years have I seen a talent such as he. Oh di Stefano was imperial; lightning quick, all strutting pomp, stunning with grace and elegance and he could kill you from anywhere. Pele strode supreme at the World Cup, his elasticised magnificence he's such a supreme athlete. Then there was Eusebio, all sheer power and pace. The genius of Puskas, a heady concoction of left footed dynamite and an unworldly technique brewed in a witch's potion in the back streets of Budapest.

But George?

He is simply on a different planet. His recent goal against Chelsea in the League Cup quarter finals at Old Trafford was, for me, a perfect example of why, may God forgive me, I let George run riot when I should have sold him years ago. For his greatest attribute is that he will not be bullied. The more these assassins and butchers hack, slash and maul George, he comes back for more. He never backs down. He never hides. I see him demanding the ball off Paddy and Bobby.

'Let me try again.'

The bigger they are, the more brutal, the more they threaten and bully – George destroys them. None more than Chelsea hatchet man Ron Harris. All that night at Old Trafford, Harris was in George's ear. In his face.

'You dare go past me George.'

'You are nothing now George.'

And then what happens?

Racing clear with just Peter Bonetti to beat on a mud heap, out of the corner of his eye George sees Harris roaring in to cut him in half. Now lesser mortals may have taken a shot, rather than be hit but oh no not George. He lets Harris in, he takes it, he rides it, and he dummies Bonetti then places the ball into an empty net.

Poets may have words for sunshine and rainbows and lightning over the seven seas, but for me, that night, seeing George's bravery, courage and sheer impudence. Even the finest wordsmith would struggle.

And yet away from the pitch he remains a pestilence and a pain in the backside. But George stays until he falls by his own hand. I owe his genius that much.

★

The Siege of Noble Street: At Old Trafford, on Tuesday 29th December 1970, I read out a prepared statement explaining that Wilf has been moved aside and I am back in charge until the season's end.

No longer than that. Over my dead body.

And then the questions rage and voices shout loud.

'Do you think Wilf got a fair chance Matt?'

'Did the players let him down Matt?'

'Do you blame yourself Matt?'

'Wilf is a little upset at the moment,' I say. Trying to sound convincing as possible and failing dramatically. 'He is a little down but I am sure he will be okay. Cut Wilf in half and he bleeds United. He will tell you that.'

'What are you going to do with George, Matt?'

I have been waiting for this.

'Gentlemen of the press, believe me. I will sort out George Best if it is the last thing I do.'

★

Friday 9th January 1971: 'Where is George?' I ask. As we wait on the platform to catch the train from Manchester Piccadilly to Euston, for our match against Chelsea in London.

'No sign boss' sighs Jack Crompton, shrugging his shoulders.

I have had enough.

'Send a car for John Aston, get him here. This time George can stew in his own mess.'

Across the city, George is in bed with a hangover and a beautiful aspiring young blond actress, who he had got on famously with in the Brown Bull the previous evening. She gets up and starts to get dressed. She is staring down at George who is still asleep. She picks up a pillow and throws it at him.

George stirs and the actress in Oscar winning style declares: 'I hope you do not think I slept with you just because you are George Best?'

'Of course not' George replies sleepily, with eyes still closed and a half smile on his face. 'There is money on the side. Take a few quid for a taxi.'

George tucks the pillow under his head and disappears under the covers. The girl eyes the cash. She walks over and instead of just taking the needed cab fare, helps herself to a wad of notes and slips them in her handbag. She turns around to face George, who has fallen back asleep. She blows him a kiss and smiles. 'Goodbye George'.

Thirty minutes later a frantic George wakes and realises he is never going to make the train. He makes a phone call and is told not to bother by the club. The boss will see him on Monday morning in his office. Another rollicking and fine awaits. George is in trouble again. But it is weekend and if he can't play football, then he will do the next best thing. So what the hell, he'll go to London anyway and meet up with another young actress who he is friendly with. Only this one is real class. And most importantly gorgeous beyond words. Twenty-one year-old Irish waif Sinead Cusack.

That afternoon, whilst Manchester United are battling for their First Division lives and clinching a much needed 2-1 victory against Chelsea at Stamford Bridge with late goals from youngster Alan Gowling and a winner from a revitalised Willie Morgan, George arrives at Sinead's flat on Noble Street in Islington, North London. She greets him with a hug and they go in. Unbeknown to George his presence has already been noted and one phone call later the word has gone round. Georgie boy is in town. Let the madness begin!

Within thirty minutes of George's appearance on Sinead's doorstep the first of the press arrive. His mysterious non-appearance in Busby's line up was already the talk of both front and back page hacks. Already on the scent, now they headed en masse to Noble Street. There is a knock on the door.'

'George are you in there?'

'Come on George open the fucking door.

'We're not going away.'

I am in Chelsea's boardroom enjoying a rare victory when in dashes Jack Crompton. He has been running and is out of breath.

'Jack what on earth is wrong?'

'You're not going to believe this boss. George is on the television news. He is shacked up in Islington with some actress and he is surrounded!'

'Surrounded?'

Chelsea manager Dave Sexton, a good lad, comes over. 'Everything okay Matt?'

'Dave son' I say, 'One word – George.'

He shakes his head and smiles. 'Is he really worth all this grief?'

I finish my drink. 'I tell myself he is not but then he does something in training or in a game and I dismiss such thoughts as heresy. But he is not going to ruin this day for me.'

I put my arms around both Jack and Dave. 'Let's have a drink lads.'

Like an invading army they arrive on Noble Street. Sinead shuts her curtains as the cameras flash and strangers stare in desperation to catch a glimpse of George. One young girl does so and starts to scream. It unnerves Sinead whilst George simply smiles.

'Don't worry about it' he says to her, 'think of it as good publicity for your career.' It is publicity she could never have dreamed of.

'What the hell have you been up to George?' she laughs – her jaw dropping at the scenes outside.

He shrugs his shoulders. 'I just missed a football match? Looks like you are stuck with me Sinead.'

The police turn up to check out the disturbance and cannot believe their eyes. An officer is placed outside the flat. 'As if we have not got fucking better things to do. Like catching criminals' groans an unhappy constable.

Vans arrive carrying television crews and reporters. Excited bystanders crowd around. BBC and ITV are reporting live on the tea-time news...

'Inside this house is wayward Manchester United soccer star George Best.'

'Georgie Best is on the nest' sing a gang of young lads, to the amusement of all.

George sings along inside. 'Not with me you're not George' says Sinead, 'you can stay until this madness is over but you're on the sofa.'

George really likes Sinead. He feels they have much in common. Both from Ireland, and blessed with rare talent. George can talk to Sinead like he cannot other girls.

She is more a friend, though it does not stop him trying. Sinead understands a little of what is going on inside his head for she too is struggling to cope with the early trappings of fame. But this? This is way out of her league.

★

The circus goes on all weekend. World-wide attention focuses on Sinead's front door.

'Is this the end for George?' the headlines scream out. All are asked for their opinions on the wild boy of English football. From priests to psychiatrists. What can be done with George? Teenage girls turn up and scream out their love for George. 'We love you George!', 'Marry me George!' Some put phone numbers through the door. The policeman shakes his head in disgust.

A besieged George and Sinead find it all hilarious, if a little surreal, as they watch themselves on hourly bulletins on the television news. Sinead points at the television.

'I am so glad I washed my curtains' she laughs. George is tempted to go and wave to the crowds but knowing he is already in deep trouble with the old man, thinks better of it. He will have to play this one clever. Maybe say the pressure just got to him? A heavy fine and short suspension should suffice and see him off the hook. Nothing more because George knows United need him. The old man needs him.

He fills up Sinead's wine glass. 'Sinead, do I look like a tortured genius to you?' George is wearing a huge grin.

'One day George you will have to grow up. But

not this lost weekend eh.'

She leans over and kisses him.

George smiles like only George can. Another result!

★

Manchester: Old Trafford: The following week.

'What am I to do with you George?' He is sat facing me in my office. 'You do realise questions have been asked in the House of Commons about you?' I put on my glasses to read the newspaper in front of me. 'Arthur Lewis the MP for West Ham said on 14th January. "Why should much needed police vehicles be used to assist in the escape of George Best from the media siege of Sinead Cusack's flat."'

George says nothing. Inside he is dying to laugh but knows to do so risks the old man throwing him through a window.

'This cannot go on. You are pushing me and this club to the very edge.'

'I am sorry boss, it all just got too much. I just wanted someone to talk to. Sinead is a good friend. The next thing I knew all hell had broken out.'

'For three days son you have been the headlines on both the front and back page. You have been on every television news programme and you have not kicked a ball. How does that make you feel?'

'I know I missed the train. I overslept, I...'

'Just answer the damn question George. How does that make you feel?'

'I miss playing. If I can't play football then this world swallows me up. It is too big. Everybody wants a piece of me and sometimes it just makes me go crazy.

247

It won't happen again. I promise'

'It will happen again' I argue, 'but do you know something George. I am close to past caring. And that is something I never thought could happen. So congratulations on that.'

'I will make it up to you boss. From now until the end of the season. You just watch.'

'I am fining you two weeks' wages George and suspending you for the same period. Now get out.'

George slowly stands. He looks pitiful: unshaven, unkempt and exhausted. Part of me wants to walk round the desk and give him a big hug and offer fatherly advice. But these days, I have neither the heart nor inclination. He opens the door to leave but then turns to face me.

'I know you think I am going to let you down again. And in time you will no doubt be proved right boss. But I promise you, I am going to make you believe in me again between now and May.' George smiles. 'I am going to take your breath away.'

I can't help but feel a slight grin come across my face. 'Make sure you do son.'

★

George is true to his word because for the remaining four months of the season he is simply magnificent. We drag ourselves up to eleventh spot inspired by a host of stunning goals by our beguiling Ulsterman. None better than the one against Tottenham Hotspur at Old Trafford that will live with me forever more.

From twelve yards out and with the Spurs defence in disarray, the ball falls to George who assesses the situation and chips a shot of such precision and audacity over Pat Jennings and two defenders stood on the goal line. He drops the ball with a sorcerer's touch just inches over their heads and under the bar.

To see such riches almost makes the aggro and grief George has caused me over the years worthwhile.

Almost.

30 - A GLASGOW KISS AND A GOOD MAN FROM CORK

The Glasgow Kiss: Paddy Crerand enters the cramped Celtic boardroom following their narrow quarter-final defeat by Ajax, in the European Cup. He is there on a mission. A good friend of 40 year-old Celtic manager Jock Stein, Paddy looks around and immediately spots him on the other side of the room. Being Paddy he does not stand on ceremony.

'Hey Jock.' Hearing his name shouted loud, Jock turns and spots his old mate. A huge smile comes over the older man's face. Paddy reaches him and they embrace warmly.

'Paddy Crerand you scoundrel. Who let you in here?'

'How are you Jock?' smiles Paddy. The United man leans in close and whispers into Jock's ear. 'I need a word in private.'

Jock looks around. He whispers back. 'Five minutes and meet me down the corridor in my office.'

Paddy makes his way to Jock's office, who true to his word soon follows. 'Why the cloak and dagger Pat? What can l do for you old friend?'

'I come with a message from Matt Busby.'

Jock smiles. 'Well you can tell Matt that no matter how much I like him, he is not having any of my players.'

Paddy grins and shakes his head. 'It is not your

players the old man is after Jock.'

'Then what is it the old rascal wants?'

Paddy points his finger towards him.

'You.'

★

In great secrecy myself and Jock meet at night time in Haydock near Liverpool. He climbs into the back of my Mercedes and we shake hands.

'It is good to see you Matt.'

'You too, son. I supposed you know what we are doing here?'

'Well I don't suppose it is to talk about our two great city's weather.'

I laugh. 'Well what do you think Jock. How would you like to be the next manager of Manchester United? The pay is £15,000 a year plus bonuses. And huge transfer funds to buy whoever you need to put us back at the top.' This wage on offer is infinitely more than Jock is earning at Celtic. We have done our homework.

Jock smiles. 'Who would not want to manage United? But l have one serious reservation Matt.'

'Go on?' This intrigues me.

'Well you have players that are legends and are adored by your supporters. Bobby and Denis are not getting any younger. Now they are both great lads but l would need them out of the door before I arrive. How could I walk in to Old Trafford and immediately sling the axe and get rid, because that is what I would have to do. Straight away I am a bad guy.'

'What about George' I ask, 'do you think you can handle George?'

Jock smiles. 'Compared to Jimmy Johnstone I think

you will find George is a monk. George will not be a problem. I can straighten him out. It is the other two. I need to vanquish the ghosts of the past. No matter how glorious. If I was to accept your generous offer Matt, you would have to ensure they are out of the picture.'

Jock is talking sense. The idea of George being a monk amuses. But for me to finish the United careers of Bobby and Denis would cause much heartache and pain that I could do without at my stage in life. Though for the sake of this club I will do it. For Jock is the right age, has the right values and he possesses an inner steel. Born a miner's son of Bellshill, Lanarkshire like myself, the work ethic, fire and passion comes from within. It is inherent. He is my natural successor. Jock Stein is tailor made for Manchester United.

I smile. 'Okay then Jock. We will speak again soon,'

We shake once more. Jock gets out. The vibes are good. Jock loves the big stage and they do not come any bigger than Old Trafford. I am sure he will agree to my offer.

Once this man arrives in Manchester I feel I will finally be able to sit back and get on with more tedious but much less strenuous aspects of my job knowing we are in safe hands.

★

Jock is heading back to Glasgow in his car. His mind racing, he is excited; he is scared but mostly uneasy. Meeting Busby always makes him feels like he is in the presence of a living legend. They are close but Jock has heard the stories that he can't leave well alone. Like a sculptor forced to retire from his life's work but watching his apprentices from the sidelines as others struggle to complete his masterpiece.

Jock knows he will be inheriting a heap of trouble. But if he gets it right United remain one of the world's biggest clubs. He knows he could rebuild it given time.

Then there are his feelings towards Celtic and his family to consider. His wife's love of Glasgow. Jock knows she will not want to move. He can hear her words now. 'Why Jock, they love you here. Our family love it here. This is our home.'

Our home.

The next day I receive a call from Jock saying he is not coming. He claims his family are settled and he is not prepared to uproot them. I am not so sure. I am angry and privately I confess to Paddy that I believe Jock used us to get more money out of Celtic. Paddy believes not but in my mind it appears I have received a Glasgow kiss and so the search goes on but I do have one more iron in the fire.

The Man from Cork: Forty-five year-old Leicester City manager Frank O'Farrell is on his way to a secret liaison with Manchester United's legendary Sir Matt Busby and their chairman Louis Edwards. Already he has spoken at length several times to Busby over the phone who has offered him the Old Trafford job. £12,000 per annum and a three year contract.

The softly spoken Irishman is a football man of former West Ham United stock. A thinker about the game. A modern coach but above all a good man. A good Catholic whose decency and insistence on doing business the right way means he feels no guilt in his dealings with United for his contract with Leicester is up.

The Old Trafford job intrigues him. Frank knows the place is a train wreck, overrun with ageing superstars, wracked by inner fighting and unrestrained egos and George Best running riot in his attempts to drink Manchester dry but Frank also knows he is capable in his own calm, methodical manner of putting them back on the right path. He views them as a club that has lost their way.

The bible says 'You are all my brothers.' Frank can deal with footballers. He can manage and he can organise.

United still have phenomenal individuals who continue to perform off the cuff. On their day they remain a potent force but those days are growing rarer. This is 1971 and talent alone is not enough anymore. Frank will right the wrongs, so praise the Lord and pass the tactics manual.

I like Frank. He is straight forward and honest. A religious man with sound values and a good grounding but I know they breed them hard-headed in Cork. He is a no nonsense character and that, at this moment, is what is required. I look in his eyes and I see compassion but I also see fire, and a bristling passion to succeed.

I hear also when dealing with troublesome players Frank can be cast from iron. His much in-demand goalkeeper Peter Shilton was put in his place by Frank when sulking about not getting a move.

A righteous man. A good man from Cork. I don't

need Frank to save souls, I need him to turn this club around. With a whispered prayer and crossing of fingers, I think we may have our man.

The meeting takes place in Louis Edwards' silver Rolls Royce in a quiet Derbyshire country lane. I am with Louis in the front, Frank is in the rear. He leans forward to shake both our hands.

'It is good to meet you both' he says.

'It is grand to meet you also Frank' I reply.

'Hello Frank, I have heard a lot about you lad. All good,' adds a smiling Edwards.

I continue. 'We are sorry about the secrecy involved here Frank but we need to keep the press at bay until we have something more concrete to tell them. Have you had time to mull over our offer?'

'I have Mr Busby and I am extremely flattered. Thank you too Mr Chairman. Can you just confirm it for me please?'

'It is £12,000 a year Frank with bonuses.'

'Hold on a minute Matt' interrupts Louis, 'I think you have made a mistake there old pal. The wages are fifteen grand a year, plus bonuses.'

Frank looks a little taken aback.

I glare at Louis but he is totally oblivious to what he has done and said.

'So what do you say Frank. Do we have a deal?'

'We have a deal Mr chairman. You too Mr Busby.'

There must be a part of Frank thinking that I have just tried to stiff him out of three grand?

A huge grin lights up Louis' face. 'Well that is just bloody great son,' he shakes Frank's hand with great enthusiasm.

I offer mine and Frank takes it.

'Welcome to Old Trafford son. And from now on call me Matt.'

'Thank you Matt,' replies Frank .

Without a hint of a smile and I believe with just a tiny hint of wariness.

31 - WELCOME TO UNITED

I am showing Frank around Old Trafford. He is telling me that his father was a train driver and before he became a footballer Frank's first job was shovelling coal on the railway footplate, back in his native Cork. He is softly spoken, affable but I sense a steely-eyed toughness about him. I am impressed.

We are having a new office specifically fitted out for him just down the corridor from mine. He stops to look for a moment. One of the workman calls out, 'Good luck Frank mate.'

Frank smiles. 'Thank you' he replies, before rejoining me.

We enter my office. I sit down whilst he remains standing

He is staring at me.

'Something on your mind Frank?'

'Well Matt, it is just this office. It is the manager's office is it not?'

'It is' I reply.

'Well I am the manager not you. It gives off a bad impression and I really must insist, with all due respect, that you move out and I have this room.'

Knowing there is little choice if he is to succeed, Frank has clearly decided there is nothing for it but to lay down a marker. He waits for my reaction. I am momentarily speechless but it is just as well for it gives me time to think.

'Why do you ask this?'

'Matt let's be honest. The players still regard you as the boss. Well if I am to succeed with the task you have handed me I must be the boss. They must be under no illusions that the buck stops with me. If I drop one of them, your boys, Bobby, Paddy or Denis shall we say and you are only ten yards down the corridor sat in the manager's office, what do you think is going to happen? They are going to come running to you. It is only natural, for you are all they have known.

'No, I need this office. I need to stamp my authority from the start.'

He has guts I will give him that. And maybe a point.

'I have already promised you no interference Frank. But, very well, if you think it will help you and is for the best, then I will arrange to have my things moved elsewhere later today.'

'Thank you,' he sighs, 'that was not easy for me to ask.'

'I understand, lad.' I smile. He has annoyed me but I will be damned if I am going to let him know.

★

It is a beautiful July morning and the entire United squad are stood waiting to be introduced to their new manager on The Cliff training pitch.

'Frank who?' quips Denis.

'He cannot be any worse than the last one the old man picked,' says Willie Morgan.

'You would not be saying that if Wilf was stood here Willie son' adds Paddy Crerand.'

'All mouth Morgan,' shouts Brian Kidd. 'You never gave Wilf a chance.'

'Who asked your opinion?' snaps Morgan to Kiddo.

'Why do I need your permission?'

'Right that's enough' orders the captain, 'Brian and Willie, leave it. What kind of impression is the new manager going to have if you two are squaring up on his first day? At least pretend to be civil. You can kill each other after training.'

'Here he comes,' smiles George.

'Next,' shouts out Denis, much to everybody's amusement.

Across the pitch walks Frank in a smart dark suit with his assistant trainer in a tracksuit, forty-one year-old Malcolm Musgrove.

'Who is the other bloke?' asks Paddy who is standing next to George.

'No idea.'

'Me neither,' adds Denis.

Right, stand up straight lads' shouts Bobby. 'Eyes front.'

'Shall we clap him in Bob,' laughs Denis.

'He looks like a fucking banker' whispers Willie, almost to himself.

But Alex Stepney hears and sniggers, 'more like a funeral director Willie.'

'They are dressed like a bunch of bloody convicts, Frank' says Musgrove. In reference to the United player's rag tag training kit.

'Just keep smiling Malcolm,' replies Frank, himself grinning wide, 'this lot will suss you out faster than it takes to blow your nose.'

The two stand before the players.

'Good morning, lads' begins Frank, 'it is good to

meet you all together. I will be seeing you all personally but for now, I just want to say a few words. This man here is Malcolm Musgrove. He is my voice and answers to me and nobody else on the training pitch. Now you will find me a hard taskmaster, but a fair man. If you do right by me, then vice versa. I know at first it will be difficult to adjust to my methods but I assure you, we can do great things here. You are still great players. A little more organisation, fine tuning and extra physical preparation and mark my words. You can win the league.'

Frank is smiling but appears a little unnerved as all eyes are staring upon him. There are no smiling faces, just glum solemnity.

'I will leave you now in the capable hands of Malcolm.'

Franks turns to leave and hears Malcolm's barking voice shouting out.

'Right boys, let us see what you have got. Five times around the pitch, jogging. Come on now.'

Malcolm claps his hands.

Nobody moves. Until Bobby speaks up, 'come on boys, you heard the man.'

Bobby jogs off and the other slowly fall in behind. Willie comes across to Malcolm.

'Welcome to United.' He smiles wryly before running off and joining the rest.

'My God' says Musgrove, watching them go, 'what have we got ourselves into?'

★

Frank is sat in his office when George knocks on the door and enters.

'You wanted a word, boss?'

'Yes come in George, sit down. How is training going? Are you feeling fit and ready to go?'

George nods. His mind clearly elsewhere. Franks senses this.

'Are you a religious man, George.'

'I believe in God if that is what you mean?'

Frank smiles. 'That is a good answer but it is not the one I was looking for. You have been blessed with a wonderful talent son, one so rare that it could only have been handed down from our Lord. Now I know of your lifestyle and it is one I strongly disapprove of. But you are still a young man. You are twenty-four years old and have the capacity to change. If you do, if you curtail the booze and the ladies, I guarantee you can lead this club back to glory and make yourself without doubt the finest player in the world. I promise you that George.'

George smiles wide. 'Are you trying to save my soul boss?'

'No' replies Frank, very gently. 'I am trying to save your career. And ultimately your life. So what do you say? Are you going to join me on this crusade to put United back where they belong. And earn for yourself everlasting glory?'

'I will think on it,' says George. Obviously taken by his new manager's words. He likes his fellow Irishman. He seems a decent bloke.

'Good lad' says Frank, finding it hard to hide a grin. He knows if he gets George onside, anything is possible. 'The Lord works in mysterious ways George,' adds Frank, 'Maybe it is time to find another path to ensure your place in the kingdom of Heaven?'

George nods as if in agreement.
But he would not put any money on it.

32 - RESURRECTION

Be it divine inspiration or tactical genius Manchester United are a club reborn and come December they find themselves five points clear at the top of Division One. Frank O'Farrell is being hailed a saviour, and Sir Matt Busby tells all who listen, 'Frank is my greatest ever signing.'

As for George, he is away with the angels. From afar Frank always knew George was special but he never believed just how much until witnessing him up close – day in, day out.

But then he finds himself muttering, like Matt and Wilf before him, 'Thank God for George' as the Ulsterman creates footballing miracles on weekly basis.

There are many moments to treasure and to behold. A hat trick at Old Trafford against a West Ham side marshalled by Bobby Moore but ripped apart and spat out by George in a 4-2 win. The Hammers left Manchester not knowing what had hit them. The England captain saying to George afterwards, 'No need for that George, I thought we were friends!'

A top of the table clash at home versus Sheffield United when George takes on and beats half the Yorkshire side whilst running across the penalty box, before letting fly a shot that screams into the far corner and electrifies the stadium. An ageing scribe in the press box is heard to instruct a young stringer, 'Don't write down the time, son. Write down the date.'

It is quite simply a resurrection. But despite the

many plaudits and the bookies stopping taking bets on Manchester United to win their first title in four years, Frank is worried. He fears it is all an illusion. George is carrying the side, he is winning games, earning win bonuses and covering up for a multitude of under achievers. He is seemingly on a one man mission to bring back the glory days. Frank calls George in and ups his money to put him on a par with the club's biggest earner Willie Morgan. A fact that left him speechless on first being told.

'Keep it going George' says Frank. 'I am so proud of you.'

And then, just when the trophy cabinet at Old Trafford was being dusted down in preparation, the lights went out on George and United's season.

The root of the demise can be traced back to the week leading up to Manchester United's game at Newcastle on 23rd October 1971 when an IRA death threat was made on George's life, because of an alleged £3,000 donation to a Protestant organisation run by Ian Paisley.

With the troubles in Northern Ireland spiralling out of control, the police took this matter extremely serious and placed George's Bramhall home under twenty-four hour surveillance. George's normally cool and calm demeanour disappeared and not surprisingly he became a nervous wreck.

Frank called George into his office to give him the option of continuing playing. 'Look George it is totally up to you. If you do not wish to travel to Newcastle I will support you whatever. The club will abide by your decision.'

'I want to play boss,' he replied without hesitation.

'I have no choice because if I don't there will be death threats every week. Where would it end?' He laughs, 'Typical isn't it? I have a chance of a Saturday off and I chose to play.'

Frank cannot help but smile and admire this young man who despite having the world fawning at his dancing feet remains, at least to him, a down to earth decent lad from East Belfast.

The coach trip to Tyneside sees George assigned two Special branch officers.

'Under no circumstance Mr Best, sit near the window,' one dramatically informs him. Not that George needed telling.

'Well no offence George but I am not fucking sitting next to you!' exclaims Paddy!

'Thanks Pat,' sighs George.

With St James's Park surrounded by high rise flats, dozens of police are assigned with high-powered binoculars to scour rooftops for potential assassins. Whilst inside the ground forty undercover officers are placed in the crowd for the match, which United win 1-0, with George sensational throughout, scoring the winning goal.

At the post-match press conference defeated Newcastle manager Joe Harvey shows a wry if dark sense of humour by declaring of George, 'I wish they had shot the little bugger!'

George himself said afterwards when being congratulated on his constant movement by Frank. 'What do you expect boss, a moving target is harder to hit.' The journey home sees the team coach escorted by two police cars.

The nightmare does not end there because the

following week a woman near George's house claims she was approached by two sinister Irish gentlemen one of whom appeared to be carrying a pistol. Events take an even worse turn when the *Manchester Evening News* receives an anonymous letter stating that 'George could expect a knife in the back if he returns to Belfast to play in the forthcoming international for Northern Ireland against Spain.'

By now George's head has gone. His nerves shot to pieces. He falls off the wagon that he had had been dangling on and off since his chat with Frank pre season. George does not so much hit the bottle as disappear in to it and so starts the beginning of the end of arguably the greatest player in the history of the British game.

Saturday 1st January 1972
West Ham United 3 Manchester United 0

If for the opening half of the season Frank O'Farrell experienced the best of Manchester United, then for the second he was forced to endure the worst excesses of a football club tearing itself apart from the inside. The smile fell from his lips as United were exposed for the joke they had become. Get after them and they would melt like butter on a hot knife.

After a horrific 3-0 beating that could have been so many more off West Ham at Upton Park, United collapse like a pack of cards. Frank is shocked at how easily his team have folded in London's East End. His worst fears realised. This lot are an accident waiting to happen.

Up to that stage they had still only lost two league games. George's seventeen goal haul and Frank's tactical master stroke of a midfield trio of Alan Gowling, Willie Morgan and Bobby sweeping all before them. They had been driven on by talented but badly ageing legs, and a force of nature called George Best. Now it was if a light had been switched off. The colour had drained from red to grey and none more than George.

Normally he adored the London crowds, playing up to the cockney wide boys with their wise cracks and showing off in the 'Big smoke'. But not today, for George was not up for the fight and could not get off the pitch fast enough at the final whistle.

George needs a drink.

In the dressing room he looks around for faces no longer there. Nobby, Shay and Jimmy have gone, Denis is struggling badly now with injuries and Paddy is back home stuck in the stiffs because Father Frank believes him simply too slow to play in the modern game.

In their place are lesser mortals, men who George thinks put more energy into mouthing off in the dressing room than they do when things are going against them on the pitch.

Also, if the boss upstairs is reluctant to act, then why should he bother? Matt is never seen these days. George smiles at the irony. Himself moaning about the old man not showing up? And so George vanishes from sight to reappear briefly into public gaze with the present Miss Great Britain, the beautiful nineteen year-old Carolyn Moore.

For seven days and seven nights George goes off the rails. When in this mood he simply does not care and is unreasonable to the point of being unreachable. The booze and the women become all consuming. He can see no further than the bottom of a glass, or a pretty blonde, brunette or red head. He is photographed with Carolyn in Tramps nightclub in London, obviously the worse for wear. Newspapers claim they are in love and planning to get engaged. George laughs on reading this because he falls in love every night with a different girl in a different bar and club and town. Sent from God, blessed as a footballer, a hopeless romantic and a tragic drunk.

Hungover, depressed and knowing reality hits you in the face like a speeding train, George reports back to Old Trafford to face the wrath of the manager. Frank views this wrecked human being before him. Stinking of alcohol, unshaven with bloodshot eyes, yet smiling defiantly. This is a side of George he has previously not witnessed.

'My God George what have you done to yourself?'

'Come on Frank' he smiles, 'you know you need me.'

'I am not interested in you as a footballer. I want to help.'

'Look at me Frank, do you really think my soul is worth saving?'

'I am not worried about your soul George. How are you feeling?'

George shrugs his shoulders. Frank notices a tear in his eye.

'Look, from tomorrow you train morning and afternoon for two weeks so I can keep an eye on you. Now I am also fining you for that same period. Finally, and I don't want no arguments about this, you are moving back to Mrs Fullaways and away from that ridiculous eyesore you call home in Bramhall. Non negotiable, okay?'

George cannot believe what he is hearing. Frank obviously means business. Part of him so much wants to help this man who he genuinely likes but George knows he cannot trust himself anymore, so how can he possibly promise anything to anyone? Especially to someone like Frank who he has already grown to admire and respect.

'Go back in digs! Boss I am twenty-five years old!'

'Well you best start acting like it don't you think?' replies Frank.

Bereft of an answer George simply nods.

'Right then' says Frank. 'Welcome home son.'

33 - REMEMBER YOUR SINS NO MORE

I watch with mounting fear as our season implodes. We have now lost seven games on the run and have fallen from the title race with an almighty bang. We have to stop the rot. I am not sure of Frank's character. I think maybe, he is not one of us. He is a good man, just not of United stock. He never asks for my advice. I send word through Les Olive and today I have a meeting with Frank to ask why.

We are in 'his' office. He has rearranged the furniture. My desk no longer set to look down upon the person sat opposite. Also he has put in a couple of armchairs with a bottle of whisky on a nearby table nicely at hand. I assume this is for my benefit. He leads me over to the chairs but I turn down his offer of a drink. I get straight down to business as we sit.

'Frank why do you never ring or come to see me?'

'I am not sure I understand Matt?' he replies, 'I have always used the proper protocol. I telephone the chairman on a daily basis. I just assumed he would pass on any relevant information.'

So that's it? Frank really has no idea. I smile.

'What you have to understand Frank, is that Louis does not have much experience in handing out advice on footballing matters. From now on, with things turning a little rough, speak to me.'

Oh now Frank gets it. This man still runs the

football club, not the chairman or board. Sir Matt Busby remains in charge of this mad house.

'Very well,' he says, 'I will make a point of keeping you informed.'

Make a point? This annoys me.

'Aye you do that son.'

There is then an awkward silence as we stare at each other. It appears to me Frank does not have much else to say so I may as well wrap this up.

'Okay then' I say standing up. He does similar, 'you know where I am if needed.'

He nods.

'Good day Frank.'

'Good day Matt.

I leave 'his' office. I am not sure. I really am not sure.

As defeats mount the blame game in the United dressing room falls on one man: George. Although he is performing no worse than the others, his utter inability to toe the line in both training and during the game is alienating him from even those he classes as good mates. None more than his old lodger from Mrs Fullaway's, David Sadler, who receives a mouthful of abuse from George for daring to suggest he takes training a little more serious instead of turning up drunk.

Or just not bothering to show at all.

'You have got some nerve, Dave. How many times have I put a fucking win bonus in your pocket?'

Sadler could not argue.

One incident on the training pitch when George

keeps fooling around with a free kick incenses Bobby, who after Musgrove simply shrugs his shoulders, as if to suggest, 'What can I do?' Bobby finally snaps and goes to see Frank in his office, but is given short shrift.

'You are the captain of this club and have over a hundred England caps to your name. If you cannot sort him out, what chance anybody else?' Bobby stands open-mouthed. Frank continues. 'Now if it happens again just push him off the ball and tell him to behave. Slap him around the head. Be a man Bobby! Be a captain!' Bobby just stares into space. Few apart from Jimmy have ever spoken to him in this manner. 'Now is there anything else?'

Bobby snaps out of his state of shock.

'No boss that is all.'

'Good' replies Frank, 'please shut the door on your way out.'

On Wednesday 19th January, at Old Trafford, in an FA Cup third round replay, the home side are on the verge of going out at the hands of Southampton. Manchester United have not played well all evening. The crowd are frustrated, tensions are running high.

Then enter George who, with time almost up, in his first game back since suspension, latches onto a Bobby Charlton pass and hurtles into the Saint's penalty area. Surrounded by desperate defenders, who had spent the evening kicking lumps out him, George somehow dances and jinxes his way through a wild array of lunging tackles, and death-defying last gasp lunges to fire a shot off and equalise.

1-1 and Frank turns to Musgrove to exclaim, 'How did he do that?'

In extra time ∙ an inspired George tortures

Southampton and forces them to run up the white flag and beg for mercy. They can stand no more as United finally run out comfortable 4-1 winners. He is simply unplayable.

George is among the scorers once more and celebrates by aiming two fingers towards the press box. Those who claimed he was finished are handed a timely reminder that when pushed and when needed, Best remains United's saviour.

Frank is struggling to comprehend what he has witnessed this night from his troublesome Irishman. The beauty and the bravery and the beast that lurks forever within are on display in what is still the greatest show in town.

He thinks of a Bible passage: Isiah 43-25-26. 'I, even I, am he who blots out your transgressions, for my own sake, and remembers your sins no more.'

'Thank you son' Frank says quietly, as the crowd sing George's name.

'Thank you.'

Saturday 19th February 1972:
Leeds United 5 Manchester United 1

One of our darkest days on the pitch unfurls with unflinching pain as Don's white shirts play keep ball and decide to embarrass us even more in the closing moments of this one-sided contest. I am fuming at the lack of heart and desire on show amongst the red shirts.

It has been a disgraceful performance by Manchester United and totally unacceptable. Whatever is happening in the dressing room, whatever is being said or coached is not working. Hanging on by our finger nails up until half time, the second half turned into a deluge as Leeds stepped up a gear to leave us breathless. Their football was incisive, cutting and magnificent with Peter Lorimer, Billy Bremner and Johnny Giles on a different level. A hat-trick from Mick Jones and further strikes from Lorimer and Clarke are no more than they deserved.

Don seeks me out in the board room afterwards. 'This is the day it changes Matt. Your lot have had your time. The power is with us now.'

Then he wanders off before I have a chance to answer. Maybe just as well for I am getting on a little now. It would not look good for someone in my position as a Manchester United director if I laid him out flat.

Frank also comes to see me as we wait to board the team coach taking us back over the Pennines.

'We need to buy Matt. And we need to do it now.'

'Get them' I say.

Frank wastes little time and signs Aberdeen's stylish young defender Martin Buchan for £125,000. Also we clinch a £200,000 deal for the fast and elusive Nottingham Forest winger Ian Storey-Moore. This one causes ructions with Brian Clough at Derby County. Brian thought he had Moore. Even to the extent of showing him off at the Baseball ground. Little did he know that although young Ian's signature was on the contract, he did not have Forest's. Quick thinking by Frank saw us step in to steal Moore under Brian's nose and send him apoplectic with rage. His phone call to me was memorable in many ways.

'Now I am not going to swear Matt because you are a Sir and I like you. But nobody does this to Derby County and most of all to Brian bloody Clough and gets away with it. I will get even with your Old Trafford lot if it is the last thing I do. But you look after yourself Matt and love to Jean.'

And then the line went dead.

Lovely man is Brian.

★

Having at one stage looked set to romp the league, Manchester United finish in a traumatic eighth place. The wheels came off in spectacular fashion after Christmas and Frank is left contemplating a summer of upheaval. Never in his worst nightmares did he realise the true extent of the challenge awaiting him at Old Trafford.

And top of his list, what to do about George?

Patience is a virtue with which he is blessed but Frank knows time is running out for George. There can be no more chances. Come the next incident Frank will be forced to sell him. For George will no doubt be used as the dagger to stab him with by his detractors at the club.

One in particular.

Frank's uneasy relationship with Busby causes him grave concern. The public image of the kindly grandfather figure is not what he has found. This is a man Frank feels is struggling to let go of the reins of power at Old Trafford. He knows behind his back the players refer to him as 'little boss' and Busby as 'big boss' and poor Malcolm may as well be a training cone on The Cliff pitch for the amount of notice the senior players take of him.

He comes to Frank constantly. 'Frank this lot are unbelievable! They are like a dysfunctional family and don't know who to stab in the back first. The atmosphere is poisonous. Bobby does not talk to anyone, Willie and Alex whisper, scheme and connive in the corner like naughty schoolboys. George is George and Denis is living on the bloody treatment table. I am telling you now, you do not need a trainer, you need a psychiatrist, a priest and a damned fire fighter!'

It promises to be less a summer wind for Frank O'Farrell than a raging tempest. One to test his character, his temper and most importantly his faith. For almost as soon as the season finishes, George, resembling a beach bum, announces to the *Sunday Mirror* on holiday in Marbella that he has become a nervous wreck and admits the not inconsiderable matter that he is downing a bottle of vodka a day.

Frank closes his eyes on reading this and says quietly: 'Oh George what have you done?

Psalm 31:16 'Give me the sunshine of heaven in my soul and I will defy the tempests of earth.'

34 - MESSAGE IN A BOTTLE OF VODKA

Marbella Skol Hotel: 20th May 1972: George Best wakes up alone. What the hell! Freedom! For the first time since he was sixteen nobody is telling him what to do. He rubs his eyes and climbs out of bed. George gazes out of the window at the crystal blue Mediterranean ocean. 'Beats the fucking Irwell' he smiles.

Today he has a meeting with Her Majesty's Press who have followed him over looking for stories and fawning on his pearls of tormented wisdom. George has decided to retire, at least for the moment, although he never mentioned it is only temporary to the *Sunday Mirror* who have just paid him £4000 for the exclusive.

The session with the press is taking place around George's hotel swimming pool and the outside bar. His barman and new best friend Juan, ensures an constant supply. The journalists crowd around him. Dressed in a vest and shorts George is laughing.

'I have an announcement lads. You may want to sharpen your pencils.'

'Are you becoming a priest George?'

A voice calls out from the gathered audience. 'Not exactly' he grins, 'but I am retiring. I am no longer a footballer and that is final. I could not face kicking another ball,' he declares to the open-mouthed sun drenched motley bunch of press hacks.

With a bottled beer in hand, his fourth of the day at just gone twelve o'clock, he continues: 'I want to rest, write my autobiography and go into business as a clothes designer.'

'Do United know about this Georgie?' asks the man from *The Express*.

'They do now!' he smiles.

George takes a sip from his bottle. 'I am sending them a message in a vodka bottle!'

★

I am meeting with Louis and Frank in the boardroom to discuss who else but George Best. 'Should we send someone over there?' inquires Frank.

'No let him sweat' I reply. 'He will come back of his own accord once sober and thinking straight.'

'I am not so sure' says Frank. 'It feels like we are giving up on him. As a club United should be seen to do the right thing.'

'Matt knows best Frank lad,' interrupts Louis, 'If George does change his mind we have his registration which means he cannot play for another team. We just sit tight and wait for him to come crawling back.'

'I must insist' continues Frank. 'George has serious problems, but he is a genius and last season without his goals we would have been in a perilous position. We owe him.'

This man is seriously starting to grate. 'The right thing? You are in no position to insist Frank,' I add sternly. 'You must remember your place in Manchester United. Louis is the chairman, then me. As for owing George, I have never heard anything so stupid in my life. The boy has had more chances to shape up than any other player I have known. You would do better to worry about next season. The team have not exactly pulled up any trees. We employed you as a football manager not a social worker.'

'Or a priest' joins in Louis.

Frank says nothing. He simply stands and takes his coat off the hanger and without looking up says, 'Well if that is all gentlemen, I will bid you a good day.'

With that he is gone out the door.

'I don't remember you saying the meeting was over Matt?' says Louis, 'he's a funny sod.'

'Let him go Louis,' I reply. My mind already thinking ahead. Frank needs a good start to the new campaign, otherwise, I will be forced to do the right thing.

The Prodigal Son: Just two weeks later on 2nd June George returns to Manchester with his tail between his legs, pleading to be given another chance. He meets with Frank in his Old Trafford office, who is seriously alarmed at his physical condition. A heavily bearded, red-eyed George cuts a sad figure and appears to have gained at least a stone and a half.

'Why George, why do you do this to yourself?'

'I'm fine boss. I will easily lose the weight in pre season training. You don't have to worry about me.'

'I am sure you will sweat it out' replies Frank, 'but I am more concerned with what is going on inside your head. Now the board have issued three conditions which you must adhere to if you wish to continue on as a Manchester United player.'

'Anything' replies George, 'I just want to get back

to playing.'

Frank looks at his list. 'Firstly you report back three days before the others so we can get a head start on getting you back into reasonable condition.'

'No problems' smiles George.

'The second is you see a psychiatrist.'

'No chance' says George instantly. 'I am not having anyone screwing with my head.'

'Then it is over George,' Frank points to his door. 'You may as well leave now. These are the conditions laid down. You either go along or go away.'

A clearly reluctant George looks horrified but knows he has no choice.

'Okay then and what is the third?'

'Number three is you move in with Paddy Crerand and his family for a month or so until we feel you are ready to be trusted on your own again.'

'Does Paddy know about this?' Frank nods. He is smiling.

'He and Noreen are looking forward to having you.'

'I bet they are' sighs George.

George's new found domestic bliss proves short lived and despite Paddy's protestations for him to tough it out, he moves back to his Bramhall residence. An incident on the opening night at the Crerand's leaves George in no doubt that despite being a welcome guest, this was not a hotel.

Noreen asks George what he fancies for his breakfast the following day.

Thinking he is set to be waited on, George answers

'Eggs and bacon would be lovely thanks Noreen.' The next morning George wakes and goes downstairs to find awaiting him on the kitchen table, two raw eggs and four rashers of uncooked bacon.

As for the visit to the psychiatrist, this proves equally calamitous as George spends most of the hour session simply laughing in his face. Any attempt to get inside his head is mocked and derided.

'You're wasting your time,' says George. 'What goes on in my head is my business, my problem.'

'But why do you do it George? Why do you do everything to the extreme? For instance, why do you drink so much?'

'I don't agree that I drink too much.'

'In what way?' replies the psychiatrist, finally believing this immensely talented but hugely flawed and fascinating human being is at last starting to open up.

'Well it is only possible to have one drink at a time!' smiles George, before bursting out laughing once more.

The psychiatrist gives up.

35 - FOOTBALLING CAMELOT

It begins with a visit to the man who can't be moved. Bobby pulls up outside the old man's house in Chorlton-cum-Hardy. This is the first time he has ever been here. An invitation from Sir Matt himself to come and share with him just what is occurring in the dressing room.

United have endured a horrific start to their 1972-73 campaign. They opened with three straight defeats, drew the following four and were then beaten twice again to find themselves marooned at the foot of the table.

It is a crisis that the players have reacted to in typical manner by blaming everybody but themselves. George is top of the list, with the manager and his assistant a close second. Despite being no worse than any others, George is sadly now looking human. A self-inflicted fall from grace, he is fed up beyond all measure by the inner turmoil and is close to giving up the fight.

Himself, Bobby and Denis no longer speak and he is sick and tired of being bawled out after games and in training by men who only a short while ago would only have made it into Old Trafford by buying a fucking ticket. Such is George's despair and anger towards his team mates he spends the evening of Bobby's testimonial against Celtic at Old Trafford throwing eggs at his picture in the Brown Bull.

For George now it is like the name of his boutique, Que Sera Sera, what will be will be, because he simply does not care anymore.

An equally frustrated Denis is at war with the world and everybody in it but the manager especially drives him insane. Those precious few times when Denis is able to scrape himself off the treatment table with his shot knees, Frank insists on playing him right up front, when Denis now believes his best position is slighter deeper.

Frank knows best! Denis cannot even talk to him to plead his case because Frank now insists players have to make an appointment to see him!

As for his sidekick Musgrove... Denis neither respects nor listens to him. This is not the Manchester United of the sixties; the passion and flair, the bonds of friendships, the glory. The United of the old man and Jimmy. This place now turns his stomach. It is United in name only. The reality being everybody is so busy back stabbing and gutter-sniping they have succeeded in ripping out its heart. Old Trafford has no soul left.

Bobby knocks on the old man's door, Jean answers. 'Bobby love, it is so nice to see you.' She kisses him on the cheek. Bobby steps inside.

'Now pass me your coat. He is waiting for you in the living room. How are Norma and the girls?'

'They are well thank you Mrs Busby,' replies Bobby, as he hands it over.

'Oh Bobby please. After all these years, call me Jean please.'

★

I am sat down when Bobby appears. I stand to greet him and shake his hand.

'Bobby lad, come in, sit down.'

'I'll go and put the kettle on' says Jean. 'I'm sure you two have a lot to talk about.'

Jean leaves the room and I lean in close to Bobby.

'Now son from the top, what is going on?'

'Frank has lost it boss' the words almost spewing out of Bobby's mouth. 'We never see him. The tactics are all over the place. We are all about defending now, keep it tight. Don't concede. The players that he is buying and the young kids from the reserves they are simply not good enough. And then there is George. He is soiling our good name. He does not try a leg in training. Every morning now when he bothers to turn up he is still drunk! It is just not fair on the other lads.'

'Forget about George, Bobby. It is Frank I am interested in. So, in your opinion the players are not putting it in?'

Bobby shakes his head. 'It is a different world. It is not like the old days when we could have a bad day, then George or Denis would pull us out of the mire with a stroke of magic. They can't do it anymore. Something has to change and quickly, otherwise we are going down.'

Bob will not say it, but it is now clear what has to happen.

Frank has to go.

★

Thursday 5ᵗʰ December 1972: A night on the tiles in London which causes George to miss training is the final straw. One non-appearance too far that finally sees Frank give up and officially ask the board to place George Best on the transfer list. They agree and a two week suspension follows.

And then the world goes crazy with the sensational news that for £300,000 George Best could be had.

Not turning up was the end for Frank, who felt betrayed with George's recent comment after being hammered 4-1 at home to Spurs, 'If Manchester United are relegated I will ask for a transfer.' Well he has got his wish now, thinks Frank. This added to a recent incident at Reubens nightclub in Manchester when George was accused of punching a twenty year-old waitress means the manager's patience has snapped.

Frank is surprised at how swiftly Busby and Edwards agree to his request of getting rid of George. Maybe they too have finally grown weary of this beautiful if ultimately too painful thorn in their side? Frank does not feel guilty, for nobody could have tried harder than he to help.

His conscience is clear. God will understand.

On speaking to the newspapers explaining the decision, Frank remains diplomatic to the end. 'We have had to consider many things, including the future and morale of the club and discipline of the players. I have tried all the time I have been here to support George Best. It is very disappointed and upsetting because he is still a great player and a good lad. He has just not behaved like a top professional should.'

George responds to this life changing episode by splashing out £11,000 on a white Silver Cloud Rolls Royce.

★

Nine days later: It was a phone call George did not expect but one that sees him head to Old Trafford for a secret meeting with the old man and the chairman.

He is told 'Speak to nobody of this but make sure you come along for it will be worth your while.'

George arrives and heads straight for the boardroom. I am in there waiting with Louis.

'Leave the talking to me' I tell him. George enters. 'Sit down George' I say. 'We are going to keep this short. Manchester United are willing to give you one more chance. What do you say?'

At first he cannot believe his ears. George really believed he had worn the red shirt for the final time. Close to tears he tells Busby. 'I never wanted to leave boss. I could never imagine playing for any other team.'

'Good lad. Welcome back'

'I am surprised Frank has agreed to this' muses George.

'Well let me worry about Frank, George,' I reply.

So this is the endgame? This is how the great Manchester United operate. Without his knowledge George has been welcomed back into the United 'family'. A phone call from a journalist being the first Frank knew. But he knows what is at hand here. He understands. This is nothing more than a deliberate plot by Busby and the board to undermine his position and make him resign.

Oh it is clever. Sinister, mean and cruel but so clever. But Frank is not going to grant them their wish. One thought does scare him though. Manchester United have always been regarded in football as the good guys, a footballing Camelot where chivalry and honour went hand in hand with genius and glory.

But if Busby and his crowd are the good guys, then just how underhand and callous are the bad?

36 - A NICE DAY FOR AN EXECUTION

Do I feel guilty? I feel I am doing right by Manchester United. This is nothing personal. Myself and Frank may not always have seen eye to eye. I know he is a genuinely good man but I have to act. To do nothing and let us drift into the New Year, I have no doubt will result in our relegation and I cannot allow that.

I will not allow that.

And so if it means me being billed as the bad guy then so be it. For this is a hard profession, Frank knows, he understands, he has been around. The wrong man at the wrong time. It was my mistake. I have to make this right.

I just need to pick my time and my moment. No doubt, sooner or later a results on the pitch will hand me the perfect opportunity.

Somewhere soon Frank's last stand will occur and sadly it will fall to me to end his time amongst us.

★

An incensed Frank O'Farrell seeks out Busby at Old Trafford. He storms into his office.

'This is not right. Bringing George back and undermining my position.'

'Come on Frank' I reply. 'The prodigal son. You of all people should understand that? We need George. We have let you spend a fortune and what do we have to show for it? We are rock bottom of the league.'

'If you keep looking back Matt this club will never move forward. You see United as a family. Through right or wrong. To err is divine. To forgive equally so. You live in the past to protect the present. But you cannot see what is truly going on because you are blinded by love. Munich was fourteen years ago. Life has moved on. United must also.'

Now Frank has gone too far.

'Do not talk to me about things you know nothing of Frank, things that you could never understand. There is a reason for the Memorial clock on the forecourt. That damned Munich afternoon. The blood in the snow. My boys' blood. I still see their faces every day around this place. I hear their voices. Laughter in the corridor. I go outside and there is nobody there. Just distant whispers. The only other person around is you. Sat in your ivory tower, writing letters, answering mail. Preaching to all you cross in that sanctimonious tone of yours. I do not live in the past. You are wrong to say that and I hold you in utter contempt for it. And neither does this club exist in the past. How dare you? We simply refuse to let the memory of those taken from us fade away. Now if that means 'protecting' as you say, the family members, picking them up when they fall, then so be it. George is family. He is back in. You? Well you can please yourself. I couldn't care less anymore.'

Frank is ashen faced. He can see the hurt in Matt's eyes. What Matt fails to realise is that Frank does understand. He feels the passion and the pride. The grief and the loss suffered at Munich. The fact he does not go around wearing his heart on sleeve and proclaiming 'Glory, Glory Man United' every day, does not mean he cares any less.

I calm down a little. Frank looks taken aback and remorseful but I cannot find it in my heart to feel sorry for him.

'Everything I do Frank, is for the good of Manchester United. We have been living on a life support machine since 1958. Winning the European Cup four years ago was no rainbow's end, I realise that now. It was nothing but a respite. Nobody can take a hit like we did and not fall from the stars and crash and burn. Well we are not at the bottom yet Frank, but we are close and I see my job as just buying time. Doing everything in my power to postpone the inevitable. Now if you don't mind I have work to do and would like to be left alone.'

Frank smiles. But inside he feels desperately sad for this man, for it is clear to him now that Busby is still on the plane.

'I am sorry for your pain Matt. I really am.' With that he leaves the office.

Why do I feel like I have just been to confession? I am surprised Frank did not make me say five Hail Marys and five Our Fathers?

This man has missed his vocation in life and should be wearing a priest collar not a tie around his neck.

Selhurst Park: Saturday 16th December 1972
Crystal Palace 5 Manchester United 0

Another George no show as once more he is either sleeping off a hangover or lying in a gutter. When we needed him most he has broken my heart for the last time. I care little now for him. But I still care about this club and in one of the most pathetic performances by a United side I have ever witnessed, we collapse 5-0 to the only side worse than us in the division.

I am speechless, embarrassed and angry. The players should have faces as red as their shirts. It is blatantly obvious they are not playing for the manager.

I cannot delay this a second longer. I have someone in mind to replace Frank. He is a wide boy. He is passionate, a loveable rogue. A lad. He is sly, devious and ruthless when required. Perfect for what lies ahead. He is a character, a Gorbals corner boy from Glasgow's mean streets. He knows no fear. He builds exciting young teams, he knows the game, he plays within the rules on it, off it I have my doubts. But I am willing to take a chance. He is not Frank, far from it. If Frank is the good vicar, then the present Scotland coach, forty-four year-old Tommy Docherty, is the turbulent priest.

And he will be the next manager of Manchester United.

I watch on as the United players are filing out of the dressing room for a meal and something to eat before the coach drive back home. None will meet my eyes. Except one, Willie Morgan stops and comes over.

'Denis will not get changed boss. He is still sat there in his kit. He won't speak to anybody.'

'Where is Frank?' I ask.

'He has just left him' Willie replies. 'Denis was just ignoring him. It is like he is in a trance.'

'I will go and have a word.'

Denis has been substitute but came on early for an injury. Sadly he looked a pale shadow of his former self. As I enter he is sat with his hands on his knees staring into space. I sit down next to him and put my arm around his shoulders. 'Frank makes me substitute. He does not think I am even good enough anymore to play with that rabble. How bad am I boss?'

'Come on Denis, son. It's just been a bad day at the office. They happen.' He turns to look at me and smiles.

'Maybe George is a lot smarter than we think not bothering to turn up?'

'George has burnt his bridges today Denis, for the last time. As have other people. I promise things are going to change. Now do me a favour, get changed and go and join the rest of the team. For me son.'

He nods. I am sure Denis knows what I am hinting at. His eyes staring at me. I stand to leave but as I do say, 'what we have just spoken about, keep it under your hat Denis. The world will know soon enough.'

I have discreetly asked my Scottish lads Denis, Martin and Willie whom have played under Tommy at international level and they heap fulsome praise upon him. All rave about his tactical nous and his man management ability. Fair but hard.

'A reformed character boss,' Denis did say to me.

'What do you mean reformed?' I ask.

'Oh it was just in the early days when Tommy had a bit of a reputation as a rum sod. He liked his slice of the cake. But that was a long time ago.'

I have no idea what Denis is talking about and decide I do not want to know. Tommy fits the bill.

As it happened Tommy was at the Palace game on a scouting mission. Ironically he was sat behind Frank who got him the match ticket. They are good friends and Frank is godfather to Tommy's daughter. I met him at half time in the board room when we were already two goals down and looked set for a good hiding.

'We have big problems Tommy,' I told him ushering away to a quiet corner.

'Aye I can see that,' replied the Glaswegian.

'Let us have a chat after the game. What do you say son?'

'Nothing wrong with a chat Matt,' he smiles.

Along with Louis, we arrange to meet afterwards away from prying eyes and prowling journalists. A gaggle of them are following my every move. They know it is just a matter of time and I am in no mood to disappoint them.

'I am not going to mess around Tommy,' I say later, 'the job is yours for the taking. £15,000 per annum, a club car and a three year contract.'

'I am very honoured Matt, but remember at this moment you still have a manager.'

'Not for much longer Tommy lad' adds Louis.

I jump in. 'I will deal with Frank. We need you Tommy. You are just what this club needs. It will be like turning round a giant tanker and we may have to fall further before it happens. But I have huge faith in you. What do you say?'

I offer him my hand and he takes it.

We have our man.

'Now you just sit tight Tommy and we will be in touch later in the week. I have unfinished business back in Manchester.'

★

The Midland Hotel, Manchester: Monday 18th December 1972: Frank knows he is in trouble because he has not even been invited to the top table at Bobby's testimonial dinner. Rumours are ablaze around the room that the manager's sacking is imminent.

Frank is sat with his wife Anne, who is clearly uneasy. Her husband gazes over to the top table where Bobby sits with Busby, Louis, their wives and other directors, plus various member of this Mancunian Catholic mafia.

Protective and loyal, Paddy McGrath foremost amongst them. Good men, thinks Frank; always polite and courteous to himself and Anne whenever their paths cross, but there was also an awkwardness, something he could never put his finger on in conversation. Now he knows.

He was always the outsider who Matt did not trust. Obviously he has been whispering in their ears. 'He is not one of us', 'he is going', 'I made a mistake but I will sort it'... Well Frank is not one to run from a fight and even though results on the pitch are proving disastrous he has the comfort of a three-year contract. If they want to plunge the knife in then he is going to make them pay dearly in pounds and pence for the pleasure.

Martin Buchan approaches Frank. He leans down and says quietly into his ear. 'They are scheming something up boss. I just want you to know that if they get rid of you then I am off as well.' Martin is a bright individual, he has class and style and is not one for back stabbing. He hates what is occurring in the dressing room. He knows they are all gunning for the boss, who Martin thinks is a good guy and does not deserve what is going on behind his back.

Frank smiles. 'Thank you Martin, I really appreciate that but you must not do or say anything. This is football son. This is how it ends. You must look after your career. You and similar lads of your character have got to stick around at United. Take it back from the parasites and the malingerers. You will be captain here one day Martin Buchan and that will make me proud.'

★

Tuesday 19th December 1972. Frank is at The Cliff when he receives a phone call to go to Old Trafford for a special board meeting with the chairman Louis Edwards. Malcolm Musgrove and John Aston Senior have also been summoned.

'Looks like this could be it boys' says Frank. Outside on the forecourt reporters hover like vultures over a dying man's staggering last steps. It is an unusually bright winter's day, the sun is shining in a beautiful clear blue sky.

'A lovely day Frank,' quips a journalist as they get out of the car.

'Nice day for an execution don't you think?' replies Frank, as the three men head inside.

Les Olive is waiting for them outside the boardroom.

'Frank, Mr Edwards will see you first. Frank turns to his two assistants. 'This should not take too long.'

Olive smiles but it is the expression of one who knows there is grave news. Both appear mortified. Aston senior has been with United since the end of the war. He knows nothing but this club. This man was a member of the legendary 1948 FA Cup winning team. His son plays for the club. He cannot believe it is all going to end like this.

Musgrove is resigned to be given the sack, he'll be delighted to let someone else deal with this madhouse. Another month here and he'd go crazy.

Frank enters the boardroom to find Louis Edwards and Matt Busby waiting for him. Busby will not meet his eye.

'Frank lad' begins Louis. 'I am afraid it has not worked out. We are relieving you of your duties.'

'You mean you are sacking me?'

Louis nods solemnly.

'Why are you sacking me?' asks Frank.

'No reason' replies Louis, shrugging his shoulders but obviously taken aback by the question.

'Mr Chairman I am not leaving this room until you give me a reason for my dismissal.' Frank is already thinking ahead to the settlement of his contract. He no longer trusts these people. Louis looks frantically across to Busby. It appears Frank has done his homework. I nod back across to Louis to tell him.

'Well Frank' continues Louis. 'It is because of our league position. The results have simply not been good enough. It is over.'

'I see' replies Frank. 'Well I must insist then that this be recorded in the minutes. What about my assistants Malcolm and John? Malcolm is an extremely capable coach. As for John. Well you look after family here don't you?'

He stares across towards me. I am not prepared to give him the courtesy of a reply.

'You are all going together Frank. It is a clean sweep,' replies Louis. Frank shakes his head in abject disgust.

'And last night, your decision not to put me and Anne on the top table was because you knew this was happening today. What kind of men are you? A night of the long knives. Everybody in that room knew except me. But to be honest gentlemen I am glad to be away. There is no magic about this place. There is no myth, no angel dust. Just old men clinging onto a fallen dream with a mad lust for power. Right then,' Frank stands up. 'I will let you get on with your dirty work. I am sure you will excuse me if I don't wish you good luck in the future.'

'Come on Frank,' implores Louis. 'You are a man of the world. You know the game. We are second from the bottom of the league. What choice have we got?'

Frank smiles. 'The good guys? My God! Father forgive them for they know not what they do.'

★

That same day a letter arrives in the post at Old Trafford from George Best. After a full week on the drink and in no fit state of mind or body to think straight, never mind play football, George pens his thoughts in an open letter to the United board.

It is a long, lingering, rambling epitaph that says more about the writer than its intended target. This wonderful waste of talent still had so much more to offer. A shooting star roaring across the skies for ten years that enthralled everyone caught in its path, before finally exploding and breaking up into a thousand tales of heartbreak, wild nights out and a depressing what if?

> *Gentlemen of The Board,*
> *I had thought seriously of coming personally and asking for a chance to speak at the board meeting, but once again I am afraid when it comes to saying things*

face to face, I might not have been completely honest. I am afraid through my somewhat unorthodox ways of trying to sort my own problems out I have caused Manchester United even bigger problems.

I wanted you to read this letter before the board meeting commenced, so as to let you know my feelings before any decision or statements are issued following the meeting. When I said last summer I was going to quit football, contrary to what many people said or thought, I seriously meant it, because I had lost interest in the game for various reasons. Whilst in Spain I received a lot of letters from both friends and well-wishers, quite a few asking me to re-consider. I did so and after weeks of thinking it over, I decided to give it another try, I came back hoping my appetite for the game would return, and even though I like to think I gave 100 per cent in every game, there was something missing.

Even now, I am not quite sure what. Therefore, I have decided not to play football again and this time no one will change my mind,

In conclusion, I would like to wish the club the best of luck for the remainder of the season and for the future. Because even though I personally have tarnished the club's name in recent times, to me, and thousands of others, Manchester United still means something special.

Yours sincerely,
George'

Unbeknown to George, not that it mattered, even before the board were aware that this letter existed, the decision had been taken to get rid. This last disappearing act ended any lingering hopes that he would ever shape up. Or grow up.

So far as I am concerned myself and Manchester United have wiped their hands and hearts clean of George Best. He is back on the transfer list. And whether he goes to City, Chelsea, Tottenham or Timbuktu, they are welcome to him.

Frank and his boys gone. George out the door. It is time for a new way of doing things at this club. A new face. Manchester United requires open heart surgery.

It is time to call the Doc.

37 - SET THE HEATHER ON FIRE

Friday 22nd December 1972: I am walking with Tommy Docherty around an empty Old Trafford. He appears in awe of the old place. Already Tommy has been a breath of fresh air at his opening press conference. The newspaper boys love him. They sense a star is born and for the foreseeable future, and more I hope, a decent headline will not be a problem.

Previously with Frank their biggest problem was what to use in their copy. With Tommy it will soon be what to leave out!

'One thing Tommy, I think it might be a good idea to appoint someone from within the club to work alongside you. Someone like Pat Crerand, don't you think?'

Tommy is no fool. It is wise not to upset the old man at this early stage, even though he hates the idea. For Crerand is on on his list to be got rid of. But he will play the game till the time is right.

'A great idea, Matt. Paddy is a good lad.' Tommy looks around at the vast empty grandstands. 'What an arena, Matt. You can almost hear the ghosts of the past, the greats. The roar of the crowds as they watched their heroes. Edwards, Taylor, Denis, Bobby, George. We will get it back, I promise you.'

'That is why I brought you here, Tom. But first we have to learn to walk again before we can run with the big boys. And that is what I want to talk to you about.'

'Go on,' says Tommy as we reach the corner of the

Stretford End.

I turn to look at him.

'Now these are desperate times son. I cannot afford to mince my words. I want you to build a side in your image. Whatever it takes, whatever you have to do because United cannot afford to be relegated. I know you are a street fighter and if you have to hit low, so be it. You cheat, you lie and you steal. You scrap and you bite and you fight until we can fight no more. But most of all, you win. Do I make myself clear? The gloves are off Tommy. No referee, no rules. You keep us up.'

Our new man wastes no time, Tommy speaks to the *Manchester Evening News*. 'There are players here not up to Manchester United standard. I am not going to allow anyone, no matter who they are, to perform on their reputation.'

His own boys will be arriving soon. Many from across the border. United desperately need an urgent blood transfusion and it will be Scottish red.

Tommy's opening game is away at Elland Road against treble chasing Leeds. Fighting and scrapping for every ball, a creditable 1-1 draw is earned. Leading with a first half Ted MacDougall goal, we appear set for a remarkable victory over the league leadersbefore Allan Clarke sneaks home a last minute equaliser past Alex Stepney.

Reality bites hard though three days later when United are outclassed 3-1 at Derby County to be sent crashing to the bottom of the table. Tommy has decided to trust his judgement and his own countrymen to produce the flair, passion and desire so badly missing at

United in this desperate time of need.

I tell him to go out and get them. Backed by the board Tommy splashes out £120,000 to bring in Arsenal's George 'Stroller' Graham, an accomplished midfielder who he compares to the great German playmaker, Gunther Netzer.

High praise indeed even if the comments cause a few raised eyebrows in the boardroom. But we have made our commitment, so let us wait and see. The next day he travels to Glasgow and returns home with £100,000 worth of Partick Thistle's hard and reliable full-back Alex Forsyth.

Republic of Ireland international midfielder Mick Martin is drafted in from Irish league club Bohemians. Six foot two and eyes of blue Jim Holton is bought from Shrewsbury Town on the recommendation of ex United goalkeeper Harry Gregg. Harry has done us a huge favour with this boy. He cannot speak highly enough of him. 'This boy is a diamond Matt.' Also he gets the price up to £80,000 from our original £40,000 offer. But we owe Harry more than words and I am happy to pay it.

And then the one that shocks the footballing world and has my good friend Bill Shankly on the phone threatening World War Three. Glasgow Celtic's diminutive if hugely talented forward Lou Macari is stolen from the grasps of title chasing Liverpool at the last. I take a deep breath and as Louis Edwards crosses himself before signing the cheque, we pay a monumental fee of £200,000 for Macari. Bill is not happy with me, but Tommy is ecstatic and almost overcome with such backing.

'We will do our part Tommy,' I tell him, 'you make

sure you do yours.'

For a first team trainer Tommy plucks for an old playing colleague from his Preston North End days. On New Year's Eve the loud, passionate, opinionated and tactically proficient scouser, forty-four year-old Tommy Cavanagh arrives from Hull City, a double act that I am sure when roused could cause a riot in an empty church. Cavanagh swiftly becomes a controversial figure at United – there really is no in-between. If Tommy rates him that is good enough for me, but Cavanagh's use of colourful language and endless profanity on the touchline is a problem behind the scenes. I have already had complaints he is upsetting the many priests and vicars who sit around the dugout. Traditionally handed free tickets by me, many a blushing clergy man cross themselves both for Tommy's and United's soul as the relegation battle rages on.

On the field results finally start to improve.

The medicine is starting to work as come March's end Manchester United have won four, drawn five and lost four of Tommy's thirteen matches in charge. Prior to Christmas Frank's record had been a depressing five wins in twenty. Safety is finally achieved and we finish a rotten campaign fifth from bottom but seven points clear of relegation.

The Doc is deemed to be a miracle worker by our fanatical supporters, who already adore him. And he them. At times he is almost reduced to tears by the passion exploding and erupting from the Stretford End and around the ground. 'The greatest supporters in the word' he labels them. The board are also suitably impressed with Tommy, albeit a little uneasy with his expensive penchant for lashing out their hard earned cash on what Louis calls, 'anything in a kilt'. We are christened Mac'chester United in the press but no one here cares. Least of all Tommy, for despite many scares along the way it is mission accomplished.

For now our supporters are breathing a little more easily. But despite the huge sums spent, a huge dose of mediocrity still exists within the squad. Uncertainty regarding the future remains. United have not exactly set the heather on fire for five years now and we do appear on a slippery slope.

Only the heartiest red soul believes that next season results will vastly improve. Tommy knows he is in the biggest fight of his life and is prepared to do whatever necessary to ensure United survive in the top league. The gloves are off. He is ready to break hearts and rip this club apart to keep it alive. No one is safe.

I hold my breath, I close my eyes and look the other way.

38 - SHADOWS AND DUST I

The Ballad of the Holy Trinity (Part One)

Tommy wears a wry smile. He has just been given carte blanche by the legend himself to rip this club apart. A cull. Tommy knows what is required and he possesses the tools of the trade to be successful. No name too big. Blow away the cobwebs and shake the world beneath their feet. In time they may scream 'who will rid me of this turbulent priest!' They may run to the legend but he will not listen. For Tommy is going nowhere.

'You can rely on me Matt. I can assure you that you have the right man.'

Bobby: Saturday 10th March 1973: St Andrews, Birmingham. Bobby knows. He is running and running but it is if his legs are made of stone. The more he tries, the harder he breathes. There is no impact on the match, no long searching pass, no thrilling runs through the centre of the park, no lashing drives that skim the surface or soar through the sky like a thunderbolt into the top corner. It is if a great tenor has opened his mouth and the slurring voice of a horribly drunken pub singer emerges.

Bobby is a mere ghost in a red shirt.

Eager, nay desperate, to help his team mates in this fearful relegation struggle but playing like he has chains and not boots on his feet, Bobby is a hindrance. None say anything to him, these new boys show great respect but Bobby can't live like this. He feels that he is not only cheating his team but himself.

What Nobby called 'the bounce' – that unworldly, mystical quality great players possess, when the ball appears magically attracted to them. Well it is now ignoring Bobby. The ball is keeping its distance. The love affair they have endured since he was fifteen years old is over. Bobby runs and runs but he is going nowhere except, he has just decided, into retirement.

United are well beaten again. A 3-1 loss. After the match Bobby says nothing in the dressing room. He feels no guilty eyes upon him, just a sense of desolation among his fellow red shirts at the loss. These lads care, thinks Bob.

Tommy has revitalised a pride in the club, if not the qualities on the pitch. That night he speaks to Norma. He tells her what is on his mind.

'Only you know Bob,' she replies softly.

The next day Bobby arranges a meeting with the manager at Old Trafford. He explains to Tommy that the time has come. He is going to retire at the end of the season. Tommy stands and shakes Bobby's hand.

'I will inform the board Bobby. Can I just say it has been an honour and privilege to be associated with you. If only for a short time.'

'Thanks Tommy' replies a glum looking Bobby. He turns to leave. Tommy beams. He cannot believe his luck. Thank Christ for that, he thinks. Tommy takes out his list and crosses Bobby Charlton's name off. That is a bullet saved and one less legend to worry about.

★

Bobby decides to head inside the stadium and just sit quietly for a while. To hold his emotions together. Bobby's head is full of memories, good and bad overloading. He feels dizzy and sits down just above the home bench. It is where he sat with Jimmy Murphy for the game following Munich against Sheffield Wednesday. Where Jimmy whispered into his ear as United began their fight back out of the abyss. Where they refused to slip gently into that dark, dark night. Instead they fought kicking and screaming against all reason to not just survive but prosper.

'Stay by my side son,' Jimmy had said, 'I need you. I have never needed you more.' He so wishes Jimmy was here now.

And then a voice which startles Bobby and makes him think he is hearing and seeing ghosts. 'Hello Bobby. What brings you here on a Sunday?'

It is Jimmy Murphy.

Bobby smiles wide. 'Jimmy' he exclaims, 'it is good to see you old mate.'

'Well you will be seeing a lot more of me. Tommy has brought me back into the fold for scouting duties.' Jimmy eyes Bobby closely. 'What's up son?'

'I've just told Tommy I'm calling it a day at the end of the season. I just needed a few moments to compose myself before I head home. I don't want Norma to see me upset.'

Jimmy sits down. He pulls out a cigarette, lights it and inhales. He smiles. 'It only seems like yesterday you were lining up in the tunnel down there for your debut against Charlton Athletic. From the beginning myself and Matt never had any doubts about you, son. You were a certainty to make it to the top. That day when your second hit the net Matt turned to me and said, "You have done it again Jimmy. We have got ourselves another golden apple."

'I have never been more proud Bobby. From that first moment to the last you have handled yourself with sheer class. Despite all that has gone on over the last years, you have been Manchester United's saving grace. And let me tell you something else,' he continues. 'The lads who lost their lives. They will be equally proud. Can you imagine what Duncan would be saying to you today?'

'Well done chief it was a great innings' smiles Bobby.

'Or knowing Dunc something along those lines!'

A tearful Bobby wipes his eye. 'That was United for me, Jimmy. Before the crash: Duncan, Eddie, Wilf, Tommy, you, the boss. They are who are in my thoughts when I think of Manchester United. We lost it after the crash. Whatever we had – that sprinkling of gold dust. We never got it back despite all what was achieved.'

Jimmy shakes his head, 'We are still falling from that crash Bobby lad. We have not hit the ground yet. There will be worse to come before it gets better.'

'How are things with you and Matt these days?'

Jimmy rolls his eyes and sighs heavily. 'We don't speak. He has his hands full I suppose. He does not need me anymore. But I am always there if he does. He knows that.'

'What happened Jimmy?'

The old man goes to light another cigarette, 'We grew old son. And somebody made the decision to get back on that plane. Like you say, the best of times.'

'Do you still think about it? Not so much the crash,

but those early days? Paradise…' smiles Bobby.

Jimmy thinks for a moment before replying. 'It is alive in my heart son. Sometimes I will be sat here alone and I swear to God I see the lads training on the pitch. Duncan will wave up to me. I wave back but there is nobody there. Shadows and dust. Bobby lad. Shadows and dust.'

'Maybe this place is haunted?' says Bobby.

Jimmy smiles. 'I would not say haunted. More blessed.'

Bobby nods in agreement. 'Blessed is the word I would use. We were blessed once Jimmy.'

'Aye we were lad.' He takes a huge drag of his cigarette, 'we most certainly were.'

Saturday 28th April 1973: Robert R Charlton steps out in the red of Manchester United for one last time at Stamford Bridge, to a rousing reception from all in the crowd. As he walks onto the pitch a barrage of photographers and cameramen surround him.

His 606th game. He looks emotional but Bobby is holding it together. He does not like fuss but today he is undoubtedly the centre of attention. Both sets of players form a circle of honour around the centre circle. The thousands of United fans present raise high their scarves to salute and sing their captain's name. The applause rings loudly in his ears. Waiting for Bobby to present him with a silver cigarette box is Chelsea chairman Brian Mears. A gentleman to the end he shakes Mears' hand and says: 'I could not ask for my final game in London anywhere better than Stamford Bridge.'

And so Bobby exits in the manner he began: with

grace and style. Just for a second before kick off, Bobby glances towards the heavens. He smiles and says almost in a whisper so no one can hear.

'I hope you were watching lads'

39 - SHADOWS AND DUST II

The Ballad of the Holy Trinity (Part Two)

Denis: Friday morning at The Cliff and Denis Law
has been called to the manager's office. He knocks and
goes in. He appears anxious. Tommy is sat at his desk.
He smiles. 'Don't look so worried Denis. Lawman
you are in good hands. I am going to look after you. I
promise. You spoke up for me with Matt to make sure I
got this job. I owe you. There is a job here for life when
you retire. Plus a testimonial. You can trust me Denis.'

This is a load off Denis's mind. He is thirty-three
years old and has no wish to leave Manchester United.
He knows his knees are close to giving way beneath
him. These days he retreats to the treatment room until
late Thursday to give himself as much chance possible
to be ready for selection on the Saturday.

He does not see this as cheating, more preparation.
Too many times over the years and seasons past he has
taken jabs and played when in no condition to. No one
could ever accuse Denis of 'swinging the lead'. This is
a man who missed a European Cup final because the
old man asked 'Take one for me Denis. Just one more
jab', and he did, and another and another. Now he is
paying a painful price.

Time to look after himself now, he has earned the
right.

'Thanks Tommy' says Denis, 'I really appreciate

that.'

'Well we have to look after our own Denis lad. I need people like you here at this club. Loyalty means everything to me. Now why don't you get yourself away for a few days? A change of scenery might recharge the batteries. I need the old Denis firing. So take a break. Go home to Aberdeen and play some golf. Get the handicap down.'

Denis is genuinely touched by Tommy's attitude. He feared the worst when asked to go and see him. He feared the end of the road. A free transfer and thrown away with the garbage. But Tommy is showing himself a gentleman.

'I will do that' smiles Denis. I won't forget this Tommy.'

Tommy grins wide. His eyes blinking fast. 'I am sure you would do the same for me Lawman.'

The next afternoon Denis is with friends stood at the bar in the golf club in Aberdeen. The BBC's Football Focus is playing on the television. A picture of him appears and the commentator announces, 'Old Trafford is in shock today after it was confirmed that Denis Law has asked for a transfer.'

For a moment Denis cannot take it in. And then reality dawns. The boy from the Gorbals has stitched him up. All eyes are upon him in the club. Drinkers at the bar and sat at tables stare. Denis seethes. He smiles through gritted teeth.

'Don't believe everything you hear on the television lads. I never said such a thing. But I have learned a valuable lesson today. If Tommy Docherty says it is daytime you can bet your last pound it is night.'

He takes the first train back south and a taxi from

Piccadilly station straight to Old Trafford. The taxi driver clocks Denis in his mirror. 'So you are off then Denis. Don't blame you mate, a sinking ship that lot. I'm a blue myself. Come and play for us. We'll treat you right. Not like them. Living in the past Denis. I blame Busby myself. Poor Frank, he never had a chance. The place is full of fucking ghosts. Come home son. Come back to Maine Road.'

Denis listens but does not reply. He simply stares out the window.

Tommy is not around but I am at my desk as a frantic Denis knocks on his door. 'Boss I need a word. That bloody Docherty has told a pack of lies. I never asked for a transfer. He is trying to get me out the door.'

I put my pen down. 'Denis, I can't interfere. Have a word with Tommy, man to man. He is fair and has my full backing. I am sure you can both come to some sort of agreement.'

Denis cannot believe his ears. So that's it then. Ten years of his life over and sealed with a treacherous lie. This cruel game. The so called glory – a myth, an illusion. The reality being it is littered with crooks, cheats, con men and two faced bastards who appreciate you only while you fulfil a need but then spit you out like a bad taste in the mouth. Worse, it is those so called friends and those you considered close to you who set you up for a fall and then kick you when you hit the floor.

Denis is annoyed because he has always considered himself a decent judge of character. He always saw them coming in the past but he never saw Tommy coming. And it has cost him badly. But what disturbs him more, he never saw Busby either. All those years, Denis knows now, he wanted him out, so why waste breath and energy on a fight he cannot win?

It is at the traditional Footballers Writers lunch in London on the Thursday before the FA Cup final that Denis bumps into Manchester City manager Johnny Hart. The talk is not surprisingly of Denis's free transfer. 'If you are interested Denis, we would love to have you at City. Before you dismiss it so easily just think for a minute. It would mean not having to move house, only the colour of your shirt would change. And it is not as if you have never worn it before. Sleep on it, let me know?'

Denis is intrigued but a little pensive. Play for United's greatest rivals? It's not as if other clubs are banging down his door to sign him? After the way Docherty has stitched him up and the boss refused to intervene he owes Manchester United nothing. They have had their piece of flesh. United Family? Denis thinks if they are family he would be better off being an orphan. To Hart's surprise Denis offers him his hand.

'Nothing to think about Johnny. I would love to sign for City.'

Hart smiles wide and the two men shake. In one instant red becomes blue...

40 - SHADOWS AND DUST III

The Ballad of the Holy Trinity (Part Three)

George: As if events are not bad enough at Old Trafford, word reaches me that George is in serious trouble. He has suffered thrombosis of the leg whilst in Spain that almost killed him on the flight home. Thank God George is now recovering in hospital. Hopefully this acts as a wake up call. I have followed his life since he left United like everyone else; on the front pages of every newspaper and television bulletin. Every escapade, drunken brawl, police arrest, court appearance, scorned woman, irate husband, broken heart and empty wine bottle. I cannot help but care about George. And though it may sound crazy, after all that has occurred, I still miss the boy.

On entering his hospital room I try hard not to look shocked, but George's appearance almost makes me gasp out loud. His bloated, heavily bearded face, his deep sunken bloodshot eyes. George looks fifteen years older.

'My God George what are you doing to yourself?'

'Hello boss.' George smiles but he is clearly in distress. I sit down.

'You can't go on like this George. This is your body fighting back. Things will only get worse. You need to get yourself into some kind of decent condition son. And cut out the booze.'

His sad and weary eyes are on me but I know he is not taking the least bit of notice. Nothing changes.

'How are things at Old Trafford?' he asks in a whisper.

'Not good' I sigh. 'Tommy has the boys fired up but we lack a spark. We are losing too many games. I fear the worst.'

'We had some good times didn't we boss? It was not all birds and booze and you hammering me in your office.'

'I will not lie to you George. There were moments when I could easily have strangled you but there were also times when you made me forget about the crash. For that I will always be truly grateful and I'm here for you if needed but unless you start to help yourself the path ahead will prove a tormented one. Now if you want to live to be an old man like me. To play football with your children and grandchildren and bore them with talk about your goals. Your magnificent performance in the Bernabeu and the Stadium of Light, you have to act now whilst you are still capable. Do it George. do it!'

He looks at me with an almost resigned air that speaks of it already being too late.

I stand to go.

'I have to get back. I hope you are back on your feet soon son.'

George says nothing, and then just as I reach the door he calls out.

'Boss.' I turn around, 'I promise I will give it a go.'

I smile.

'Is it not time you were playing again George?' With that I leave the room and the idea hanging in the air. What on earth have we to lose?

★

It was a hint from Busby that it might be worth a gamble. Not so much a last throw of the dice, more Tommy thinks, like sticking a rocket up a donkey's backside in the hope it might win the Grand National.

So far as he was concerned it was crazy.

Another example of Busby's inability to let go of the past but he would go along with it for, as sure night followed day, Tommy knew George would fuck it up like he did everything else.

With Paddy Crerand acting as a go-between, George meets Tommy in Paddy McGrath's house in Altrincham. The two know each other reasonably well. They first met in the sixties in a Spanish bar and enjoyed each other's company. They greet each other warmly with a handshake and embrace.

'George you look fucking terrible' laughs Tommy.

'Thanks Tommy you don't look too good yourself' smiles George.

George is on the mend but is seriously overweight and the huge bushy beard that adorns his face ages him greatly.

Tommy glances towards Paddy McGrath who gets his message, 'Pat son why don't me and you go and grab a cup of tea in the kitchen and leave Tommy and George to chat.'

Crerand nods and the two men leave the room.

Tommy waits until they are both well out of earshot.

'Alright George, no bullshit. Do you want to give it another go?'

'One last time, Tommy. Just to see if it is still there. I am going to need a month, maybe two to get in shape but I will work like a Trojan. I will train morning and afternoon. You have my word.'

'Okay George here is my take, I don't like this, I think the world of you as a person, but I have enough on my plate at the moment without taking on the baggage signing you up will entail. But I believe you really want to make this work and even a half fit George Best is still worth taking a risk on. So I have three conditions.

'The first you get yourself fit. You sweat off the booze and crap that is in your system and get down to a fighting weight. The second – once you are up and running, if you are doing the business, one thing I will not have is you turning up for training in the morning stinking pissed. It sets a terrible example and it undermines my authority. I can't have that. So instead you come back in the afternoon and you make up the lost hours. Okay?'

'And what is the third?' asks the Ulsterman.

'The third is simple. Just don't fuck with me George and we will make this work.'

George looks Tommy straight in the eyes. He nods. 'Don't worry Tommy, you are not my type!'

George smiles. The two men laugh. They shake hands and the greatest comeback since they found the stone removed from Jesus's tomb is under way.

★

Manchester United suffer a horrific start to the 1973–74 season which opens with a 3-0 mauling at Arsenal. United are not just beaten by the Gunners they are horribly outclassed and as openings go it is akin to the leading man forgetting his intro then throwing up all over his audience.

Results do not improve – just three wins in the opening eleven league games spells disaster and events have degenerated to a point where Tommy Docherty, who once considered the return of George Best as nothing more than an emotional afterthought by Busby, now believes if the fallen genius can produce a modicum of the talent he possesses, it could improve United's chances of staying in the First Division.

George resumes training on 10th September 1973 and true to his word, works like a madman to shed the extra pounds. But he is not there yet and is surprised when his manager suggests: 'We need you George'

'Don't rush me Tommy. I need more time.'

'There is no time, George. The boys need a spark, anything to ignite a fighting chance. Come on son you owe this club, you owe me and you owe the old man.'

George glares at Tommy. The last comment was below the belt. He is not ready and fears being embarrassed.

'We have a friendly in Ireland on Wednesday against Shamrock Rovers. Come over and give it a try, see what you think?'

George looks across to Paddy Crerand who appears unsure. But George knows he is being backed in to a corner.

'Okay, I'll do it.'

'Good lad George. Trust me son you are going to be hero, a fucking hero.' Tommy makes his leave, whistling with hands in pockets – he is convinced this is the right decision.

George glances again at Paddy.

'I don't trust him, Pat.'

'Join the bloody club, George.'

★

On Wednesday 15th October 1973, 25,000 are packed into Dublin's Dalymount Park, and there is only one person the Irish crowds have come to see. His face adorning the match programme, George's every touch is cheered to the rafters. A 2-1 win for United is irrelevant for it is all about United's number eleven. The touch and eye for a pass appears unspoilt. At times a beguiling flick or a flash of instant control causes gasps of wonder and delight. There are tears of joy and relief amongst many Irish based reds who feared their boy had gone forever.

The lightning speed is no longer evident but there appears enough left on show to believe this comeback is no token gesture.

A friendly pitch invasion occurs before the referee calls time. All are racing towards one person as George finds himself swallowed in a sea of love. A young boy puts a scarf around his neck. George appears overcome. The nerves and emotion of being back home and in the red shirt catching up with him.

Tommy and Paddy Crerand watch on. Paddy is grinning wide. He is delighted to see his good mate back in the fold.

'Good lad George' he says almost to himself. 'we missed you pal.'

'I have seen enough' says Tommy. 'He plays on Saturday against Birmingham City.'

Three days later George receives another heart

warming welcome as a packed Old Trafford welcomes back their prodigal son. The Stretford End sways, rocks and ebbs. They sing out his name.

You can sense a desperation in the air for George to exhibit his full dazzling array of talents but it is soon obvious to all that the searing pace has gone and speed of thought and quickness of feet are now his main weapons. George drops deeper, he drags opponents towards him, sucks them in then a slight of foot or slipped pass through a needle's eye raises the crowd and sets United on the attack.

Not surprisingly George tires in the second half and receives a huge round of applause, not just off home supporters but Birmingham fans, on being substituted. By this time United lead 1-0 with a penalty put away by, of all people, the goalkeeper Alex Stepney.

This sums up United early form, for Alex is top scorer with two goals! Sadly the victory over Birmingham is only a mirage and a brief respite from the storm as United go on to endure a terrible first half of the season. George flatters to deceive.

He is trusted by Tommy in a playmaker role but there are moments when George plays a pass and his teammates are simply not good enough to read it. This is starting to drive George to distraction. Even at walking pace he is in a different class to anybody alongside him. The frustrations grow, defeats mount. George is a winner and teams are coming to Old Trafford and not just beating United, they are putting them to the sword.

It is hard to take. Temptations mount. On the week leading up to Christmas George opens a nightclub in Manchester. Slack Alice explodes into life and a legend is born in Mancunian folklore. His head is turned.

On New Year's Day the last humiliation, a 3-0 drubbing at QPR when United appear to throw in the towel much to George's disgust. He too gives up. The home supporters give him the bird. George's head is down. In the dressing afterwards he swiftly gets changed and disappears saying nothing.

Tommy watches him leave. He knows the gamble has failed. It is time to end it.

The following Wednesday George enjoys a late night at Slack Alice and fails to make it to training on the Thursday morning. He telephones as arranged with the manager and fixes to make up the time later that day at the Cliff. George turns up and goes through a rigorous three hour session.

Coming up that weekend Manchester United are at home to Plymouth Argyle in the FA Cup. George is looking forward to it in the hope that against lower league opponents he can impress a little more.

However come Saturday on arriving at Old Trafford at just after two o'clock, he gets a message that he is wanted in the referee's room. On entering George finds Tommy and Paddy stood waiting for him.

'What happened on Thursday, George?' asks the manager. A little taken back George does not answer. Tommy continues: 'You have let me down, son. I am leaving you out because you missed training.'

'What are you talking about?' replies George. 'We had a deal remember, if I missed training in the mornings I could come back later in the day. We shook hands for God's sake!'

Tommy shakes his head. 'You are out of order George. I said nothing of the sort.'

His piece said, Tommy walks out leaving a stunned George and glum faced Paddy stood staring at each other. 'This is a joke Pat. I had a deal with him. He is lying, I swear to God.'

'Go home George' sighs Paddy. 'Calm down and come in Monday. I will have a word with him.' Inside Paddy knows George is telling the truth. Docherty has struck again. He wants rid.

'Don't bother Pat I've had enough. If I cannot get in this team what's the point? No more and this time I mean it.' George has tears in his eyes.

For once Paddy is stuck for words. He is choked. 'Think what you are doing George. You are a long time retired.'

'It's over Pat.'

George walks past his friend and out the door and he disappears in a hazy blur of booze, gambling and women. Not necessarily in that order.

George Best never puts on a Manchester United shirt again.

★

Busby: I hear no evil, I see no evil.

Tommy smiles: It is like receiving a blessing off the Pope.

Busby: I tell myself thy must be done.

Tommy smiles: 'Fight dirty, do whatever' he told me. I do not need telling twice.'

Busby: To go on we must be cruel to be kind.

Tommy smiles: Clean it all up. Exorcise the ghosts of the past. The living red dead.

Busby: We need new blood to reignite passion and fire for that which has waned.

Tommy smiles: Sever the ties of past glories. Old stars do not retire here, they rot. Seek out the weak and destroy their spirit and show them the door.

Busby: I pray my appointment of Tommy and my blindness as he wreaks carnage is viewed by almighty God as a necessary evil.

Tommy smiles: And I the avenging angel now sit at the right hand of the legend, this Father of Football. A living saint. And I say unto him, I will execute your wrath but you must promise to watch my back. For you have sold your soul to the Red fucking Devil.'

41 - WHEN THE LIGHTS WENT OUT

In the Spring of 1974 Paul McCartney and Wings release Band On The Run. The Sting starring Paul Newman and Robert Redford wins the Oscar for best movie. Billy Joel is singing about a Piano man. The Watergate scandal rages on as Nixon attempts to lie and scheme his way out of a hole. The worlds' tallest building, the World Trade Centre, opens in New York City where it is claimed she will stand 'forever more'. In Great Britain industrial strife is wreaking havoc and as a three day week blacks out the nation into a candle lit existence, the lights are set to go out on Manchester United Football Club.

Saturday 13ᵗʰ March 1974:
The Battle of Maine Road.

With City and United struggling at the wrong end of the table, Welsh referee Clive Thomas would have had more use of a bell than a whistle as red and blue clash in one of the most vitriolic derbies of recent times. Both sides forget about the ball and decide to kick lumps out of each other.

On the terraces it is equally violent with scuffles constantly breaking out between supporters. United's infamous red bedecked hooligan following intent, it appears, on tearing apart their rival's ground brick by brick.

Back on the field no quarter is given or asked

as tempers explode on the ball and off it. Private vendettas and petty feuds simmer dangerously and it all culminates in a remarkable Wild–West type brawl on the touchline involving City's Mike Doyle and United's Lou Macari launching into a full scale boxing match!

The diminutive Macari refuses to back down and goes hell for leather with the infamously 'red hating' Doyle. After a short if brutal exchange of punches both men are dragged apart by linesmen, team mates and staff from the benches.

Thomas has no option and shows each the red card but they refuse to go. Instead Doyle and Macari stand their ground, testing the referee's authority. After consulting a policeman Thomas blows his whistle and orders the teams off the field. In a shameful episode Manchester football is being dragged through the gutter. Maine Road is in uproar. What happens next? Will the match be abandoned?

Minutes later the teams reappear minus Doyle and Macari. By this time police lines are formed around all four corners of the ground. Whether this is to protect the players from the supporters or the other way round is uncertain. Unsurprisingly the game finishes 0–0 with points shared if not pride. Not on this day.

★

With events at Maine Road still fresh in the mind, I call Tommy in for a chat. Relegation is looming large. All season we have fought hard and scrapped for every ball, but a dearth of class has been obvious and now it appears just a matter of time before the trapdoor opens and we fall through.

I fear a case of when and not if? So why do we not go out in the style for which United are renowned? We have attempted to play like the rest of the barbarians to save ourselves and it has failed miserably. Tommy has tried everything, he keeps our trust whatever happens in the next defining weeks or so.

I put it to Tommy 'We never say never at this club but I have to admit it does not look good. I understand why you have had to change United's traditional style because we are in a war but why not let us have a go for the remainder of the season? What say we switch back to 4-2-4 and maybe, just maybe, the footballing gods may shed a little sunshine on our fading hopes and grant us a miracle?'

'Why not?' replies Tommy, 'we have tried everything else. And I am probably out of the door at the end of the season anyway, aren't I? I am not a fool Matt, I know how this works. I know the signs. But I want you to know there are no hard feelings, because I cannot expect anything less after what has gone on.'

'Nonsense Tommy, this was written in the stars a long time before you showed up. You are going nowhere, son. I want you at Old Trafford so long as I am around. If we do fall then next year we will need you more than ever to inspire both the players and crowd. Trust me, your job is safe. But do me this one favour. Let us charge to the sound of the guns instead of going meekly. There are nine games left before the lights finally go out, let us give them something to remember Manchester United by.'

Tommy cannot believe his luck. Convinced he would be shown the door like Wilf and Frank before him, now the old man must be listened to and for the final eight games they will go hell for leather. Besides, Busby may have a point. It is against Tommy's natural inclination the way he has had to set United up these past eighteen months. It suits him to change.

★

Tommy comes across Paddy Crerand in the Old Trafford corridor. 'So he has not given you the boot then?' says Paddy.

'No, sadly for you Pat.' The two are joking, to a point. Neither trusts the other. Paddy cannot stomach some of the underhand methods employed by Tommy to get people out of the door. Some of them like George and Denis, are good friends. Now Tommy has to admit to this man who he cannot wait to be rid of that Busby wishes the same as he.

'You will be glad to know the boss wants us to go all out in the games left.'

Paddy smiles '4-2-4 you mean?' He has been in Tommy's ear for months now to revert back to United's traditional style, but all to no avail.

Tommy grins. 'What is it with you Busbyites? This is not Disneyworld, Paddy. You lot have lived on another planet for too long. This is the real world. The Manchester United way has gone. These days we kick, run and boot the fucking thing like everybody else in our situation. We have been battling for our lives. There was no other choice. No other way. You are indoctrinated with this pass and move to a red shirt garbage! The old man is not God. We are still going down Pat, Jesus Christ himself cannot save us from that. Busby admits as much.'

'If you don't get it Tommy, then I cannot explain it.

Besides in two months' time you will be gone anyway, so I would not worry too much about it.'

'Oh no,' smiles Tommy, 'I am going nowhere. He has told me my job is safe. If I was you old son I would watch my back. You can't trust anybody here these days.' He winks knowingly and walks off.

A stunned Paddy watches him go. He had heard the rumours about how Tommy went about his job but to see it from close in. The lies and the treachery - it turns his stomach.

★

In a mad, crazy, last-gasp cavalry charge Tommy Docherty's United go all out in search of salvation and to stave off relegation. It gains instant results for just when the nails are being banged into the Old Trafford coffin, a sensational 3-1 win at Stamford Bridge against Chelsea offers hope where previously none existed.

Tommy's boys are magnificent. A stunning, long range, rasping drive from Willie Morgan puts United in front and two second half goals from youngsters Sammy McIlroy and Gerry Daly seal a most unexpected if welcome victory.

Tommy is delighted after this victory. He tells the waiting press: 'We have tried to play tight, to play defensively and it has not worked because it goes against our natural game. You may as well ask a cat to bark! So from now on Manchester United will go forward. We will attack and damn the consequences!'

'We have a chance Matt,' he says to me afterwards. 'Keep playing like this and we have a chance.'

What follows over the coming weeks defies belief as seemingly freed from unnatural defensive shackles, we rediscover our verve and attacking instincts to score thirteen goals in a six game spell and gain ten points out of a possible twelve.

A thrilling 3-3 draw at Burnley is followed by three straight wins over Norwich, Newcastle and a 3-0 hammering of high flying Everton at Old Trafford. A tight, uncompromising point is hard earned against a fellow relegation struggler Southampton at The Dell and suddenly redemption. A chink of light shines. If not a miracle, then a huge slice of luck is required to stay up but so long as we keep winning it could happen.

It really could.

On Wednesday 15th April 1974 Manchester United travel the short distance to Goodison Park to take on Everton, a side we have only recently beaten with some ease on home territory. United have to win and pray that Birmingham City, our chief rivals for survival, slip up at home to Queens Park Rangers.

As half time approaches we are the better team at Goodison and look more than capable of gaining two invaluable points. Then news filters through from the Midlands that Birmingham have scored not once but twice in swift succession and suddenly Tommy's boys appear nervous.

A tense second half unfurls and as we try manfully to regain our first half swagger, disaster strikes when Everton's Mick Lyons ignites the home crowd and sends the vast United following into despair. It finishes 1-0 and with Birmingham victorious the most frightful scenario now exists with just two games remaining.

Norwich City are bottom with twenty nine points

whilst United are above them on thirty two. Occupying the third relegation spot are Southampton with thirty four. Just outside the drop zone are Birmingham City clear by one. United still have a lifeline, but it is slim. If Birmingham lose at home to Norwich and we win our last two remaining games then the Midlands club would fall and not us.

It is too close to call.

United's next game? At home to Manchester City and a certain Lawman, now wearing blue, set for a date with destiny. I cannot believe Denis will be in the mood to spare us if the opportunity arises. It appears that our story is almost over. All that remains is to thank you for partaking in this journey and to tell you now of how Manchester United finally fell to earth.

42 - FROM THE STARS

Old Trafford: Saturday 27th April
Manchester United v Manchester City

Manchester awakes to a bright morning sun in late spring, with snatches of early summer on show. A city divided, one half praying for salvation, the other desperate to deny them. A Mancunian showdown of the like this fair city has never experienced.

Families and friends ripped apart. Eyes opening with both dread and joyful expectation. For the blues, this is not a question of loving thy neighbour but burying them. For the reds, they can only pray a season of torment and mediocrity can suddenly transform itself into something resembling a miracle.

Few hold out hope.

I am at the ground early. It has just gone eight in the morning and for obvious reason I cannot sleep. I walk into what I thought would be an empty stadium but I am wrong. One figure is sitting alone high in the stand.

It is Jimmy.

I take a deep breath and make my way up towards him. He smiles on seeing me approach.

'Hello Matt. You cannot sleep either I would hazard a guess?'

I sit down next to him.

'How are you doing Jimmy?' I pass him a newspaper

from my coat pocket and point to a headline. He reads it out loud.

'Tony Book to make King Denis City's Captain for the day.'

Jimmy laughs. 'Shrewd. A good way to fire the Lawman up.'

He hands it back.

'Let us hope that tonight you are singing "It's a wonderful world" eh Matt?'

'I have not sung that for a long time, Jim. Somehow I don't think it will be getting an airing anytime soon.'

He nods. 'At least the cats will be happy.'

I laugh. 'Look Jimmy, I have been meaning to get in touch. It was just with everything that has been going on. It just never felt like there was time.'

'Don't worry about it old pal. I understand.'

How can he be so understanding. Why is he such a decent man? 'But I do worry about it. It is wrong. We go back a long way.'

'Matt, please, there is no need. There is nothing to apologise for.'

'I should have done right by you Jimmy. I should have kept you close.'

Jimmy takes out a hip flask from his pocket. He is smiling wide. 'Whisky, medicinal purposes. Calm the pre match nerves.'

'This is prescribed from your doctor?' I grin.

'My doctor drinks more than me. Mind you he is a red so no surprise there after this season!'

He passes it to me. I take a nip and hand it back. Jimmy does likewise and replaces the top. We both go quiet for a minute then Jimmy breaks the silence.

'I saw a good winger yesterday at Tranmere

Rovers. A smart lad; clever, fast and a good crosser. Steve Coppell he is called. I told Tommy to go check him out. The lad is definitely for us. He will play for England one day.'

'They blame me for this mess Jimmy.'

'Who blames you?'

'Everybody: the supporters, the people who work here at Old Trafford. Nobody says anything to my face but I see it in their eyes.'

'Nonsense, Matt. Everything you have ever done is for the good of this club. If you made mistakes they were honest mistakes.'

'I am so sorry for what happened between us.'

Jimmy smiles. 'Hey we are sat here aren't we? It is eight thirty in the morning and we are sharing a hip flask. Now where I come from that is what good mates do. Not pals, friends.'

I can feel tears forming in my eyes. I do not deserve the friendship of this man. If God has given Manchester United a little grace then it was sparing him the trip to Belgrade. For once the angels turned away and gave us a break.

'We should never have got back on that plane Jimmy.'

He looks at me. His eyes a window to my tortured soul. He can see the hurt and pain. The sorrow and the grief. The dreadful feeling of loss.

'Like I said before Matt,' he takes another swig of the whisky, 'an honest mistake.'

He passes me back the flask. I glance at Jimmy but he is staring out across the stadium.

'So many ghosts.'

★

Denis arrives at Old Trafford and getting off the Manchester City coach he is mobbed by United supporters. 'Hope you are keeping well Denis', 'Missing you Denis', 'You are still the king Denis', 'Make sure you don't score today Denis!' He is busy signing every autograph book thrust in front of him, when he feels a hand tugging on his arm.

'Come on Lawman, we have got a job to do'

It is Mike Doyle. Here on enemy territory he is receiving merciless stick. 'I hate this fucking place Denis. It gives me the creeps. Let's make sure we put this lot down today then no need to bother coming here next season.'

Denis smiles but inside he is churning. He has already spoken to the manager Tony Book about being left out. He responded by giving him the armband! A red heart in a blue shirt.

'Make sure you go in the right dressing room Denis' laughs Francis Lee, as they enter Old Trafford. Everywhere people appear to shake his hand.

His is a fixed grin but it is a joker's smile. Denis is dreading this game like no other. So many memories, good friends: Paddy, George, Shay, Nobby, Jimmy. His initial anger after the harrowing exit towards the old man has vanished. Now all Denis remembers are the good times. There is one he would dearly like to make suffer. Though in wreaking revenge on Docherty it would only in turn break the hearts of so many he cares about. But Denis knows his is an instinctive talent. He simply cannot help himself. If a chance arises then may God and all the angels in heaven forgive him because he will take it.

★

As kick off draws near Old Trafford resembles a nervous, fraught arena and no place for the faint or half hearted. 57,000 gather and erupt in a cauldron of noise as both teams come on to the pitch.

The Stretford End explodes into a frenzied mass of red and white defiance. If this is to be the day they fall from the stars, they will go down breathing fire and screaming out the two things their underachieving team has not been able to take from them.

Pride and Passion.

The thunderous roar that greets the men in red is one of mortal defiance. On this wooden fortress, where boys become men, fuelled on Double Diamond and Watney's Party Seven, these red legions raised on glorious tales of yesteryear. Of Edwards, Taylor and Colman - those taken too soon and then Best, Law and Charlton.

Their songs sung with such gusto across the land. Loyal, fanatical, troublesome - 'downright hooligans' the authorities scream. All together now for one last carnival of sorts. Nobody ever promised them a happy ending. Six years of trouble and strife have put paid to that but as the outside world waits to read the last rites on Manchester United Football Club, those who hold it dear are damned if today will be their last stand.

This is not a disaster, nobody more than United supporters understand this. Dying is a disaster. Losing a team at the end of a runway is a disaster. Whatever happens today, whichever way the wind blows, United will rise again.

★

I take my seat with great reluctance and I'm still

thinking of Jimmy's parting words. Does he hold me responsible for what happened or is it just the emotion of today? For never have I seen this place so wracked with nerves. Grown men finding it hard to talk. The atmosphere is raw. This is not about football today, this is life. People queue to wish me luck.

Me?

I'd give a penny for Wilf and Frank's thoughts at this moment. They have seen the reality beyond the glory and the facade. A wise old man who has watched with a kind eye and warm heart over a prosperous kingdom. Giving out pearls of wisdom that belonged in another age and such was the esteem in which I have been held that nobody dared to suggest otherwise.

Few have dared to say, 'Hold on a moment Matt, those days are over. We are in big trouble here.' The Father of Football: this ridiculous title foisted upon me but then I never complained. I enjoyed the plaudits, it was good for the ego. When the reality was I had human frailties. Maybe more than most. I broke hearts and hurt people. I was not so paternal with both of those boys I sacked. I closed my eyes when Tommy went chopping dead wood. I cut off their heads when the going got tough. Every journey has an ending and this is ours.

This is what it has come to.

Denis heads into the centre circle to shake hands with United Captain Willie Morgan and is given a standing ovation by all four corners of the stadium.

'Behave yourself today Denis' smiles Willie.

Denis shakes his hand but says nothing. His emotions in turmoil. His heart racing.

The 90th Manchester derby is under way.

Manchester United's 36 consecutive seasons in the First Division is on the line. They twice go close in the first half. A Jim McCalliog effort is cleared off the line by Willie Donachie and Sammy McIlroy sends a header just wide of the post. United are trying everything but it is all effort and hustle. Everything is rushed.

A first half littered with mistakes unfurls. City are sleepwalking, occasionally causing heart attacks on the Old Trafford terraces by meandering into United's half. Suddenly there is a huge roar from the terraces as news filters through that Norwich have taken the lead at Birmingham! The noise level rises. Red voices scream towards the heavens. It is if a passing train is roaring past your face. There is hope, slim but a real sense the day may end well.

City come forward and Denis Tueart slides in Colin Bell to fire a shot from twenty yards that screams past Alex Stepney's post.

The nerves return, this lot have woken up.

More news from St Andrews and it is enough to stop you breathing. Birmingham have scored twice in quick succession. Kenny Burns and Bob Hatton. The City fans roar with delight whilst the red hordes reel. The momentarily glimpse of salvation has gone.

It was asking too much. Like standing in front of a firing squad and praying they would miss.

Half time comes and goes, a strange sense of trepidation has settled over Old Trafford. Something is going to happen. Nobody knows what, but it is in the air.

A United corner, mayhem ensues and City defenders scramble the ball away after Gerry Daly looks certain to score. But no, it goes on and the clock ticks forever down. The home side are almost spent and the visitor's sense it is time to end their pain.

Tueart crashes a fine effort against the crossbar. City are now rampaging, Tueart again is foiled at the last with a magnificent stop by Stepney. United are on their knees.

There are nine minutes left to play and the stage is set for the return of The King.

Midway inside the City half Mike Doyle tackles Willie Morgan. He passes to Summerbee who in turns send Colin Bell racing through the centre circle into acres of space. As the United defenders retreat Bell feeds Francis Lee, who is pushed wide in the penalty area. Hovering nearby is Denis.

Lee's cross finds him and from eight yards Denis instinctively backheels it and the ball flies low past Stepney into the net.

The roar goes up from the City supporters.

Denis's face says it all.

'My God what have I done?'

EPILOGUE

Bari, Italy 1943

Sergeant Major Busby is listening in as a seemingly mad Welshmen addresses twenty-two soldiers, partaking in what is nothing more than a kick about.

'Calm down Jimmy!' one of them exclaims, 'it's only a bloody game!'

'Only a game!' he replies with eyes blazing. 'Let me tell you something lad. Cricket is just a game. Tennis is just a game. That stupid baseball what the Yanks play is just a game. Football is so much more. Throw me the ball!'

The young soldier passes it to Jimmy and he holds it up.

'You see this? This is a magical thing. You treat it well, you cherish it and it will never let down. It only asks one thing of you. That you treat it with respect. That when you play you give your heart and soul. Because that is what football is. It comes from here.' Jimmy smiles and thumps his heart. Around him the soldiers stand mesmerised. 'Now you lot get back on that pitch and you show this ball that you care.'

Jimmy throws it back to the young soldier who is grinning wide.

'Will do Jimmy.'

'Good lad' he replies.

★

My mind is made up. This is the man for me. I approach him.

'Jimmy, remember me? We played against each other before the war.'

His face breaks into a huge smile

'Of course I do. You're Matt Busby.'

'Jimmy, I have a proposition for you. When this mess is over I have been offered the manager's job at Manchester United. Now at the moment they have no team and the Germans flattened their ground back in 1941 but I have a dream Jim. I believe with you by my side we can do special things. You have the passion that I am looking for. We will in time build our own team. We will use young players. We will shock the world with our football. It will be beautiful. It will be winning pass and move and give it to a red shirt football. They will not see us coming Jimmy. I promise you. So what do you say?'

Jimmy stands in shock and admiration. Here is a man just like him. My God, he thinks. There are two of us!

'I would love to Matt. It would be my honour to stand by your side.'

Jimmy offers me his hand and we shake on it.

'Good lad Jimmy. Together we will not just take Manchester United into the heavens.

We will take them beyond the stars.'

THE END